DI

Praise for
Ruth Logan Herne

"The author exudes warmth and grace and love on each page of this novel, and the set-up for the next book leaves readers hungry for more."
Romantic Times reviewer Carrie Townsend for 4½ Star Top Pick
Home on the Range

"Back in the Saddle is an uplifting and heartwarming story about two wounded people using the power of faith to find the courage to change. A dramatic ranch setting, rich characterization, and a beautiful love story make this a book to savor. This is a strong beginning for what promises to be an exciting trilogy. Ruth Logan Herne is my new favorite author!"
New York Times bestselling author Karen White

"Heart and hope combine in Ruth Logan Herne's sweet tale of old wounds and ties that bind. Where faith and forgiveness are present, old scars can be healed and new love can bloom. Sometimes, you really can go home again."
Lisa Wingate, national bestselling author of The Story Keeper and The Sea Keeper's Daughters

"From the first pages, readers will be drawn into the community of Gray's Glen, the amazing cast of characters, and the lives of the hero and heroine. Angelina and Colt fill the pages of Back in the Saddle with a romance that will have readers wanting to know their past, their future, and the story that intertwines their lives. Ruth Logan Herne takes us on a journey that we will want to continue!"
Brenda Minton, author of the Martin's Crossing series

At Home in Wishing Bridge

ALSO BY RUTH LOGAN HERNE

At Home in Wishing Bridge

RUTH LOGAN HERNE

Waterfall
PRESS

Published by Waterfall Press, Grand Haven, MI

www.brilliancepublishing.com

Amazon, the Amazon logo, and Waterfall Press are trademarks of Amazon.com, Inc., or its affiliates.

ISBN-13: 9781503904088
ISBN-10: 1503904083

Cover design by Eileen Carey

Printed in the United States of America

This one's for Karen. With love. Thanks for being you and loving us. We couldn't ask for better!

CHAPTER ONE

"Lay a hand on her and you die."

Thea Anastas had once heard an expression about blood running cold.

Now she was living it in a run-down shack that brought back far too many terrible childhood memories.

Goose bumps dotted the nurse practitioner's arms. An adrenaline rush pumped her heart into an angry rhythm. She wasn't sure if she should lock eyes with the aged dementia patient facing her with a knife or ignore her completely, but when the white-haired old woman slashed the air in a very convincing move, indecision was no longer an option.

Focus on the old woman and the child. Disregard the squalor and smells and so many old buttons being pushed at once.

Sage advice. She swallowed hard, gathered her courage, and held the deranged woman's gaze. "Are you her grandma? I'm from the doctor's office. We heard Shannon was sick, and we wanted to help." Calm voice, neutral tone, low key. That's what she'd learned in her psych rounds years before, and while she'd felt well rounded enough to hang a family practice shingle, years of education melted into a puddle at the sight of that knife. But that was her problem. Not the old woman's.

Unfortunately, dementia patients weren't psych-method friendly. Anything could exist in their world—and often did. Thea reached for her phone to call for backup.

"A gun! A gun!" The old woman charged forward, then back, waving the knife. "I'll take us both to Jesus before I let you shoot her! Get back! Get back!" Like a scene from a Stephen King movie, the old woman let out a howl, arm raised, knife gleaming.

Stay calm. Don't look at the knife. Pay no attention to the knife.

An impossible task when she'd met knives before, in South Philly. Squalor, too. But that was a long time ago. She drew a breath through her nose to calm her racing pulse. "A phone, Mrs. Willoughby. Just my phone to call the doctor. Shannon's sick, remember?"

For a few seconds, Thea thought she'd broken through the addled woman's haze, but the knife slashed once more. The longer days of spring offered oblique light from a west-facing window in the hills of Wyoming County, New York. It backlit the old woman, but the angled glow put Thea at a disadvantage. She reached for her phone again and took a step back.

"You go! You go! You go!"

She couldn't leave a child in these circumstances, but angering the old woman further could make things worse. She backed out the door and dialed.

"9-1-1. State your emergency."

"This is Thea Anastas, the nurse practitioner from Hillside Medical. I'm trying to treat a critically ill child at 17072 County Road 27, but I'm being threatened with a knife by an elderly woman. I need help, ASAP."

"Is the child in danger?"

It sure looked that way. "Yes."

"Are you in danger?"

"Yes. It's a big knife and the old woman is out of touch with reality. We have a critical mental-health situation compounding a grave medical condition for the child. Every minute counts."

"Wyoming County sheriffs are responding. Do you want to stay on the phone with me until they arrive on scene?"

I want to treat my patient and go home. She didn't give voice to the thought. She tried to peer through one of the windows, but the sun's glare made it impossible. "No. I'm going to try to talk her down. Again."

She'd no sooner hung up the phone than it buzzed with a text from Darla, one of the Wishing Bridge EMTs manning the volunteer firehouse down in the village:

Try singing Amazing Grace. It's Dotty Willoughby's favorite.

Nurse Practitioner Killed While Singing Hymns.

The probable headline filled Thea's head as the rising voices of spring peepers serenaded the marsh surrounding the old cabin.

But since talking and reasoning hadn't worked, singing a song was worth a try. "Amazing grace . . ."

She moved forward, singing softly, hoping the old lady wasn't a music critic because Thea wasn't known for her vocals.

The old woman hadn't moved. She stood rock-still, a sentinel, knife held high, staring down at the grievously sick child.

". . . a wretch like me . . ."

As Thea moved back into the doorway, the old woman stirred. She brought the knife higher, and with a marksman's arc she sent that blade flying through the air to land like a spear in the doorframe to Thea's left.

Heart attack time.

Another shot of adrenaline surged through her.

Calm disappeared in the gleam of that flying blade.

And just when she thought she'd have to tackle the old woman to save the child's life, a birdlike chirp joined her in song.

"I once was lost . . ." The old woman sounded like a cartoon parody, but her face . . . *oh, her face* . . . eased into the sweetness of old-time reverence as she sang.

"But now am found . . ." Thea continued the hymn softly as the crazy woman transformed before her.

"Was blind, but now I see." The old woman pierced her with a tight look of expectation.

3

The second verse.

What was the second verse?

A deep voice chimed in from behind her.

That meant Deputy Hale Jackson had arrived, and then an alto accompaniment joined in as well. Lita Szabo, an EMT from Wishing Bridge. For long moments it was as if the whole stinking choir section was about to have a sing-along with a child dying on the floor.

The kid came first, no matter what, and Thea had been delayed long enough. She moved to the little girl's side as a red blinking flash announced more help.

The flashers put the old woman back into a frenzy. She screamed and charged forward. She darted right, then left, trying to get to the knife in the wall.

"I've got her, Thea." Hale wrapped two strong arms around the aged woman. "I called for an extra ambulance for Dotty. You take care of Shannie."

Hale Jackson, newly engaged to Thea's wonderful friend Kelsey, had become a rock to lean on in tough times, and he knew his hymns. Right now Thea was real grateful for that.

The old woman keened as Hale took her outside. Somewhere in the background, the hymn recommenced in pew-worthy harmony.

But as Thea gently probed the child's turgid abdomen, she was just as sure she might lose the little girl on the floor.

"What've we got, Thea?" Lita slipped into place at her side, then grimaced when she recognized the child. "It's Shannie. Oh, baby girl, what's happened to you?"

"Probable burst appendix, immediate transport to the children's hospital in Rochester."

"On it."

Brian Teague wheeled a gurney into the bare-bones house, a generous term for the shack surrounding them. Two buckets held water from spring rains, water that dripped through the sagging roof. While Brian and Lita secured the little girl for transport, Thea called the hospital to make sure a pediatric surgeon was available.

She finished the call as Lita and Brian trundled the gurney down the broken path to the waiting ambulance.

The child moaned, then writhed in pain.

"Oh, baby, sorry." Tough-as-nails, pragmatic Lita whispered words of comfort. "I'm so very sorry."

"Who can we call?" asked Thea when they'd tucked the gurney into the bed of the rescue wagon. When Lita looked blank, she waved to the house. "Family. For both of them. Who can we call?"

"There's no one to call," said Lita, and the deep note in her voice underscored the words. "No one at all."

No one to call.

No one to comfort this child.

No one to see to her care. Her well-being.

Reality hit Thea worse than the old woman's blade ever could have. Thea knew being alone. She knew being threatened. She knew being abandoned. And with God as her witness, she would never let that happen to a child again. Not on her watch. "Go. I'll follow."

"Thea, you look worn out." Brian poked his head out the window while Lita closed the access doors.

Thea was worn out. Not because of the work involved. She thrived on work. It was the need surrounding her in the tucked-away corner she'd happened upon three months before. She wasn't supposed to be here. Backwoods medicine wasn't on her agenda, yet here she was. She waved to Brian as she moved to her car. "Nothing a double shot of espresso won't cure. I'll meet you there."

Hale had corralled the old woman into the back of his SUV cruiser. He gave Thea a sign that he and his cousin Garrett, another county sheriff's deputy, had things under control.

Thea gave him a quiet nod and climbed into her small SUV. She'd traded her pricey sports car for more practical wheels when life and luck had taken a steep decline in mid-December. And here she was, treating patients in a tar-paper shack, avoiding knives and crazy people.

Been there. Done that. Didn't expect to do it again. Ever.

But she had. And she'd survived. As she drove down the rain-slicked gravel drive to the county road below, she realized anew why staying in Wishing Bridge had been a dangerous choice back in January. This little town and its discordant mix of people needed her, and if there was one thing Thea Anastas had learned to avoid, it was being needed. By anyone.

Her phone rang. She recognized the Hillside Medical number and took the call on Bluetooth. "What's up, Ethan?" Ethan Brandenburg was her somewhat grumpy current medical partner in a nonpartnership arrangement made out of pure necessity and accidents of timing. Divine timing?

Uh, no.

Accidental timing was a far more accurate assessment.

"Where are you?" he asked.

She heard the sounds of children in the background. His niece and nephew, two California kids orphaned the previous year and not exactly happy with their new normal. Constant sun had graced their lives until they moved here. Now they dealt with snow, ice, sleet, rain, and then more snow. And no parents, a huge tragedy of grave importance in all three lives. "Heading to Children's Hospital to follow up on a tragic case. And praying there's a coffee shop nearby."

"Starbucks on Mount Hope Avenue," he told her. "Opposite the College Town shopping complex. It's right around the corner from the ER. Mara, can you stop criticizing him, please? He's nearly three years younger than you. Cut him some slack."

"I hate him," the girl retorted, loud enough for Thea to hear, and that was probably intentional. Mara wanted everyone to know how desperately unhappy she was, and she was remarkably successful in her goal. "And I hate you."

That was most likely directed at her poor uncle.

"I hate everything about this stupid place," the girl went on. "There's some slack for you."

Oh, Mara. Troubled child or not, she'd upped her brat game exponentially lately and was giving her uncle/surrogate father a run for his money. To his credit, Ethan didn't sigh and didn't fuss, which left Thea wondering if there was such a thing as too much patience.

"Who were you seeing, Thea?"

"Dotty Willoughby's great-granddaughter, presenting as burst appendix. Seriously sick kid. Grandmother tried to kill me. A good time was had by all."

"You went without an escort? Did you forget Hale's warning about going into the hills alone? There's danger on some of these back roads. Why didn't you call for an escort?" The county sheriffs had agreed to accompany them to medical emergencies in the backwoods region for that very reason.

"A grandmother and a sick child. Who'd have jumped from that to danger?"

His silence said he would have, and Thea was too tired to argue. "Stupid move on my part. The good thing is the knife missed me. The bad thing is I think she missed me on purpose, just to prove she didn't have to miss me."

"Thea."

"Starting to rain, have to hang up." She disconnected the call quickly. She didn't need Ethan to scold her for being careless. She'd figured that out all by herself. And with only three months left in their unintentionally combined practice, she needed to extend feelers for a new position. Rochester, maybe? That would work if she wanted to stay close to her friends Kelsey and Jazz, the two women who'd helped her achieve some level of normalcy as a teen. Now that they'd reconnected, a part of her didn't want to let go.

Was Rochester a big enough city to keep her happy? Keep her on task?

She'd been big-city bound all her life. That had been the dream, the goal, until the University of Pittsburgh megapractice had downsized in December, leaving her jobless. She'd come north to help Kelsey and her new baby, then stumbled into this job when Ethan's older partner had gotten sick and Ethan had needed temporary help. Thea was totally transitory and a board-certified nurse practitioner in family practice, so it made sense, but once the former partner died and time stretched on, she was finding it harder to keep her distance. That could become a problem because, except with Jazz and Kelsey, Thea always kept her distance.

She swung into the coffee shop drive-thru thirty-five minutes later, parked outside the ER, and hurried inside with her coffee in hand. "I'm the nurse practitioner that sent in Shannon Willoughby. Peds patient, approximate age seven, possible burst appendix."

"There's no Shannon Willoughby on record," the data-taker behind the desk said.

"Thea?" Brian Teague motioned to her from beyond the check-in station. "They took her right up for surgical consult. Have you been here before?"

She shook her head.

"Go through security there, and the pediatric surgical waiting room is just beyond. Tell the liaison who you are."

She started to follow his directions, then turned. "Brian. What's her name? I tried Willoughby at the desk and they had nothing."

"Carter. Shannon Carter. Dotty Willoughby is her great-grand-mother and the only family on record."

Lita had said as much, but that couldn't be possible. Could it? "That poor old woman is her only family? And her guardian?"

"I don't think anyone realized how bad Dotty's gotten." Brian folded his arms, troubled. "She doesn't come off the hill too much, and

I think the long winter kept her housebound. On top of that, Shannon might not have been going to school. She was on the homeschool list a year ago. She had an aunt who was supposed to be teaching her, but the aunt overdosed fifteen months back. Shannie might have slipped off the radar completely. And that makes this partially our fault for lack of follow-through."

An aunt that overdosed. A demented great-grandmother. A hovel of a home on a backwoods gravel path.

"Well, she's on the radar now, with possible mortal results." She strode away, thoroughly angry that, once again, the system had let down a child. She'd been that child once, and no one deserved that kind of gross neglect. She didn't pretend understanding, because when it came to kids' welfare, carelessness deserved no understanding.

She alerted the liaison to her presence, that the child's great-grandmother was indisposed, and that she was staying. And then she curled up in the waiting room.

This wasn't her norm.

She'd been on the other side of the waiting room door for years, treating patients, but tonight she wasn't on staff. She was a guardian, standing by so one little girl wouldn't wake up in a strange place alone. And if she could make this sacrifice for every abandoned child in the world . . . she'd do it.

CHAPTER TWO

Ethan spotted the folded sheet of elementary-school tablet paper on his narrow desk at home. He picked it up and opened it, then wished he'd left it alone.

Things I Hate The Most

The title was in bold block letters done in rainbow marker shades. Should he be heartened that his seven-year-old niece thought enough of the list to make it attractive?

Not when he was listed at number one, followed by their house, the town, her brother, God, the school, and gym class.

She'd left off her teacher, Kelsey McCleary. That was a good thing, right? That the angry girl had developed some kind of relationship with someone? And it wasn't as if pediatric therapists were readily available in the area. He'd taken her to one in Mount Morris, and there was another in Warsaw, but when she refused to get out of the car, he learned to pick his battles. If taking her was more of a struggle than the reward reaped by going, he'd avoid the fight. Right now he'd do just about anything to avoid the fight, which made him feel like an abject failure as a surrogate parent.

Mara's voice cut in from behind him. "I can't believe we're going to be in this stupid, ugly town for three more months. I'd rather be anywhere else. With anyone else except you."

He turned to face her. She'd taken a shower as instructed, but not without a fight, whereas her little brother worked overtime to be sweet and nice. That only angered her more, because she clearly wanted a united front as they raged against the fate that had taken their parents in a brutal car crash the previous year. "We're stuck, though. You. Me. The kid." He aimed a smile at Keegan, and the boy grinned from the far side of the room. "It's not much longer, Mara. Then we'll move on. A new place, a new start. All of us. You'll see."

"*You'll* see!" she promised as she whirled and flounced away. "You'll see exactly what happens if you try and take me there! I just want to go home, and I've told you that a million times!" she shrieked. "I just want to go home."

Of course she did, but home didn't exist anymore. Not like it had.

He understood her meaning clearly. She wished her parents hadn't died, she missed her Southern California blue-sky existence, and she didn't want life to have turned upside down and inside out in one fateful moment. But it had. And there was nothing he could do about it. He'd already taken a year sabbatical from his cardiology-related genetic research to give the kids time to adjust before he jumped into a long-awaited opportunity.

She stomped off to her small room.

Keegan crept over to him once she was gone. "Uncle Eefen."

"Come here, little man." He reached out, hauled Keegan into his arms, and held him.

"Sissy scares me." The boy whispered the words, as if saying them out loud or having Mara overhear them would be really, really bad, and Ethan was pretty sure the kid was right. "She's so mean, Uncle Eefen."

"She's mad, Keegs."

"Well, she could stop bein' mad sometime, couldn't she?" Keegan lifted two defined, arched eyebrows—his mother's eyebrows, total Brandenburg—and met Ethan's gaze. "I wish she would stop being mad. And I wish we could stay here forever, Uncle Eefen. I wuv Mrs. Shirley and my teachers and my frogs so much. Can't we just stay here forever? Please?"

They couldn't, no, because Ethan had already put his research appointment on family leave hold for a year. Chicago had given them time to adjust, citing the cruel circumstances of the double loss, but if he didn't accept the position in June, it was off the table. He'd been aiming to make a difference from the time he was a kid, from the time he had kissed his sick little brother goodbye. He couldn't mess it up now. "We'll get a house with a yard in Chicago," he promised Keegan. "And maybe even more frogs." The early spring chorus of tree frogs had enraptured the little guy, and when he saw one of the tiny frogs actually change color on a low branch, he had fallen instantly in love.

Keegan didn't argue with his uncle.

He never argued. Maybe that was as bad as always arguing. How would Ethan know? And who could he even ask to find out?

Keegan went off to bed, chin down. He dragged a satin-trimmed blanket alongside him, like a *Peanuts* character. He trudged on quiet feet, then disappeared into his room. He didn't call for Ethan to kiss him good night.

Ethan would do it anyway, but the somber look on the boy's face hit him with force.

He was a disappointment to both children in separate ways. Currently he was kind of a disappointment to himself, too. Not to mention the staff at Hillside Medical, soon to be out of work.

His phone rang. Seeing his younger sister's number on the display made him hesitate.

He'd always gotten along better with Alexis, their older sister. He and Alexis had shared a similar ambition and drive to be the best they could be.

He barely knew Eva. She'd been raised by their mother after the divorce that followed his brother's death. Broken dreams. Broken hearts. Broken lives. His mother had taken Eva and moved to New Mexico when the girl was quite young, and he could count on one hand the number of times he'd seen her since. What kind of family did that?

His.

He answered the phone in a quiet voice. "Hey, Eva. What's up?"

"I just wanted to check in and see how things are going. Are the kids asleep?"

"Are the kids asleep" was code for "I want to tell you what to do, but I'm far too busy with my minimal existence to help." Advice from the childless younger sister still trying to find herself in the Pacific Northwest wouldn't get him far. "In bed. Not asleep. I have to go hear their prayers."

That made her laugh. "Words I never thought I'd hear coming out of your mouth."

Him, either. But Alexis had left him a personal note, asking him to bring the kids up in a church, embracing a belief system he couldn't accept. He was a man of science. Science liked proof. But for Alexis . . . *for these kids* . . . he'd do what he was asked to do. "Things change. So do people."

"Hey, I'm not against the idea. It's the hypocrisy of the whole thing that bothers me. But if it helps Alexis's kids settle in, I'm all for it. I was wondering if you could pretend you're not my brother and write me a recommendation for a job."

Which most likely meant she'd left her former employer on bad terms. "You mean lie."

"I mean gloss over the relationship status and highlight my good points from the perspective of a former employer."

"I'm not your former employer."

"You paid me to keep quiet when your girlfriend came to visit once. I think that qualifies."

"Eva." He crossed the room, tipped the curtain, and gazed at the stark nothingness of the cold, wet March night. "It doesn't. Get the job on your own merit or apply elsewhere. Didn't the ice-cream place give you a reference?" She'd been hired to help run part of a large family-friendly destination outside of Portland, famous for its farm-fresh dairy treats.

"I had to downsize that job. They wanted too many hours. It's finally spring and I need time to explore the coast. It's vital to my being."

"Well, gainful employment is vital to mine, and I've got two kids waiting for me to tuck them in. Gotta go."

"Listen, Ethan, I know you're busy—"

The understatement of the century.

"But if you would—"

"I can't lie, Eva. You know that. And I can't keep the kids waiting any longer." He hung up the phone.

It rang again, almost instantly, like he'd known it would. He didn't pick up. He had enough on his plate right now. More than enough.

Eva had been a surprise addition to the family after his brother, Jarod, died. When his parents split up a few years later, he and Alexis stayed with their father. Eva had stayed with their mother. No one offered the older kids a choice or asked their opinion. Their mother simply packed up Eva and their belongings and moved a thousand miles away, leaving her older children with their curt, self-absorbed father. Ethan didn't understand it then. He didn't try to understand it now.

In the end, his mother had died from a drug overdose labeled an accidental death, and his father had assumed custody of Eva. But by then, Alexis and Ethan were grown and had moved on to lives of their own. Lives not governed by drama . . .

That had been their promise to one another as they matured.

Yet here it was, on his doorstep, more drama than he'd ever thought possible.

Prayers.

He hurried into the kids' respective bedrooms too late to say prayers or hear them. Mara was sound asleep but hadn't thrashed around enough to wipe her tear-stained cheeks dry yet.

Keegan lay curled up, his blanket caught between his thumb and his fist, thumb firmly in his mouth.

Should a four-year-old still be sucking his thumb? Ethan didn't know. But he should know these things, shouldn't he?

He sank onto the living-room couch. It was fairly old and nasty, but the basement apartment had come furnished, and he'd figured that made sense in their case. But did it? Would he irreparably harm two innocents by living in a clean but kind of drab apartment for twelve months? Probably.

He put his head in his hands, needing sleep. Needing help. Needing—

He was failing them.

He was failing Alexis.

He was failing himself and pretty sure that if someone took a survey of his patients, they'd give him a low grade, too.

A text came through just then. From Thea. Staying to see this through. Unsure of outcome. Social services called in. A mess. No foster-care placements for postsurgical care available. At wits end right now because this kid will have nowhere to go when they release her.

He stared at the text.

He wasn't sure if it was the tone or the words or what, exactly.

It sounded different. Different from the pragmatic get-the-job-done woman who'd come on board when he desperately needed help in late December. She worked hard, did well with patients, and minded her own business with barely a word in his direction, which is how he preferred things. *Keep it simple. Keep it temporary. Maintain your distance.*

He reread the text. The urge to call her niggled him.

He set down the phone.

She'd think it was weird, and maybe it was, but between her words he sensed something else. Deeper. Thought provoking.

Of course talking to anyone when he was dead tired wouldn't be in his best interests.

He grabbed his pillow from the closet, threw it on the couch, and tugged a blanket up under his chin. He'd given the bedrooms to the kids and didn't love sleeping on the couch but did it just because. And he was tired enough most nights that it really didn't matter where he laid his head.

CHAPTER THREE

Stop now and turn back. Jazz Monroe's brain loved to scold as it deemed necessary. Even when it was quite unnecessary. *You're being obsessive. Let's not do that, okay?*

The leggy former supermodel crested the current forested hill and had to pull herself up short. The urge to keep going, keep running, pushed her, but the mental warning was right. Tipping herself into compulsive mode would do no good.

Running gave her a rush. It gave her control in uncontrollable situations, unless she allowed the running to become an uncontainable situation, and why add fuel to that fire?

One more hill . . . The rolling forest tempted her forward with its lure of physical success, but the lures didn't own her any longer.

She turned and retraced her path toward Wishing Bridge. She had never been able to run freely like this while working the international modeling circuit from Manhattan. There was always someone with a camera or a cell phone to grab pics and blast them across the Internet.

Here there were trees and regular folks who thought it was interesting to have a supermodel in town, and that was about the extent of it.

The village lights began to wink on as the sun sank lower in the western sky.

Spring was here.

Not fully apparent yet. The gray-barked trees remained leafless, and the steady drizzle sogged the ground beneath her feet, but she didn't need leaves to tell her change was in the air. Longer days. Brighter sun, more intense. And no job, still.

It was time.

She stayed on the path, curving through the forest preserve, aiming for the glimmer of town.

She needed something to do. Something to keep her hands busy and keep her among people.

You've got money. You could go back to school. You could get an education.

Money wasn't a problem. She'd been highly paid for a lot of years and saved whatever she could. With modeling perks, she'd been able to invest. It wasn't money that pushed her to work.

It was simply work. The need to be involved with something now that she wasn't slave to a starvation diet to stay center stage on the modeling circuit.

She slowed her pace to begin her cooldown as she neared the town. The last leg of this run took her down Main Street, past a line of old-style small businesses and straight to Wyoming Hill Road.

"Hey, Jazz!" A teen girl waved to her from across the street.

She waved back, smiling.

"Lookin' good, girl!" Avis Washington, a local midwife affiliated with a Rochester hospital, slowed down as she drove by. "Give my best to Maggie and Jeb, all right?"

"Will do!" She turned up Wyoming Hill Road, walking now. She didn't hurry, letting her heart and lungs slow down gradually.

"Are you soaked right through?" Her friend Kelsey, the reason she and Thea had ended up in Wishing Bridge back in December, was on the front porch of the Tompkins house, waiting for her.

Jazz shook her head as she climbed the stairs. "Naw. This material wicks moisture away and somehow manages to insulate the body at the same time. Clever stuff, right?"

"I'll say. And I'm going to warn you ahead of time. Your phone's been blowing up with texts and messages."

"I know. That's the reason I stayed out longer than usual." She let Kelsey precede her into the quiet house. "Rage Fashions and Bellisima have both offered my former agent unbelievable contracts to coax me back to represent their lines. And I'm actually tempted, Kelse." She bent and stretched her fingertips to the floor, then flexed her legs. "I love being here, but I'm starting to go stir crazy. Maggie's healthy enough to watch the baby, and I'm going to go mad if I don't get busy. The last thing I want to do is model. And yet that's the first thing that comes to mind because, unfortunately, it's the only thing I know how to do. And isn't that a sad commentary on my life?"

"Wait." Kelsey held out a hand. "Wait right there, let me get some streamers. Maybe some balloons. And some high-protein food." She made a face as if high-protein food was a lot of fun. "I didn't know we were having a pity party tonight. Must have missed my invitation."

Jazz stared at her.

Kelsey stared right back, then arched a brow. "Please tell me you're not on this negative-thinking kick over being one of the world's most sought-after supermodels for nearly nine years? Because an elementary-school teacher like me might have trouble identifying with that."

Jazz groaned. "I'm turning into a whiner."

"A little bit."

That was the best thing about true friends. They didn't let you get away with stupid stuff like whining about being rich and beautiful. "Smack me, okay? Where's Thea?"

"Staying at the hospital to monitor the condition of a very sick little girl."

"And now I'm officially mad at myself." Jazz pointed up the stairs. "I'm going to shower, stop whining, and count my blessings. Where are Maggie and Jeb?"

"Tuesday-night bowling league."

The normalcy of that made Jazz smile. "That's perfect. I forgot it was Tuesday. Hey, instead of cooking, how about if we take Hayley over to the diner? I don't want to cook, you worked all day, and the Tuesday special is Chicken French."

"Which I love." The baby began to stir in the portable crib they'd set up in the living room. "I'll feed Hayley now and maybe we'll get enough time to eat. But I'll bring my nursing cape just in case."

"That works. Give me twenty minutes."

"You've got it."

Jazz hurried up the stairs. Twenty minutes to get ready, including her shower. In New York, she hadn't dared poke her nose outside her apartment without full makeup, but that was her personal hang-up. Fear of losing the edge, losing her spot, losing her audience and her contracts had ruled her life.

Not here.

Here she ventured out like a normal person. She met folks and chatted with them as if she'd been doing it all along. Here she was just Jazz, one of the gals living at the Tompkins house, and she loved being able to claim a normal identity. But now she needed a job.

"Have you thought about volunteering someplace?" Kelsey asked as she drove them toward the diner a short while later. "The schools are always looking for classroom help. And your experiences could really help high school girls see both sides of body-shaming issues."

"I've thought about it." She'd been thinking about a lot of things. Too many things. "But then I look around and see how many people are struggling here. For jobs. For food and rent. To make ends meet. Why would they want a tall, skinny black girl with plenty of money in the bank telling their kids what to do?"

"And there's that self-image monster, rising up to swallow you whole again." Kelsey spoke softly as she pulled into a parking space.

Kelsey was right. Jazz didn't see herself as a successful business-woman. She knew the truth. Models were contract employees; they rarely got to think for themselves. She'd been more like a puppet for years, following orders. *Wear this. Flaunt that. Stand here. Walk there. Roll that shoulder, Jazz! Swing those hips!*

"You managed the rigors of a butt-kicking job, dealing with creeps left and right while making yourself financially sound. That takes skill, hard work, and intelligence. You don't need letters after your name to show that you're smart. Sometimes you can just *be* smart. Do you think intelligent women suddenly appeared on the landscape when they finally let them attend college?" Kelsey waited as Jazz detached the sleeping baby's car seat from its base, then smiled up at Jazz. "I think you've got more than money in the bank, Cinda." She used the name Jazz's grandmother had called her as a little girl. "I think your wealth is in your knowledge and it should be shared. One way or another."

She held the door so Jazz could enter the retro-outfitted diner.

Chaos reigned inside.

A cook was calling out order numbers. A frazzled woman was trying to deliver drinks to a table and got upended by a naughty preschooler who knocked into her on his way to the bathroom. A second waitress balled up her apron, flung it onto a customer's table, and shrieked "I quit!" before tugging a jacket from the hook rack near the entrance and storming out the door.

Jazz didn't hesitate.

She'd waitressed in a Manhattan diner for two full years before hitting the big money in fashion.

She tucked the baby into a booth with Kelsey, winked at her friend, and strode forward toward the very surprised and upset restaurant owner near the cash register. "Give me an apron, a pad, and a pencil, Vern. I'm here to help."

If Vern Strokos thought it weird to have Jazz step up to the plate, he didn't voice it. Wordlessly he handed her all three things as customers grumbled around them.

She faced the cook through the pass-through. "Can you refresh what's been sitting?" In other words: "I can't give customers cold, congealed food and make them happy."

He eyed her, then the plates, and offered a grudging nod. "Give me five."

Five minutes.

She could do a lot of schmoozing in five minutes. She took the side the waitress had abandoned and moved quickly from table to table.

Light and breezy. Conversational tone. Don't linger and chat, reassure and move on.

She remembered the order of events like it hadn't been ten years ago. More like it was yesterday.

And by the time Kelsey had eaten and unobtrusively fed the baby once again under the shield of a nursing cover, Jazz had not only jumped in and helped out, she'd pocketed over thirty dollars in tips, the gratitude of the Strokos patriarch, and one more thing:

A job.

A job she did well, almost as well as runway walking.

Jacinda "Jazz" Monroe . . . diner waitress.

CHAPTER FOUR

Jill Jackson ladled up two bowls of hearty stew while Max Reichert withdrew a tray of warm rolls from the oven. "This smells amazing, Jill."

She carried the bowls to the old maple table in her retro kitchen. "Stew and bread on cold, wet nights. Nothing better than that, is there?"

"In the right company, that is." He winked at her and she laughed at him.

"That flirting will get you into trouble someday." She angled a knowing and skeptical look his way, a combination she did well after raising two boys on her own.

"Not much chance of that, because I only do it with you," he assured her.

"Because I'm safe." She buttered a roll as she acknowledged their friendship boundaries. "I've sworn off men. You've sworn off commitments. We go through life in self-designated neutral zones."

"And all this time I just figured we were friends." He grinned at her.

"We are." She handed him the buttered roll because she had a servant's heart and she was a great gal. The kind that someone should have loved and cherished and held close to his heart for decades. Unfortunately her husband had been a lying, cheating schemer, so she had raised Hale and Bennett on her own, living her life avoiding personal relationships with men and helping others. Max wasn't blind to the parallels between their stories, only *he* wasn't the injured party. He was the one that had inflicted the injury way back when, and how does a solid Christian man fix that?

He couldn't.

He'd tried years ago, when his selfish desires had ruined his marriage and his relationship with his beautiful daughter. He'd failed. They wanted nothing to do with him. End of story.

When you wreck lives because your ego gets in the way of your family, then you bear the consequences. For a long, long time.

"How's that big old Queen Anne coming along?" Jill asked after a sweet blessing. She dipped her roll into the bowl and bit it, then smiled, happy with such a simple thing. "Comfort food. My favorite."

"Agreed. And I'm glad Bennett was able to bag a few deer last fall, because nothing makes a heartier stew than well-trimmed venison." He took a drink of water before he answered her question. "The house on Maplewood is pretty much done. Thank you for recommending your niece to do the painting. That left me free to work on the other property I bought across the road."

"That yellow Dutch colonial that went neglected for so long?"

"That's the one. I'm still in demo mode there, but it's coming along. That's a house meant for a family. The two apartments in the Queen Anne are ready for occupancy, and most of the medical offices are situated. Another few days of this and that, then the kitchen. I'm hoping it will help draw a doctor into town. Ethan and Thea will be leaving in a few months, and a town needs medical care to help keep it solid."

"You've done your part," she told him. "I'm expecting God will do the rest."

"I can't argue with that," he agreed. "Somehow things have a way of working out, even when I'm pretty sure I'm staring impossible in the face."

Jill leaned forward and held his gaze. "The word 'impossible' isn't in your dictionary, Max. The very thought makes you work harder, and that's a rare and wonderful trait."

"Just a job, Jill."

"Mmhmm." She kept eating. "You're talking to the woman who just opened a beautiful store on Main Street. With your help."

"Well, Hale bankrolled it and helped with demolition, so we've got him to thank, too."

"I sent him cookies."

Max laughed. That's all Hale would expect or want. He'd been an NFL quarterback with one Super Bowl ring to his credit before he suffered a career-ending injury. Now he was back home in Wishing Bridge, working a growing beef-cattle farm with his brother, Ben, and wearing a deputy sheriff's uniform. Not because he needed to. He had enough money to finance a couple of small-town lifetimes.

Hale was doing it because he wanted to. Big difference. "I expect he shared the cookies."

"You know him well."

"Wedding plans moving along?"

Jill got up and filled two coffee cups. One for him. One for her. "Yes, because Kelsey doesn't care how much money Hale has in the bank, she wants a simple wedding, a simple reception, and a dog."

Max laughed. "Sounds like a good match, doesn't it?"

"Oh, I hope so." She put her hand over Max's, and he tried not to think of how perfect that felt. Her hand on his. The sweet look of utter sincerity in her pretty light-brown eyes. "When Hale realized his first wife cheated on him, he was devastated. I don't think he'd ever considered that kind of thing in the realm of possibilities, but when you're at the top of anything—sports, TV, Hollywood—things get weird. There's temptation everywhere."

"There's always temptation everywhere," Max said. "It's just dressed prettier as the paychecks increase."

"Well, I don't foresee a problem with Hale and Kelsey," she said as she finished the last of her roll. "They seem made for each other."

Max had heard those words before. Thirty-five years earlier. And then he'd been too busy working the NYPD and running weekend contractor jobs to be the husband and father he was supposed to be. Someplace in there the drinking had started . . . and it hadn't stopped until he'd hit rock bottom with his family. The eventual change to being a New York State trooper got him out of the city and away from old temptations. But the change came too late to regain his family.

"They're smitten, that's for sure. And Kelsey's baby is winning hearts all over town, isn't she?"

"I can't wait to take her walking in that pretty stroller." Jill smiled, and the warmth in that smile, her warmth, made him wish he didn't have so much to atone for. Most folks might find it easy to go off and build a whole new life as if the first one had never existed.

Not him. Besides, Jill deserved the best. She'd gotten the short straw once. Didn't deserve it then. Didn't deserve it now.

"I'll show her the flowers and the trees and we'll listen to the birds. When Hale's ex-wife took little Michael away, she took my heart right along with him," she explained. "I know Hale did the right thing, but it was like someone ripped out a piece of me to have that little fellow whisked off to a whole new life in California. A whole new father. I hated seeing the pain on my son's face," she went on. "I'd get so angry, Max, because I couldn't fix it. I couldn't fix his knee when it blew out, but that's life. Change happens. But to have your child taken away, that was wretched for him, and for me. So when I hold Hayley, when I give her a bottle or make her laugh, it's like she's healing my heart just by being here. Being part of us."

"No one ever wants to say goodbye to a child." The image of Gwendolyn, his little girl, waving goodbye from the back seat of a Manhattan taxi, with tears streaming down her cheeks. Calling his name . . .

The image haunted him almost as much as his bad choices.

Jill squeezed his hand lightly. "Go to her, Max. Try again. You know it's eating at you from inside. What's the worst that can happen? She says no, she doesn't want to see you?"

He hated this conversation.

They'd only had it a couple of times before, and he wasn't sure if he hated it because Jill was right . . . or because he was wrong. "I've tried, Jill. When you hurt someone badly enough that they throw you out of their lives, it might be best to just leave it. Maybe that's the only gift I can really give Gwennie these days." Gwen was married now. She had two kids of her own, a boy and a girl that would never know Max. Never look up at him and call him Grandpa. His heart broke a little more every time he thought of that, so he tried not to think of it too often. Only with every sunset. Every moonrise. Every morning, noon, and night.

But everyone had regrets. His just went deeper than most, and that was one hundred percent his fault. "I think it's best to let her live in peace. It's not like she couldn't find me if she wanted to." He flicked a glance at Jill's laptop on the nearby desk as he stood up. "There's no such thing as being invisible these days."

"That's for sure." She stood, too. "Thanks for having supper with me."

"Thanks for the invite. Eating alone gets old, doesn't it?"

"Yes. Which is why it's good to have friends."

"There you go." He bumped his shoulder to hers before he walked out the door. "See you tomorrow."

"I'll make the coffee extra hot."

Now that her shop was open, he made it a point to stop in daily and grab a coffee. Sometimes a bag of doughnuts or rolls from the Amish bakery counter established in the front corner. The yeasty smell of fresh bread was already drawing people in, even before the weather turned nice. "And I'll grab a couple of hot cross buns."

She rolled her eyes and laughed.

She didn't like hot cross buns, but she'd contracted with the Amish community to run the bread bakery and supply quilts for sale. If folks weren't sucked in to Jill's eclectic Americana, they'd be drawn to the Amish side of the store, just because it was Amish and people were attracted to the simplicity of their basic life.

"I'll slice up a loaf of white bread and make toast," she told him. "With fresh butter. You keep those buns and their nasty raisins to yourself."

He walked to the truck, grinning.

She made him smile. She made him happy. He was pretty sure he had the same effect on her, but they'd declared their lines in the sand long ago and, for now, it was all right. Kind of. Except when it wasn't.

He drove home, let himself in, and whistled for Gracie. The trusty black Lab trotted his way, dashed out for a quick turn around the wet yard, then came back inside.

He had a home that was paid for. Money in the bank. Properties, friends, and a dog that loved him. There wasn't anything more that he needed, except maybe, just once more, to kiss his beautiful daughter good night. He'd trade everything he had, everything he'd done, all that he'd accomplished once he got clean, to have that one last chance.

It wasn't about to happen. He knew that.

But every day, at least once, he thought about it. And when he did, he offered it up to the good Lord above, because God had gone the distance for him many times. Max figured a little pain and suffering on his part paled in comparison.

But he'd still grab the chance if he got it.

CHAPTER FIVE

ICU. Peritonitis. High fever. IV antibiotics.

Shannon Carter might be out of surgery, but at seven o'clock the next morning, the child's grip on life was precarious. Thea had a long, wet drive back to the office, and the little girl had yet to awaken. Have to leave hospital, Shannon still sleeping, fighting infection. Will stop by house for clean clothes.

She sent the text to her friend Jazz, but it was Kelsey who texted her back. Jazz is feeding Hayley. I'll meet you at office w/clothes on my way to school. Maggie will go to Rochester and sit w/Shannon.

Thea blinked back tears.

She never cried. Well, mostly never, except during sappy Christmas movies depicting a life she'd never had even before her mother sold her to a human trafficker. But real circumstances rarely made her emotional, and if she ever had five minutes of her own, she might consider why that was the case.

Right now, tears threatened. Lack of sleep, the child's squalor or current condition . . . she wasn't sure. Maybe a combination of the three.

But as she waited for her coffee in the Starbucks drive-thru, she glanced back at the text.

It was Maggie's self-sacrifice that made her choke up.

Maggie and Jazz were watching three-month-old Hayley while Kelsey taught at the elementary school. They'd all been brought together at Christmas when a very pregnant Kelsey sailed off a snow-covered curve in a heavy storm. She'd been on her way to Pennsylvania, determined to give her precious baby up for adoption. A tie-up on I-81 had rerouted her over to the Rochester-area expressways and the turnoff for Wishing Bridge, her mother's old hometown.

She hadn't wanted to turn off there, but a lake-effect storm barreling in from Lake Erie had brought blizzard conditions to a wide swath of Western New York. The whiteouts left Kelsey no choice. And when a sudden dip in the snow-filled road sent her car plummeting into a farm field, Kelsey was trapped.

With the odds against him, Hale Jackson had found the car and Kelsey, now in labor, and had gotten her back to town in time for Avis Washington to deliver the baby. That's when Kelsey sent out the SOS to Thea and Jazz, calling in the pledge they'd made to one another a dozen years before. Three women who'd helped each other as troubled foster-care teens in Philadelphia had rejoined forces at thirty.

You're not thirty yet. You're barely twenty-nine and a half, Thea's inner voice scolded.

Almost thirty, she corrected herself as she headed back to the hills of Wyoming County. Maggie and Jeb Tompkins had taken Kelsey in while she recovered, then opened their home and their hearts to Jazz and Thea when they needed a place to stay. They were kind, good people, the sort you'd see on TV but rarely encountered in real life. Which meant that Thea either had become jaded working in the big city or traveled in the wrong circles.

Possibly both.

She pulled into the parking lot of the somewhat bleak strip mall housing Hillside Medical and parked along the edge to give patients easier access. She climbed out of her car and hurried up the leaking covered walkway, keys in hand. With a quick thrust, she tried to over-look her wet feet and pushed open the office door.

Gushing water met her head on.

The deluge soaked her from the knees down, and there was plenty more where that came from.

The Wishing Bridge fire whistle sounded just then, and she turned as a car pulled up.

It was Ethan, about to be really surprised and none too happy, understandably. He'd pulled out his phone as he parked, then looked her way, wide-eyed.

Kelsey pulled in behind him, and as Ethan headed toward Thea, the first fire truck came roaring up the street and turned into the crumbling parking lot.

He held up his phone. "Jean at the hairdresser's said we're flooded?"

Thea pointed to the stream of dirty, mucky water trailing out the door.

He stared at the dank, dark flow. "Creek water."

"So it appears."

He peered at the water, then her, then the water again, disbelieving.

This wasn't his problem. Like her, he was here on short-term assignment. The bleak office had been owned by an elderly doctor who'd passed away midwinter, leaving an unsold practice in Ethan's hands.

She'd only been in town because of Kelsey, and she'd offered to help because her job had folded.

And now—

"Oh, man, Ethan." Bud Almeter, the Wishing Bridge fire chief, joined them as more cars pulled into the patched-up lot. "I'm real sorry about this. Oakfield Creek hasn't flooded in years. I expect there's a logjam or some kind of blockage below because that overnight rain shouldn't have caused this kind of trouble." The firefighters hurried forward from various trucks, setting up hoses to pump the water out of the tired-looking offices and faded stores.

"What do we do?" Thea kept her voice soft and deferred to Ethan.

"I don't know. Can we retrieve records and schedules from inside?" he asked Bud.

"Once we pump it out, sure. Can't have you in there with electricity still on and standing water. And this might be the final straw for this old mall, Ethan. The landlord will probably declare it a total loss and take the payment. That's what smart money would say."

Thea didn't think Ethan could look more surprised. She was wrong. "Not fix it?"

The fire chief frowned. "Not much point. Decreased value over the years yet a solid piece of real estate if the building's gone. Especially if a giant firm like Amazon or Walmart decides to build a distribution center close to I-90 like the rumors say. I could be wrong, of course," he added as Sheila, the front-desk manager, parked her car off to the side of the lot.

"We have to figure out what to do for the next few months," Thea said.

"And what Becky Wolinski wants to do," Ethan replied. Becky was the former-practice-owner's widow. "No one has stepped forward to buy the practice."

That wasn't exactly a big surprise to Thea. The worn-out building and aged equipment all needed updating. But the growing patient list was a solid base for someone who liked rural medicine.

Motors roared into action from multiple sides of the old strip mall. Water gushed forth, directed away from the building, but the creek was still rising, which meant the flooding would only increase before it stopped.

"I've got two crews from other fire departments walking the creek to determine what's gone wrong. The sooner we can get it cleared out, the faster we can fix this problem."

But not fast enough to help patients today or maybe ever again.

Kelsey joined them. She'd popped open an umbrella as a steady drizzle made a bad situation worse. "Guys." She hugged Thea and faced Ethan. "I'm so sorry about this. What a mess, and at the worst possible time, when you're both trying to square things for the future. How can I help?"

~

How could she help?

A part of Ethan wanted to thank her for her concern because it was clearly genuine, but the cynical side of him longed to point out that there was nothing to do. A rural town filled with needy people, a shambles neglected by its absentee landlord, and a population with decreasing economic status because the lack of local jobs had forced young people elsewhere.

He could walk away.

He'd contracted for a year, but acts of God nullified the contract, and Dr. Paul Wolinski's death had accomplished that two months ago. He'd stayed on because that's what good men do. They don't ignore the needs or plight of those around them. They follow through on promises.

He'd also stayed because of the kids. Uprooting his niece and nephew from their lives because of grown-up changes seemed wrong. Mara was troubled enough with the loss of her parents, and little Keegan was doing so well that changing their routine seemed counterproductive. And he'd had nowhere to go, in any case. But now . . .

As water poured from multiple hoses, Ethan second-guessed what he'd thought was a good decision.

A van pulled up. Four ladies stepped out, erected a back-end tent assembly, and arranged a coffee pot, sugar, and creamers on a flip-down table. The Wishing Bridge Fire Department Ladies Auxiliary, always on the job, always looking out for others.

"Ethan, can I get you some coffee?" asked Shirley Corder. Shirley was part of the Ladies Auxiliary and also one of their patients. It used to bother him that folks called him by his first name, but it seemed stuffy to request a change, even though they'd addressed his aged boss as Dr. Wolinski.

He started to shake his head, but Thea stepped in. "Shirley, that would be lovely, for both of us. Thank you."

A gust of wind tugged Kelsey's umbrella up and away, spraying them with icy cold water. He'd thought he couldn't get colder.

Wrong.

So when he wrapped his hands around the to-go cup filled with fresh coffee, welcome warmth seeped through his palms.

"You two don't have to stand out here in the rain and the cold." Bud Almeter reapproached them. "This is gonna take a while, and no sense getting soaked. If we can retrieve your schedule from inside, maybe the gals can call folks. Explain what's happened. And we'll notify the news stations that the plaza's been shut down."

Thea raised her phone. "I keep a schedule in my Google calendar," she explained. "We can retrieve most data for today from there. But what do we tell people?" she wondered as Sheila hurried their way. "What are their options?"

"I don't know," said Ethan, but it was his job to know. Except none of this had been in his original plans. He'd accepted the simple one-year assignment to give the kids time in a quieter environment to adjust to their loss and their new situation. No ties. No harm. No foul.

That had all turned upside down.

A white extended-cab pickup turned into the lot and pulled up beside them. The window rolled down and Max Reichert motioned them to get in.

Ethan held the back door for Thea, then climbed in the opposite side while Sheila took the passenger seat up front. Ethan was about to thank Max for the thoughtfulness when Max put the truck into gear and drove back toward the village. "Max, where are you going? We've got things to do. Patients to contact. We—"

"I hear you, Doc, and I figured a little warmth and a chance to revisit that idea I had at New Year's might sound better today. Considering."

"I'd be okay with warm and dry while I use Thea's calendar to contact people," Sheila agreed. "Lord have mercy, we need spring in the worst way right about now. Not *this* kind of spring," she stressed, gazing out at the drizzle. "The nice kind with yellow daffodils and orange tulips. And leaves. I'd give anything for a touch of green. I am that sick of grays and browns."

"We're all ready for that, Sheila." Max pointed up. "From your lips to God's ears." He turned left onto Maplewood Avenue. Old homes lined the short neighborhood street, fronted by thick-trunked deciduous trees.

Max had suggested a great proposal during the holidays, an idea Ethan would have grabbed if he were staying. He wasn't, so when Max had approached him about relocating the practice out of the run-down strip mall, he'd tabled the notion. Not his practice, not his choice to make. When Max pulled into a small parking lot adjacent to a wide pink-and-cream Queen Anne colonial, Thea hummed softly. "Stellar house."

"There are some timeless places in this village," Max told her as he shut the car off. "A real nod to yesterday with an eye on tomorrow. Come on in and see what you think."

Ethan didn't dare say what he thought. It might be construed as rude, mostly because he was worn down by circumstances beyond his control. The flood was just the latest of many. "Max."

Max turned his way and hooked a thumb, but his expression was understanding. "Ethan. Give it a look. No push. It's warm and dry, and that's saying something right now. And the Wi-Fi is turned on, so Thea can pull up her Google list for Sheila without using data."

Max cared. He cared about people and their pocketbooks, and that made him a solid friend in the hard-pressed small town.

Ethan studied the outside layout as he moved forward. A ramp began at the parking lot's edge and angled up to the back corner of the wraparound porch, offering full accessibility. From the front, a long sidewalk ended at broad concrete steps that led to the front door. The steps were flanked by stone supports, while turned spindles lined the porch edges. The spindles needed some paint, and so did a few upper reaches of the three-story building, but nothing major. Max reached ahead, unlocked the door, then stepped back to let them in.

"This is charming." Thea stopped on the textured entry rug covering the foyer and looked around. "Beyond charming, Max. You did all this?"

A wide room opened to their left. To their right stood a long, solid-oak table, old-fashioned and perfect for the setting. It had been adapted with electrical outlets for technology access. Short, old-style filing cabinets fit beneath either end, making the table more desk-like. Matching rolling chairs were positioned a few feet apart. Behind the table, built-in bookcases below leaded-glass windows framed the workstation. To the right of the bookcases were comfortable chairs mixed with hard-bottomed chairs to allow for patient preference and mobility.

"I've got two exam rooms done, working on a third," Max explained. "The professional offices are rudimentary right now. But that's an easy fix over the next couple of weeks."

"You did this even though I brushed you off?" Ethan faced Max directly, and Max answered swiftly.

"Had to. If you're leaving and Thea's leaving, this town needs some kind of medical practice, and no smart practitioner would be interested in signing a deal in that strip mall. Even before the flood," he added. "I've got two ready-to-rent apartments upstairs. That monthly income will be solid, so the rent for the office space is negligible the first twenty-four months."

Max had done this before. He'd fixed up several village buildings with a dual purpose to keep business rents low. He'd helped a lot of small businesses gain solid footing in the struggling town. And he didn't do it for thanks or lust for money. He did it to help, and that made him pretty rare in Ethan's experience.

"The attic is a really solid double, and the second floor is a three bedroom with a crazy amount of room. Come see the exam rooms."

They followed Max down the hall. Freshly oiled gumwood trim framed open walnut doors. The faint smell of fresh paint wafted through the opening. Inside each room, a glass-fronted old-style cabinet was mounted on the wall, out of the reach of children. Wooden cabinets lined the lower wall, and a cleverly designed nook let the medical practitioner face the patient while making computer notes. "The exam tables can be here in three days."

"Or we move the ones from the old practice. If they're not ruined," Thea suggested.

Max waited.

Thea did the same. Even Sheila, normally full of opinions, kept quiet, but Ethan read their emotions. They'd think him foolish to wait, and he couldn't disagree. "Your timing couldn't be better, Max."

"God's timing," Max countered in an easy tone. "I put in the work knowing eventually it would get used. Sooner rather than later works for me. Do you guys want to bring over the old examination tables?"

"Boss, I'll donate a day's pay toward new tables," offered Sheila. "It would be a shame to bring those old things into all this prettiness, wouldn't it?"

"I talked to Becky on my way over," said Max. "She said she'll use some of the insurance money to fund the necessities and roll it over into the selling price of the practice when someone buys it. It makes sense," he added. "She'll benefit from the sale in the long run." He handed Ethan a catalog. "Lots of choices online."

The decision had been made, it seemed. New offices, clean and fresh, and new equipment. An old house, repurposed.

"The kitchen's set up like a staff room. Coffeemaker, table, fridge. Nothing major's been done there. I kind of liked it as is, although I'll be redoing the ceiling in a week or two."

Sheila faced Thea. "If you pull up the calendar on your phone, I'll call patients from mine. How quick can we reschedule?"

"Tomorrow," Thea told her.

Ethan swung around, surprised, but caught himself because she was correct. They could start seeing patients first thing in the morning because Max had taken the initiative a few months before.

"We could bring the old exam tables over for a few days to tide us over," she went on. "We can get rid of them when the new ones arrive, but there's no sense holding people off longer than necessary. They need medical care, and we need to generate income to cover costs."

"I love a practical woman." Max grinned at her. "My mother was like that, straight to the point."

"And you didn't find it annoying?" wondered Ethan, not masking the wry note in his voice.

"Only when I was wrong," said Max, cheerfully. "Which was fairly often. I'll see to having the tables washed up and moved over. And I'll get the landline phones connected ASAP."

"Sheila, can you see if Laura and Faye can meet at the old practice around one o'clock?" Ethan asked. "We can pull things we need and bring them over."

"I've got the cap on the truck, so I can help with that," said Max. "Makes the rain a nonissue."

Thea's phone buzzed just then. She pulled it out, worried, then the frown line between her eyes eased. "Maggie says Shannon Carter is doing better but to keep the prayers coming. The surgeon said it was one of the worst cases of peritonitis she's ever seen in a child."

"I don't recognize the name," Ethan told her. "How old is she?"

"Mara's age."

The thought of a small child that sick gripped his gut. "Who called it in?"

"The call came from an anonymous concerned party, right, Sheila?"

"Exactly in those words," confirmed Sheila. "She wouldn't identify herself and told me not to trace the call. Obviously she hadn't seen our antiquated phone system at the practice. Or maybe she thought we had an 'in' with the FBI." She wrinkled her forehead at the unlikelihood of that. "In any case, she didn't sound old, but she did sound worried. Thea was already on her way out to drop off Mr. Thornton's meds, so she said she'd check it out."

"Who will be taking care of this child?" Ethan asked.

"No one now," Thea answered as she texted a reply to Maggie. "Great-grandma is in the regional hospital and will probably go straight to a nursing home or memory care unit, and the house is unlivable."

"I had no idea things had gotten that bad up there." Regret laced Sheila's tone. "I'm so sorry about that."

"And I hate it when kids fall through the cracks," Thea told her. "This means we've got a sick child with nowhere to go. I couldn't stay until she woke up, but Jeb took Maggie into Rochester so she could sit by her. I couldn't have her waking up in a strange place, all alone."

"You spent the night at the hospital?" Ethan asked. "And then came straight here?"

"Couldn't leave her," Thea repeated. "That's why Kelsey dropped off clothes this morning."

"Not too many people would do that." *Would I?* Ethan wondered. He was ashamed to say probably not.

"Sometimes you can't just walk away." She spoke softly and didn't look up at him at first. When she did, worry had deepened the tiny line between her brows.

He wanted to smooth it away.

The reaction surprised him. The fact that he liked the thought of it surprised him even more.

Thea moved to the kitchen, pushed open the door, and looked absolutely delighted. "Max calls this rudimentary, but I'm going straight to vintage perfection. Total retro, a step back in time." Then she exchanged an appreciative look with Sheila and sighed.

Her look of longing grabbed Ethan, just enough to make him wonder what had caused the wistfulness, because Thea the NP didn't sigh. Was it the child's situation or the quaint kitchen that had inspired her reactions? Either way, his partner had a softer, gentler side that she'd kept hidden for months. He appreciated the work-first ethic she brought to Hillside Medical. She got things done and wasted no time doing it.

But he *liked* this side of her.

"It would be a shame to modernize things too much, for sure." Max followed them into the kitchen and powered up the one-cup coffeemaker. "The water will take a couple of minutes to heat up, but then it's good to go. There's creamers in the fridge. I kept stuff on hand because I like coffee when I work."

"Coffee works for me, too." Max had stopped by with coffee for him now and then. They had a coffee pot at the old site, but once in a while Max would stop in with coffees for the crew, fresh and hot from a local doughnut shop. Just because.

"I know, Ethan."

"You're a good friend, Max." Ethan turned to face him. "Hope you realize that."

Max shrugged off the compliment. "If folks look out for each other, there's a lot less trouble in the world."

"Simple truth."

"The best kind. Give me your keys to the office and the car. Since I've kidnapped you without recourse to transportation, we'll bring your cars over in case you get an emergency call out. But Thea"—Max turned toward her—"if you get another call into the hills and the deputies are busy, I'm available as needed. If there's no one who can ride along, call me. I'll make the time."

"Thank you, Max."

He raised a hand as he headed out. "We'll have what's needed over here by nightfall. This is one of those times when I'm glad daylight savings kicks in early. Now if the rain would stop, that would make things easier all around."

"So." Ethan fixed his coffee and pulled up a chair. He indicated the medical catalog. "How do we go about ordering new stuff when we might have usable stuff coming over from the old office?"

"A wish list," Thea told him.

"Just like Santa," he said.

Her expression disagreed. "Yeah. Like that."

"You didn't make lists for Santa, Thea?" Too late, he remembered that she, Kelsey, and their friend Jazz Monroe had formed their friendship in a group foster home for wayward teens.

"Not even once, but I understand the concept," she replied smoothly. "Let's start here." She handed him the book and pulled up the website on his phone. In thirty minutes they'd created a list of things needed to outfit the exam rooms and the front desk.

"What about an updated computer system?" he asked.

"Rather than the nineties-era monster desktop the girls have been using?"

"How expensive would it be? I don't want to take advantage of Becky. Can we limp by with the old one for a while?"

"I doubt it will survive the trip, boss." Sheila came through the swinging door and moved toward the coffeemaker. "It gets mad if we lift it to dust underneath."

"How about if you and I split the cost?" Thea asked, but Sheila shook her head.

"There's flood insurance," she told them. "And while Dr. Wolinski wasn't great about updating the building or equipment, he kept insurance in place. We've got the policies in the files, and Becky has copies at home, too. We won't get insurance on the building because it was landlord owned, but unless Becky changed something recently, the practice and the contents are insured."

"That's good to know." Thea bumped knuckles with Sheila. "Then we should get an IT rep in here to hook us up right away. In the meantime, my laptop will suffice."

"I'll double-check with Becky," added Ethan. "How are the phone calls coming, Sheila?"

"Half done. They'll go quicker now that I have this." She raised her to-go cup. "I do better caffeinated."

"Don't we all?" Ethan stood. "You should head home and get some sleep," he told Thea. "You look worn out. Don't worry. We've got this."

CHAPTER SIX

Tiny hairs bristled along the back of Thea's neck.

She *felt* worn out, but hearing him say she looked that way made her want to tap into hidden energy reserves. Or punch him.

Calm down. He said you look tired because you are *tired. No offense intended. Get over yourself.* "I will once we have today straightened out. Then I'll check on Shannon."

Ethan had moved toward the coffee brewer for a refill but quickly turned back toward her. "You can't drive back to the city on no sleep."

Was he actually worried about her? Or just his normal cranky self? "I'll catch a nap before I go. Maggie said she'd stay at the hospital until someone could relieve her, and Jazz is watching Hayley for Kelsey."

"I can ride along."

"No need." She moved toward the front room. "Once I've had a nap I'll be fine."

"I'm not questioning that." He followed her into the spacious foyer. "I think it would be smart to check on the patient with you since we have unexpected time today. I want to get an update on the status of Mrs. Willoughby, too, and we have two other patients at Strong Memorial. I can handle that while you keep an eye on the little girl. Mara and Keegan are set until five o'clock, so I've got the afternoon free. You go rest and I'll pick you up at noon."

"It's a good idea, Thea." Sheila handed Thea her cell phone and spoke frankly. "It's only a couple of blocks to Maggie's place, and we can have the guys drop your car off there. There's nothing to do here until we've got this set up, which means an unexpected day off."

She sounded lighthearted, but Thea knew the truth of the matter. Days off without pay were unwelcome. "Let's consider this a paid staff-development day instead. And well deserved," she added when Sheila smiled her thanks.

"Has the rain stopped?" Ethan asked.

Thea shook her head.

"Take this." Ethan handed her his hooded jacket from the rack on the wall. "No umbrella, but the hood will keep you from getting soaked."

A gallant gesture of simple kindness. "What will you wear?"

"I won't be walking," he reminded her. "And the rain's supposed to let up by late morning. I'll come by in a few hours. All right?"

She tried to stifle a yawn and failed. "Yes."

He held the door for her, and when she tugged the hood of the jacket into place before starting down the broad steps, it smelled of Ethan. His hair. His aftershave. Maybe even a little of the ever-present coffee he carried with him from room to room when not seeing patients.

The added warmth helped. It didn't keep her face from being pelted by the wind-driven drops, but at least she arrived at Maggie and Jeb's house on Wyoming Hill Road without being completely soaked.

"Oh, honey, what's happened to you?" Jazz rushed to Thea's side when she came up the back steps into the Tompkins kitchen. "You're drenched!"

"Only a little. The boss gave me his coat, and when I'm not so dog-tired, I'll be even more grateful. The office is flooded, Max Reichert has a new place ready for us, and I'm wiped out. Wake me at eleven thirty, okay?"

"Do I have to?"

Jazz's sweet, deep voice made her feel at home. Through the thicks and thins of being errant, unwanted teens, she, Jazz, and Kelsey had stuck together, buoying each other through rough times. They'd not only survived, they'd thrived in their own ways, and here they were, suddenly back together. She hugged Jazz and nodded, then climbed the stairs to the bedroom they shared. "Yes. I have to go check on Shannon."

"In that case, I will. Expect coffee waiting."

Thea smiled her thanks, and when Jazz shook her awake a full hour later than expected, she almost sprang out of bed. "Jazz. I'm late. I'm—"

"You're not late, you're fine. Ethan called and said he'd be here at one instead of twelve to give you an extra hour of sleep. Coffee's made, you've got time to shower. Barely."

It was 1:05 p.m. by the time Thea was ready, but she'd taken that five extra minutes to add a light touch of makeup.

Jazz noticed instantly. Her lips formed a small O when she arched her brows. Then she smiled, as if punctuating the reaction.

Thea ignored her. There was nothing wrong with wanting to look decent, was there? Her eyes were too tired to wrestle with contact lenses, so she propped her glasses on her head to use as needed. And so they wouldn't cover up the eye shadow and mascara, which meant she was most likely being ridiculous. Still—the reflection in the upstairs mirror looked brighter and younger when she was done.

"You look better, rested," Ethan said as Thea came downstairs. He had his now-dry jacket on his arm and a cup of coffee in hand. "Jazz made your coffee, and we're good to go. Jeb's picking up Maggie. You okay with me driving?"

"Except that you need to get home to the kids and I might want to stay."

He frowned. "Or you could trust the medical professionals at the children's hospital to keep an eye on her overnight."

She should.

She knew that. But the idea of Shannie being there with no family to care for her pushed a lot of old buttons. No kid should have to face that kind of thing alone.

"It's not like she even knows you," added Ethan.

"Or anyone there," Thea answered softly. She took the coffee and moved toward the back stairs leading to the driveway. "But being left totally alone isn't an option."

"I can drive in later," offered Jazz. "A children's hospital can't be all that bad, can it?"

Her generosity made Thea pause. Jazz had developed a fear of hospitals and death when she lost first her mother then her grandmother to terminal illnesses. She'd shied away from hospitals and sickness ever since. "You don't have to do that. Let's see how it goes, okay? I'll call you. But thank you. Shannon's release will require a full-blown plan to transition her to a new life. In the city, we know what that means. I'm not sure what it means in a rural area like this."

"We'll figure it out," Ethan said.

The baby fussed over the nursery monitor, and Jazz stepped back. "That's my cue to exit stage right."

"See you later." Thea preceded Ethan down the steps and to the car. He surprised her by following her to her side, then reaching out and opening the door.

She paused. Looked back.

Big mistake.

Her eyes met his, and he was close. Very close. It wasn't as if she meant to lock gazes with those deep blue eyes of his, but it happened, and neither one of them seemed to want to break the connection.

But she had to because what kind of fool added falling for the boss to a temp position destined to end in three months? Not her.

She blinked to separate her gaze and got into the car.

"Don't use those tissues for your glasses." Ethan motioned toward the box on the console between them when he got behind the wheel.

"Lotion treated. Keegan catches some kind of cold every three weeks so I stay well stocked."

"Not Mara?"

"No." He frowned as he shifted the car into gear. "Should that concern me? That whatever he's getting isn't contagious?"

"All depends," she told him. "He might have more sensitive sinuses, or he might just be more susceptible to recurring colds. It was a long, dank winter that never got super cold."

"You think that old idea holds true?" He gave her a skeptical look as he made a right onto Main Street. "About mild winters promoting germs?"

"I can't prove it, but it's sure seemed that way the past few years. We had a crushingly cold winter three years back. I'd just gotten my NP and the practice I worked for was unusually quiet. The old doctor said that freezing-cold winters staved off illness either because the germs died or people stayed home. He also said he didn't care which came first, the chicken or the egg, in this case. He was just glad they lost fewer elderly patients that year."

"Does it worry you to think about what we know versus what we don't?"

An insider question only shared between medical professionals because the comparison would scare most normal folks. "I try not to dwell on it and thank God that the human form is amazingly resilient. I treat symptoms as needed, intervene as required, and let the body do the rest."

"That's part of why I felt the tug to research," he told her as he headed for the expressway. "Taking things to the mitochondrial level feels like I'm doing something. Like I'm in charge. Sometimes straight medicine makes me feel like my hands are tied."

"Like God's in charge?"

"Well. Like something's in charge." He lifted his right shoulder. "I've never done the church thing or the God thing. I'm trying to now,

49

because of the kids. When I can, that is. My sister wanted it like that, and there's no way I'd shrug off her request. The rest of us just maneuvered through life as it came along."

The God thing?

Thea bit her tongue to keep at least a little bit quiet, but that only worked for about five seconds. "That God thing, as you put it, saved my life at least twice that I know of. People who used their faith to bring me to safety. To help me physically and emotionally after some fairly horrific circumstances I went through as a kid, including a gang member who got himself killed because he saved my life. God's not a *thing* to me, Ethan. He's like *the* thing. The strength. The rock. The fortress."

He frowned. "Sorry. I didn't mean to offend."

She raised her cup in a mock salute. "Congrats. The responsorial defense time of that statement might have been at record speed. I'm not criticizing you. I'm telling you that my experience has been very different. So much so that it got to the point where I couldn't imagine not believing in God. I wonder if it's like this for most people," she mused. "If you have no experience with God, maybe it's easy to shelve him? To dismiss faith?"

Ethan whistled lightly. "I should have gotten you at noon, Thea. That extra hour of sleep might have reenergized you a little too much, and you're already operating on fully charged lithium batteries every single day."

She liked getting things done. She liked moving quickly. She'd never been a downtime type of person and didn't care to start now. "The days are jam packed. And I do appreciate the extra hour of sleep, Ethan. Thank you for that."

"My pleasure." He glanced her way and smiled.

She smiled back, and there it was once more, the feeling that they were somehow connected or maybe meant to be connected.

Ridiculous, right? Only it didn't feel ridiculous. It felt surprisingly nice.

Since flirting and romance wasn't on either of their agendas, she would disregard that flash of something indefinably sweet and utterly unreachable, although the guy did make a great sparring partner.

"How's your coffee?"

"Perfect. Do you think we'll ever see leaves again?" She studied the tall, gray deciduous trees lining both sides of the expressway. "I miss green."

"The buds will pop with the first warm front. Spring's coming. Real spring, not the calendar version that doesn't take two massive, cold lakes into consideration," he added. "Between Erie and Ontario, this area clings to cold. And the end of our tenure here follows that. Have you sent out applications?"

She hadn't and she wasn't sure why because normally she was fifteen steps ahead of the game. "Not yet."

His right eyebrow rose slightly. "You thinking of staying, Thea?"

She wasn't thinking anything of the kind. "No. I'm not small-town savvy. I've always loved big, busy practices in vital hospitals, preferably connected to a university. That environment challenges me to be on top of my game twenty-four-seven. But there is a part of me that's fallen in love with this town. With the people I've met. I won't like leaving, that's for sure."

"Mara hates it here."

Thea was about to sip her coffee. She didn't. She set it down and listened.

"I know she's still reeling from losing her parents, and I realize now that the total change of setting might not have been the best choice, but I was between a rock and a hard place," Ethan continued. "I'd just been awarded a spot on a genetic-research team in Chicago based on my findings at an independent facility downstate."

"But you're a family practitioner." This wasn't adding up. "Family practice and genetic research?"

"My little brother died of the progressive cardiac problems caused by Pompe disease. He was the greatest kid and his entire life was marked by pain and discomfort and the inability to do anything we'd call normal. It made me sad for him." He paused as he changed lanes to avoid a new construction setup. "And guilty to be born healthy."

Pompe was a rare disorder of metabolism. "Oh, Ethan." She put a sympathetic hand on his arm. "A disease like that is hard on everyone, but especially the patient. I'm so sorry."

"I want to make a difference," he told her as he cruised east on I-90. "They've come a long way with medications, but like so many 'orphan' drugs, treatment cost has been prohibitively high. On a positive note, they've added Pompe to newborn screening, so now we can interrupt organ damage with treatment. That's a huge step for afflicted children and their families because diseases with no hope can really mess things up." His expression indicated he understood that firsthand, but when he didn't elaborate, Thea simply went on listening. "I was single and burning both ends of the candle to make my mark. I've always believed that research shouldn't be done in a vacuum when it affects not only one life but an entire family. And genetic flaws that result in inborn errors of metabolism affect a community because they're required to provide services. I got offered the research fellowship, accepted it, and resigned from the practice downstate, ready to bury myself in some pretty exciting things the Chicago team was working on. Things that could be game changers for some of those disorders."

"That's some heavy stuff, Ethan."

He grimaced slightly. "Then Alexis and Peter died and I inherited the kids. I couldn't uproot them and thrust them into life in Chicago when I would be expected to work night and day to launch my new career. I figured a year of small-town practice would buy me some time, the university granted me a leave, and here we are. But Mara's no better. Worse, maybe." He paused. Sighed. "And I have no idea what to do about it."

"Are you venting? Or asking for advice? And just so you know," she added, "your reply adjusts my answer accordingly."

"Both."

"Hmm." Thea stared forward, thinking. Too much honesty, fed too fast, could be as bad as an uncontrolled IV. "How's Mara's therapy going?"

"It's not."

Oops. She waited, letting him fill in the blanks.

"She refused to go, and I gave up the fight." When Thea stayed quiet, he grimaced. "I know, I should have made her go, I should have taken her kicking and screaming, but then the little guy would get all upset and I felt like a jerk, making his life miserable because he wants to protect her. And isn't that a weird turn of events?"

"It's survival," she told him. "We do what we deem necessary to endure, and it's different from personality to personality. Keegan's a giver. He longs for approval and wants to make people happy. Mara wants people to make *her* happy. She's more self-centered, so when everything was swept out from under her, she got totally ticked off. She can't fix it because it can't be fixed. Her parents are gone and she's stuck and she's crazy angry. And depressed."

"You think it's that bad?" He frowned as he eased the car toward the hospital exit. "Really?"

"Yes."

The look on his face bothered her. So sad. So troubled. His jaw went slack, but then he firmed it. "Well, we'll be gone soon. I can find a therapist in Chicago."

"Sure, as long as she doesn't do something foolish or dangerous in the next three months."

He glared forward, then at her. "She's seven, Thea."

"I could cite you cases of angry kids and what they've done, ranging from arson to physical abuse of siblings to self-harming behaviors. But I won't because I don't think you really want to hear what I have to say."

"Do you want to talk to her?"

Thea held her hands up, palms out, and shook her head. "No, sir, I don't. I made sure I took extra rotations in psychological health because I believe the body works as a unit, mental, emotional, and physical, but that taught me a valuable lesson. Treat what you can and call in the experts for what you can't. Would you allow someone who wasn't a surgeon to operate on her?"

"Don't be silly."

"Then stick with the professionals in this case, too. I'm not saying it will be easy. Mara's mad at the world and she wants you to know it. She wants me to know it. She wants everyone to know it because she's totally frustrated. But she's not calling the shots, Ethan. You are. Even the crazy difficult ones. You're in a game of tag with one player, and that makes you 'it' all the time. Not an easy job, but someone has to do it and your sister picked you. And that doesn't leave you a whole lot of choice, does it?"

"No." He flipped on the signal to turn down Mount Hope Avenue and frowned. "But then life doesn't always offer up the choices we want, and rarely do they come gift wrapped. We'll get by. One way or another." He hesitated, looking grim and somewhat unassured. "We'll get by."

He made the turn and switched the topic of conversation at the same time. "You were wondering about foster-care placements in our area."

"An effective change of subject with no segue, but I'll follow along," she told him.

Ethan grunted, swung into the parking garage, and yanked a ticket from the machine. "I ran into this problem last fall, with a case of neglect. The county services are good, but there aren't a lot of approved placement homes when you're dealing with reduced populations. And a kid coming out of surgery will need special care, so that minimizes the options further."

"What does all that mean?" Thea asked once he'd parked the car. She climbed out and slung her yellow purse over her shoulder.

"Placement in other counties. Whoever has an appropriate, if temporary, setting."

"So a different school?"

He fell into step beside her as they approached the doors leading into the children's hospital. "Possibly. Once she's healthy enough to return to school. And then she could be placed anywhere since there's no family to bind her to Wishing Bridge."

No one to care for her.

No one to love her.

No one to look at this sick child and make her feel like she was the center of their universe. Old thoughts tumbled in from a similar past.

She'd been in big-city practices for years. She'd witnessed grief and sadness and dysfunction from just far enough away that she could help without anything sticking to her. At the end of the day, she could crawl into bed and get a good night's sleep. But this one struck hard, as if urging her to do something. Anything.

They took the elevator up and headed down the left-hand corridor. A flurry of activity hurried their steps as they entered the child-friendly room.

"What's going on?" Ethan asked.

Thea assessed the scene. Labored breathing. Stiffened limbs. Fear marked Shannon's wan face as she struggled to breathe.

A thirtysomething physician's assistant looked up quickly. "Are you family?" he asked.

"Family doctor. Ethan Brandenburg. When did this present?"

"Just now," said another physician's assistant, a middle-aged woman whose nametag read "Elaina" in letters young children could easily identify. "She was doing well, then went down."

"Pulse is erratic. We need to call the surgeon," the first PA said.

"Have you done a chest film?" asked Thea. "I'm the NP at Hillside Medical. I sent her in from a home visit." It would be unusual for Shannie to develop an embolism, but if she'd been lying inert on that cold floor for a while, it moved up the list of possibilities.

"Pulmonary embolism is rare in children," replied the woman. "But we can't rule it out without a look. Call for the portable," she instructed a nurse. "ASAP."

Thea reached out to the little girl. "Hey, princess. Don't fret, okay? We'll get this fixed in no time."

Dread tightened the child's expression, but when Thea laid a hand against her forehead, when she smoothed the girl's lank hair back, out of her face, Shannie Carter reached up and touched Thea's hand.

A tear dribbled down the girl's cheek. Then another. She tried to talk, couldn't, and got scared all over again.

Thea bent low beside her. "You don't need to say a thing, sweet girl. You let us do our jobs, and we'll fix this. It feels bad because you can't breathe properly and that's scary, isn't it? But don't panic, okay? We'll get it taken care of. I promise. All right?"

Shannon didn't nod. She blinked her eyes once, as if in assent.

"Good girl. They're going to take an X-ray of your lungs, a picture so we can see what's going on inside. They'll shift you around to get a clear shot, and I'll be right here with you the whole time."

It didn't take long. Shannie was small, and the staff used great care to position her for the film. When they were done, Thea's supposition was confirmed.

"Two clots," Elaina told them. They began blood thinners right away, then a sedative to help Shannie sleep.

When she'd dozed off, the male PA stopped back into the room. He focused on Thea. "Forgot to introduce myself before and my nametag's gone missing. Dave Powell." He shook her hand, then Ethan's, before he brought his attention back to Thea. "You went straight to an embolism."

She nodded.

"Why? The rarity of that put it far down my list."

"Length of sickness, lying prone on a cold floor, inability to move for indeterminate length of time, grave peritonitis, followed by surgery and antibiotics."

"Solid call," he told her. "We'll keep her sedated overnight then see how things are progressing in the morning."

"Has the surgeon been advised?" Ethan asked, and the PA nodded.

"Yes. She'll stop in later to check her status."

Ethan redirected his attention to Thea. "Do you want to sit with her while I look in on the patients at the main hospital? I can text you when I'm done."

Thea laid a hand over Shannon's unkempt, snarled hair. "I do. Yes."

"I'll see to the others, then."

"All right. And Ethan?"

He paused and looked back.

"I'm glad you're here. Thanks for taking the time to come in with me."

"Well, it *is* my job." He swept the sick child a kind look. "But you were right, Thea. No child should have to go through stuff like this alone. See you later."

She smoothed a hand across Shannon's forehead again in a gentle gesture. "I'll be here."

~

Ethan crossed the walkway to the main hospital, thinking about Thea's gaze. Her touch. The deep compassion she felt for a strange child.

Was it her rough childhood that brought such empathy? Angelic behavior didn't get kids put into group homes, and Kelsey had been open about meeting Jazz and Thea at Hannah's Hope, the Philadelphia-area home for troubled teen girls. They'd formed lasting bonds of friendship there. Was that unusual?

He had no idea.

He'd googled it one night, just to see what Hannah's Hope was like, but it no longer existed and had left no real digital footprint.

He checked in on the patients, then called Sheila. "How's everything there? Have we made progress?"

"Significant," she told him, sounding happy. "We'll be ready to see the first patients tomorrow, I've rescheduled today's appointments, and I think folks will really love this place. How's Shannon doing?"

"Better now. Sheila, thanks for all you're doing," he continued. "And for all you do every day. You keep us on an even keel, and that makes things run smoothly. I know I don't thank you enough."

The line went quiet. Then she drew a breath. "Thank you. That means a lot to me. Probably more than you know. Oops, gotta go. Max just pulled up with the last load. See you in the morning."

He hung up and took the long route back to the elevators so he could stop by the coffee kiosk. Thea should be ready for a cup about now. He certainly was. And while he waited for the barista to make their drinks, he thought about Sheila's words.

When had he stopped appreciating a job well done? When he got his license to practice? Or was it because he'd spent the last few years working nonstop as if his plans and goals were of utmost importance? Because he used to be a nice guy. Thoughtful. Kind.

He rotated his arm to relieve a nagging ache just below the shoulder. He massaged it as he waited for the coffees, then checked the time on his phone.

Three o'clock. They'd have to leave soon for him to pick up the kids on time.

He texted Thea that he was on his way. Would she stay the night again? Would she come with him? Did she not trust the staff at the hospital?

He walked into Shannon's room. Thea spotted him, then leaned down and whispered something against the girl's cheek. Soft words, not meant for him.

She stood, gave the little girl a long, thoughtful look, then approached him. "She'll sleep the night and hopefully wake up feeling much better in the morning."

"She should, yes." He waited when she hesitated. "Are you worried because she'll wake up alone?"

"Yes, but Maggie will come back. She texted me."

"Not Jazz?" It still felt odd to call the supermodel by her first name when once he might have dreamed of being able to do that. In an alternate universe–type setting. "She made the offer earlier."

"Jazz has a big heart, but she doesn't do hospitals well, and I don't want to tip her into a funk."

"Does she tip easily?"

Thea considered the question before she answered. "I think all three of us do, depending on circumstances," she said honestly. "Kids with normal lives don't generally end up in group homes. I don't want her to do anything that upsets the balance. Jeb's family was friendly with Shannon's family a while back, so Maggie's happy to do it. Please tell me one of those coffees is for me."

"Mocha latte with whipped cream." He handed it over.

"You have no idea how happy this makes me." She raised the tall cup slightly. "I was in danger of dozing off back there."

"I would have woken you."

"Well, thank you. I think you've been hiding this gentle side beneath all the grumbling we've been hearing lately," she told him, but she wasn't scolding. She almost sounded concerned. "I wonder why we don't see that side of Ethan Brandenburg more often?"

"I've been wondering the same thing," he admitted.

"Is it having custody of the kids?" she asked as they veered toward the elevators. "I know you second-guess yourself a lot, but you don't have to be perfect to raise kids, Ethan. You just have to love them."

"Did anybody ever love you like that, Thea?" The minute he asked the question, he wished he hadn't. Her face darkened. Her jaw firmed.

Then she started walking again as if the topic wasn't important enough to discuss.

"You're good with Shannon. I see that," he went on. "And with Mara. Is that medical education or real-life experience that makes you a cut above when it comes to troubled kids?"

She faced him once they reached the elevators. "Both. And part of the reason I went deeper into psychology of families and children. There are so many needy kids out there, Ethan." The doors opened, and she pressed the button for the ground floor once they were inside. "They're everywhere. I was lucky enough to have a champion in my corner once I got to Hannah's Hope. And friends. But a lot of kids never have that chance."

"The chance to succeed?"

"The chance to be loved. Cherished. To have someone think they're special and smart and wonderful. Something every single kid should feel every day of their lives."

"Except you can't help them all."

They'd exited the elevators and walked toward the adjacent parking garage. "Then I'll be like the kid that threw beached starfish back into the sea, one by one. If you can't make a difference to everyone, make a difference to the ones you can. None of us emerge from dark beginnings unscathed, but if we take what we know and give back to others, then at least we've made things better. Not worse."

"Well, you've made things better at Hillside," he told her. "I don't know what I would have done without you, Thea. I probably would have exercised the act-of-God clause in my contract and walked away because I couldn't have handled this winter on my own. And I want you to know how much I appreciate that."

She turned as he reached for her car door. Close . . . so close. Close enough to count the gold and green flecks in her hazel eyes. Close enough for the fruity scent of her shampoo to remind him of summer days. Close enough to wonder what it would be like to get closer still.

"Thank you." She didn't flirt with him like some women would have at that moment. She gripped the handle and flicked a look across the garage and the major hospital beyond. "I never expected to like it here. You know?"

"Wishing Bridge?"

"Yes." She pretended to scowl, then sighed. "It gets under your skin, one person at a time, and it would be so easy to fall in love."

"It's a nice place. For people who like the small-town thing."

"Liking it ranked about dead last on my list, too." She climbed into the car, fastened her belt, then sipped her coffee while rain beat a relentless drum on the parking garage's metal roof. The taste made her smile. "And yet . . . I do. Maybe this is God's way of pointing me in a different direction."

He almost snorted. "Like all the stuff that happened with Kelsey and the baby and Hale and you and Jazz coming to town was meant to be?" The idea was ridiculous. Stuff happened when it happened, you dealt with it and moved on.

End of story.

"Exactly like that. Maggie's got a favorite saying. 'Wanna hear God laugh? Tell him your plans.'"

Simplistic nonsense, but he wouldn't say that to her because if there was one word that didn't apply to Thea, it was "simplistic."

So why did a woman of science buy into all that nonsense?

She laid her head back as he took the left lane toward the expressway. Clearly now was not the time to ask.

He stayed quiet. She was tired. He left the radio off and, within a few minutes, she dozed off. He let her sleep.

Kelsey had revealed her story over Christmas on national television, how her mother had abandoned her years before. A kind nation had showered her and baby Hayley with gifts, because who didn't love a great rescue story at Christmas?

And then there was Jazz. Supermodel. Internationally known. She had money, clout, and drop-dead gorgeous looks but showed all the earmarks of an eating disorder. Ethan had only seen a couple of teens like that downstate, but both cases had lodged firmly in his memory.

What about you, Thea? he wondered as he drove across the foothills of the Southern Tier. *What's your story? What drives your need to fix everything and everyone?*

It wasn't his business, but he wanted to know. Almost longed to know, and wasn't that an odd turn of events?

You're leaving.

She's leaving.

Move on.

He drove slowly, letting her rest. As he approached town, he reached over and touched her arm. "Thea. We're almost home."

The phrase felt wrong.

This wasn't home. A transient staff, a basement apartment, and a temporary placement.

"I fell asleep?"

"Almost an hour ago." He could tease her, but he didn't feel like teasing her. He felt more like caring for her. Protecting her. "I expect that mocha's gone cold."

"I'll heat it up and enjoy it inside." She yawned, stretched, and picked up the cup from the center console. "Thanks for letting me sleep."

"No problem. See you tomorrow."

"Good night."

He waited until she was inside, then drove to Jenny Harper's place to pick up Keegan and Mara. He pasted a smile on like he did every day. Keegan would come along without a problem. Mara liked to make problems where none existed. He walked into Jenny's kitchen.

"Hey. I'm here. Are there two extra kids around that want chicken nuggets for supper?"

"With French fries and dippin' sauce!" Keegan power-punched the air as he raced toward Ethan. "I would eat that every night if I could, Uncle Eefen!"

"We should be having vegetables." Mara was filling out a chart at the table. A food pyramid. She'd colored the pictures with precise strokes of sharpened colored pencils in a bright array of colors. The careful work didn't make her happy. Success at school didn't make her happy. If he could resurrect her parents, he'd do it in a heartbeat, but he couldn't, and short of that miracle, Ethan couldn't seem to find anything to break through the brick wall she'd erected.

"I hate veg-ables," announced Keegan as he thrust his arms into his jacket. "They're yucky."

"You like corn and carrots," Ethan reminded him as Jenny came into the room. "So not all vegetables are yucky."

"And salads." Mara didn't stand. She studied the chart with grave intensity. "We should be eating them, too. Raw veggies are better for us than cooked ones. Miss McCleary told us that today."

"We can buy raw produce," Ethan agreed. "As long as someone will eat it."

"Not me." Keegan knit his brow. "I like o-o-other stuff so much better."

"Mom wanted us to eat healthy." Mara stood up from the kitchen chair and nailed her little brother with a sharp look. "She wanted us to eat good stuff and grow big and strong and exercise all the time. Why doesn't anyone here do what Mom wanted? Why are you all so stupid?"

"Mara, you cannot call your uncle stupid in my house," Jenny Harper scolded as she handed Mara her jacket. "He's not stupid. He's trying to make the best of a rough situation. Most kids would be delighted to eat out as often as you do."

The fact that Jenny was right didn't bother Ethan. The fact that she sounded slightly disapproving did, because he was trying. It wasn't as if he had come into this knowing the rules. If there were rules, Mara's emotions threw them right out the window.

Her face shut down.

She crumpled her carefully drawn work into a wad and stuffed it into her book bag. Then she took her jacket without a thank you, moved to the door, and went outside to the car.

"I'm sorry, Ethan, I shouldn't have scolded her like that, but when she gets that hoity-toity attitude going, it irks me," Jenny confessed. "I know she's suffered, but so has he." She dipped her chin toward Keegan. "And he's coming along so nicely."

Ethan refused to compare the children openly. He couldn't see any good in that, and he understood childhood resentment quite well. Why feed it? "They're adjusting. It's not an easy path for either of them."

Jenny clamped her lips together. She was intentionally *not* disagreeing with him because they both knew Mara wasn't adjusting. She was barely existing.

The rain had stopped, but the dull, gray sky didn't offer a glimpse of spring. Instead it fit the mood like a perfectly placed theatrical backdrop. Except there wasn't anything perfect about any of this.

He swung by the drive-thru and ordered a kid's meal and two salads when what he really wanted was a fried chicken sandwich with lettuce, tomato, and mayo. Lots of mayo.

But he should set a good example, like his sister had. At least some of the time.

When they got home, they carried their food toward the stairway leading to the apartment.

Mara hesitated.

Ethan paused, too.

She glanced around, looking for options. When she found none, she sighed. Not an indignant, I-hate-your-guts kind of sigh, and he'd heard enough of those to catalog the variances.

This one was hopeless. Aching and empty. As if the few choices offered to a bright, witty child had been swept away, leaving nothing in return.

"I hate going down," she whispered. She stared at the steps leading to their basement apartment, then went down, through the door, but not because she wanted to. Because she had no choice.

Keegan dove into his supper. Ethan pretended to enjoy his salad. "This was a good idea, Mara. I'll make sure we have more fresh produce in the house from now on, okay? Vegetables and fruits."

She didn't pretend to care now.

She toyed with her salad. They'd used a spring mix instead of all-American iceberg. She took three bites and stopped.

"A little twiggy for you?" he asked.

She shrugged but looked guilty for pushing him into a salad purchase she didn't like. When she thought he wasn't looking, she swept Keegan's remaining nuggets a longing glance.

Ethan opened a door of quiet opportunity for her. "Keegs, let's go out back and have a catch, okay?"

"I'll get my glove!" The little guy came back with a blue-and-black miniature baseball mitt, excited. Ethan didn't clear away Keegan's leftovers. He turned toward Mara. "Do you want to have a catch with us?"

"No."

"Okay, well, you know where we'll be." He took Keegan into the fenced-in backyard. The ground was wet, but it felt good to get outside and do something. Anything. Which made him wonder what he was going to do with the kids in Chicago. Would they be relegated to life indoors because of his new schedule? Was that fair to them, or just one of life's ever-changing trade-offs?

He tossed the ball to Keegan for a good twenty minutes, then called it a day. "You need a story and some chocolate milk, I think."

"Two stories," declared the boy. He thrust his hand into Ethan's, so trusting. So endearing. *"Green Eggs and Ham* and *Where the Wild Things Are.* My favorite ones of *all* the world."

"Except for the one about baby monsters being born," Ethan noted, because Keegan loved stories. Hearing them and telling them.

"And the bunnies. I love the bunnies a lot," Keegan admitted.

The two remaining nuggets were gone when they got back inside. So was the scant handful of fries.

Was that all she'd be eating tonight?

Thoughts of his conversation with Thea struck home. Rough childhoods. Sad lives. Triggers.

He tucked the kids into bed a short while later, then went online to look up therapists. If Mara had resisted the first one, maybe it wasn't the right person. Or the right time.

He found a listing south of Wishing Bridge, but the website was nonspecific. It was a broad-based corporate website that offered an overview but told him nothing about the people who might be working with Mara. Eyeing it, he had a wake-up call.

Other than a generic business listing, there was little about Hillside Medical on the Internet. Paul hadn't bothered with such things. He thought them a waste of time. "As long as sick folks find our phone number, we're fine," he'd professed. "That's all they need."

It wasn't, Ethan realized now, gazing at the screen.

Parents and families had a right to know how a practice represented itself. It wasn't his call to make, but it made sense. After viewing the corporate website for the mental-health service, he had learned nothing valuable about the people providing the service. That made him less inclined to use them.

When his search turned up nothing more, he decided he'd call the school counselor to get ideas. There had to be help somewhere. And if not . . .

Someone should take the time to fix it.

~

"You sit." Maggie used her no-nonsense tone, and Thea didn't have to be told twice. "Supper's ready. It's a veggie lasagna and not too heavy on the cheese, but solid with roasted vegetables. I got the recipe straight off the computer, one of them sites where folks are always doing this and that to tweak things, but I don't think this needed the littlest change. Except," she went on as Thea curled up in a living-room chair and yawned, "I did use garlic on the veggies when I roasted them, and I used marinara, not straight tomato sauce. It's got that spunky taste we all like so well. And a generous sprinkling of parsley. Fresh parsley brings out the zest in vegetables, but you probably already knew that."

Kelsey came into the room with the baby and winked at Thea. "But it didn't need tweaking," she teased, laughing.

"So I heard."

Kelsey settled the baby into Thea's arms. "She's freshly washed, fed, burped, and changed, and I think I heard her ask about Aunt Thea, so I brought her right down."

"Did you do that?" Thea held the three-month-old up and smiled at her. Instantly that adorable baby smiled right back. "Oh, Kelsey, she's beyond precious. Beyond miraculous. She's just so sweet, and her Auntie Thea wuvs, wuvs, wuvs her."

"She loves you, too." Kelsey tucked twin folders into her teaching bag and took a seat opposite Thea. "How's Shannon doing?"

"A rough day, but better now. She's sedated so she'll sleep overnight and hopefully wake up to a better tomorrow."

"I can't imagine." Kelsey dropped her eyes to the baby. "Now that I'm a mother I can't imagine neglecting your kids. It was wrong when it was us on the receiving end," she told Thea, and Thea wasn't about to disagree. "But it's so out of whack from a mother's perspective that I don't get it."

Maggie came back into the room with Thea's reheated mocha. "Not everyone embraces the idea of sacrificial love," she reminded them. "A lot of folks have a me-first mind-set, and if kids come along, they're set aside because Mom and Dad are too busy with their own pleasures. It doesn't have to be drugs or alcohol, either," she said as she set the mug down. "It can be plain selfishness. A child Shannie's age doesn't stand much chance of being taken in. But I'm sure you girls know that better than most."

"I hate that you're right," Thea said. She sipped her mocha, careful to keep it away from the smiling baby. "I was hoping it might be different in a rural setting."

"Maybe worse because you've got fewer folks to offer room," Maggie said. "There's a few folks here in town that take in foster kids, but I think they're full up. That means she'll go somewhere else, most likely, and that doesn't seem right, either. Not when all her family's from here."

It wasn't right, but Thea was too tired to come up with an answer. She nuzzled the baby's face, making her smile wider. "Kelsey, you give me hope."

Kelsey made a skeptical face. "Dare I ask?"

"Because you're such a good mom," Thea told her. She kept her voice soft while Hayley patted her face. When the baby tried to steal her glasses, Thea pushed them up on her head. "I was always afraid to dream about being a wife and mother."

Maggie put an arm around her shoulders. "Such talk."

"It's not like I'm walking into this with a normal past," Thea reminded her.

"That past might be abnormal. You're not," Maggie assured her. "And you are purely in the present, dearie. Anyone who can care so quick about a strange child has got good mothering sense in my book." Maggie gave her shoulder a light squeeze. "We make our own choices, every day."

"You're right." Thea nuzzled the baby, and when Hayley made a noise of delight, she laughed. "I'm not my mother. I'm me. And I can be a wonderful mother when the time comes."

Kelsey propped her feet and sipped some water. "It's hard to trust ourselves when there's been so few good examples in our lives. But those examples come from all over." She smiled at Maggie, and the older woman looked downright embarrassed. "From Mrs. Effel at Hannah's Hope. From you and Jazz. And now from Maggie. When folks believe in you, it makes all the difference. Doesn't it?"

"Something smells real good, Mother, and this old-timer's mighty hungry." Jeb walked in and slung his flannel shirt on a doorknob less than three feet away from the coat hooks.

Kelsey laughed.

Thea cringed because she wasn't sure if Maggie found the old fellow's humor all that funny.

"Jeb Martin Tompkins."

Jeb winked as he moved the jacket where it belonged. "I fixed it, Mother, don't get in a dither. Hey, baby girl." He peered down at Hayley over Thea's shoulder. The scents of fresh air, sweet tobacco, and a hint of coffee came right along with him. "I'm not clean enough to hold you just now, but you look mighty happy with your Aunt Thea. Like it oughta be," he added, smiling at Thea.

Leaving town didn't just mean leaving Wishing Bridge. It meant leaving Jazz and Kelsey and the baby. It meant she would barely be around for Kelsey's June wedding, much less watching Hayley grow up. And Jazz . . .

What would Jazz do when Thea left?

She'd forgotten how wonderful it was to have a girlfriend around. Of course Jazz would have Kelsey and Maggie.

Who will you have?

She knew that answer. Same as she'd had for years. No one.

She'd done that on purpose, avoiding relationships. Now that she was here, though, it seemed silly to keep to herself.

The kitchen timer rang.

"I've got Hayley's little swing in the kitchen." Maggie reached out and took the baby into strong, gentle hands. "Let's get her settled and have supper because I don't think Thea's going to last long tonight."

"I expect you're right." Thea stood and stretched. "But I'll tell you something wonderful. I can't wait to wake up in the morning and go to that new office."

"Yeah?" Kelsey smiled. "Is it that pretty? Because that old one didn't have a whole lot going for it, and that's a more than generous assessment."

"It's beautiful." Thea followed Maggie to the rich-smelling kitchen in the simple, classic home. "Like this," she told them. "Timeless and clean and good."

"Your kind words make me more willing to overlook the scrapes and bangs here and there, because an old place is like an old heart." Maggie tapped a worn spot on the counter to make her point. "It's seen things in its time. And it's managed to keep right on beating. And that's something to be glad about."

The baby cooed from her swing just then. The innocent noise made them all smile.

"I guess we've got a lot to be glad about," Jeb said in a soft voice. He gazed down at the baby, then slung an arm around Maggie's thin shoulders. "You gettin' better after a rough time with your heart this winter."

"Happy to be in tip-top shape again," Maggie agreed.

"And these gals and that baby coming here were one of the best gifts I've been given. Better yet, because they come straight from the good Lord above and at the most perfect time."

Maggie smiled up at him with a look so besotted it made Thea's heart almost ache. "And we're doing all right, aren't we, old-timer?"

He kissed her forehead with a pleased smile. "That we are, Mother. That we are."

They had supper together. No one generally tarried over meals because babies didn't give long stretches for relaxation, but tonight Thea did. Sitting around Maggie and Jeb's table with Kelsey and that baby felt like they were a unit. A family. Not by blood.

But by love. And maybe that was the best kind of family to have.

CHAPTER SEVEN

Thea pulled into the small parking lot adjacent to the new practice and couldn't contain her smile. The beauty of the gracious old home invited people in. She grabbed her laptop bag, medical bag, and purse, and a generous sack of Hershey's Kisses. Nothing like chocolate to ease people through a transition. She stepped inside and paused, happy.

The women had organized the desk area. They'd gathered some homey things from the flooded practice and displayed them on the built-in bookcases behind the reception area. Thea set her laptop down as Sheila and Laura came in behind her. "You guys did a great job setting up," she told them.

"To arrange things here was a piece of cake," said Laura. "I fell in love with it the minute I walked in. Maybe now someone will decide to buy the practice in June."

Laura didn't disguise the note of worry in her voice. Jobs weren't plentiful, and no one took them for granted.

"It sure ups the game, doesn't it?"

"It's absolutely respectable, and about time," added Sheila. "Dr. Wolinski had his good side, but he squeezed every penny. It's one thing if you do that to make things cheaper for patients. He did that sometimes. But mostly it was because he couldn't part with a dime unless he absolutely had to."

Thea hadn't known him before he passed away. "I'm careful with money myself. Most of the time," she added as she set the big bag of chocolate on the long desk. "Then there are moments that call for celebration. I'm going to set my stuff in my office and grab coffee. Is Faye coming in?"

"Yes. And Ethan just arrived. How's Shannie Carter doing, Thea? Any word?"

"Stable this morning," she told them. "I'll visit her once we wrap things up here. Sheila, you said she has no family. You mean like none?"

"Her great-grandmother was the only family left in town," Sheila explained. "Dotty lost her two brothers in World War II and neither had married. Her daughter and son-in-law died in the past few years. They were raising Shannon and doing a good job of it after their daughter ran off with some drugged-up friends. The daughter passed away about a year ago. A dentist in Warsaw confirmed her identity through dental records. That might actually be the last time anyone had contact with old Mrs. Willoughby and Shannon." She frowned. "I'm pretty sure we all dropped the ball on that one, Thea."

Thea couldn't disagree. "In the city, people get lost in the numbers. Here they get lost in the hills, out of sight, out of mind."

"But it shouldn't have happened." Laura exchanged looks with Sheila. "We were her medical office. One of us should have thought to check in."

"Then we try harder next time," Thea told her. "Because life being what it is for some families, there's always a next time, Laura."

They all turned as the door opened. Ethan came inside, saw the trio, and stopped. Then he smiled, one of the first relaxed, truly happy smiles she'd seen him offer. "This is going to take some getting used to."

"I keep looking around, wondering if it's real," Thea agreed. "Yet it appears real, and I'm over-the-moon in love with Max right now."

"Max is coming by midday to show us the apartments." Laura moved to the kitchen for coffee. "I can't wait to see them."

New offices. New apartments. Longer days, brighter skies now and again.

She didn't want to love Wishing Bridge. It wasn't part of the plan, but as she crossed into the classic kitchen, she realized it might be too late, because if ever a place had old-time charm, this was it. And after years of nothing even close to charming, the quaint town was calling to her. The question was—

Did she dare answer?

~

Max strolled in just before one o'clock and jangled a set of keys. "Tour time." He handed Faye a box. She opened it and hugged him when she spotted a dozen monster-sized muffins.

"You've saved us, Max. Again."

"Muffins!" exclaimed Laura. "I am happily calling this lunch."

Ethan came up front, greeted Max, and didn't hesitate to take a chocolate-chip muffin. "I love these things."

Max raised the keys in invitation, and Ethan instantly shook his head. "Gotta catch up on things here, but—"

"Five minutes, Ethan. That's all I'm asking."

Ethan met Max's look. He didn't want to cave. There wasn't time to be messing around looking at things, but Max had saved their hides by moving forward with this project. Ethan owed him the courtesy. "All right."

They rounded the building to the parking lot side, and Max inserted a key into a thick steel door. "This entry leads to both apartments by a stairway that separates at the second floor." A landing at the top took the continuing stairs off to the left. The door of the second-floor apartment faced them.

"This is the first rental." His voice echoed as he pushed the door open. "It's got three bedrooms, great views, early-morning sun, and late-day shade." They stepped into one of the nicest apartments Ethan had ever seen. Light filled the rooms as if to spite the clouds. Three bedrooms, none of them really big, left ample space for a well-outfitted kitchen with a dining area, and a large, wide living room, aided by the curve of the house's front turret. From the front window the beauty of the old-world neighborhood nestled against the forested Western New York hills was breathtaking.

"This is stunning, Max. Really nice."

"With a spot for twirling." Max indicated the turret area with a thrust of his chin. "In case anyone's got a little girl that likes to twirl."

Ethan stared at the spot. He stared real hard, then swallowed. He glanced around. "Someone's going to love living here, Max." He got Max's drift, but how silly would it be to uproot the kids from their current place when he'd be leaving soon?

"They sure will," Max agreed. "The stairway coming up is pretty enough to make someone real happy."

A stairway up. Not down. Mara's pinched face came back to him, and the dread in her words. *I hate going down.* Could a change of venue help? Looking around the welcoming space, he knew one thing—it certainly couldn't hurt.

"Let's go see the attic."

Ethan waved him off as he finished the last bite of muffin. "I'll see it later. I've got to make notes on two patients before the next round. And Max, I can't tell you how grateful we are." He indicated the staff. "You saved us."

Max sent him an easy grin as Ethan headed for the staircase. "I'm giving God the credit on the flood. I just made sure I had an alternative ready and waiting. I did my job. And he did his."

Ethan made a doubtful face and they both laughed, but as Ethan progressed down the stairs and rounded the curved porch, the image of the clean, bright apartment nudged him. How much nicer would it be to wake up each day in a place like that?

He entered his small office, pulled out his phone, and texted Max. Can I take the second-floor apartment for the duration of my time here? I think the kids would love it.

Max messaged back instantly. Done. Move in this weekend. Need furniture?

Ethan groaned, because he did, of course. I've got a table and chairs.

Ella Barnard's estate sale is Friday. Nice place, four bedrooms, I'll hook you up. I can store things in the carriage house as needed between tenants.

He didn't deserve a friend like Max, but right now, Ethan was mighty glad to have him. I can help move things.

Good.

And just like that it was done. He'd be moving the kids to a more cheerful setting. A homier setting. A part of him, the more cynical part, wondered why he was doing this. What would three months in a new apartment accomplish?

You know what, his conscience chided. *Because no kid should have to dread coming home. Ever.*

The scolding was well deserved. He'd walked into this new normal nine months before, thinking they'd make do for a year, but that was a dumb assumption when dealing with children. Now he needed to change things up, and a cheerful, bright home seemed to be a real smart beginning.

⊶

"You gals have time to see the attic?" Max asked.

"I can't wait," Sheila said. "I've looked at this house for years and wondered why no one ever gave it the love it needed. This is awesome, Max."

"It was caught in a custody battle over an inheritance," he told her.

"Money." Sheila made a disgusted face. "Folks ruin a whole lot of things over money. It's a shame, isn't it?"

Sheila didn't see the flash of pain cross Max's face, but Thea did. It was gone by the time he turned, but she'd seen the glimpse of sorrow firsthand and it surprised her. As Max led them up the next flight of stairs, she noted the wide landing. "Clever use of space here."

"This was the tricky part," Max told her. "Offering good entrances to both units and meeting fire codes. Luckily this house is so huge I had some room to work with."

"How'd you get so good at this stuff, Max?" Sheila asked. "You were a trooper for over twenty years."

He didn't answer right away, then he shrugged. "I was young and stupid once. Back when I was with the NYPD. I spent too much time working and hanging with the guys. Generally at the local bars," he added with emphasis. "When my family left me I realized that I was a first-class jerk and I needed to change. I couldn't fix the stuff that went bad then," he told her. "So I fix other things now. Make them pretty. My atonement, I guess."

"I don't believe it," stated Sheila flatly. "Max, you're one of the nicest guys I know."

He acknowledged the compliment with a slight smile. "That wasn't always the case. Somewhere along the way I wanted to stop being a jerk."

The glimpse of pain Thea had seen . . .

Even kind, hardworking Max had regrets, and Thea understood that well. She climbed the steps into the apartment and fell instantly in love. "Oh, Max. This is perfect."

"Cute, right? Jill gave me advice about colors, then I hired her niece Charlotte to do the painting when she came home over spring break. Charlotte made some money, and I bought myself some time, because trimming out those moldings is a pain in the neck."

White trim framed pale-yellow walls around the kitchen and eating area, then continued into the turret-edged living room. Can lights lit the area from above, a touch of modern in an old-fashioned setting, and the sloped ceilings were all painted with a soft-luster white, keeping the extended room bright. The bedrooms were done in a neutral cream trimmed in white, but it wasn't the paint that drew Thea. It was the gorgeous, gleaming oak-framed windows. "This would be like living in the clouds, wouldn't it?"

"An unfortunately apt description for how our March has gone," he agreed. "Spring is coming. Maybe right along with Easter this year. And this place is within walking distance of the churches and Main Street and all those nice little shops."

Jazz, Thea thought, looking around.

When Thea left, Jazz would be on her own. Wouldn't she love a place like this to call home as she retook control of her life? She and Jazz couldn't stay at Jeb and Maggie's place forever. This could be the perfect transition.

As the other women exclaimed over the old-fashioned built-ins and the charming amenities, Thea contemplated her choices. If it was just her it would be silly to change things up because she'd be leaving soon. But it wasn't just about her.

She snapped some pics and sent them to Jazz before her first afternoon patient. Apartment for rent, 132 Maplewood Avenue, 2 BR, right here in town. Close to Kelsey and Maggie and Jeb, close to everything. Absolutely adorbs. What do you think?

Jazz sent back a string of heart emojis and one word. Love.

Ditto, thought Thea, and the three-story climb would double as a daily workout. She texted Max between patients, and when he invited her to move in that weekend, she hesitated. Was that too soon? Would Maggie's feelings be hurt? Was this a stupid choice for a woman who planned on leaving so soon? But Jazz needed a place to stay, too, she reasoned.

She finished her day and refused to think about Jazz and Kelsey staying put in Wishing Bridge while she moved on. Moving on had always been the plan. This was a stopgap. An itinerant placement. She'd set her parameters when she had first arrived because she knew she'd go crazy living here on a forever status.

Now she wasn't nearly as sure.

As she pulled out of the parking lot and glanced back, the strong, dramatic angles of the house offered reassurance. No one choosing to live in such a place could ever be considered crazy. They'd be considered smart and blessed. And that should be enough for anyone.

~

Jazz Monroe was putting down roots in a small rural town while waiting tables in a Greek diner. Could life possibly get any stranger than it was right now? And yet—it felt good. She felt good.

Her phone buzzed in her pocket. Rage Fashions had upped their offer, and her agent was having a heart attack over her refusal to come back. Hopefully Eloise would let it go soon, but Jazz knew the modeling biz. Few models walked away on their own terms. Bringing her back would be considered a coup for the Hopkins Agency.

"Jacinda, can you bag that to-go order for me?"

"Glad to, sir."

Vern grinned. He always grinned when she called him sir, and the fact that she towered over the diminutive restaurant owner made him laugh more often.

She bagged the order, saw the name Whitaker, and added two of Maggie's homemade cookies in a small waxed side bag.

"A special treat, eh?" Vern noted as he finished ringing up a customer.

"This guy orders a lot of stuff here. And his little boy is adorable," she answered. "A nice surprise for both."

"A rich woman with a kind heart," said Vern. "You're a special person, Cinda."

She'd had him put Cinda on her nametag, the name her grandmother had used for her.

Her phone buzzed again. She pulled it out to shut it off but glimpsed part of the message in the process. The vastness of the financial figures would tempt anyone.

She shut the phone off.

She should change her number. Or gain twenty-five pounds.

Her heart stutter-stepped at that thought. The image of an extra twenty-five pounds rocked her.

Shift patterns. Avoid triggers. Use mental and virtual reminders. Great tips from a very nice therapist, but in the end, the struggle was just as real now as it had been a decade before.

"Can we get more coffee, Cinda?"

She paused by the older couple's table. "Got it right here, sugar. And did I hear it was your anniversary today?"

The old woman blushed, and the elderly man's face crinkled when he smiled. "Fifty-two years today. And she's just as pretty now as she was then, ain't she?"

"Absolutely." Jazz refilled their coffees carefully. As she set the old man's mug down, he took his wife's hand.

"We've had our ups and downs, and at our age we don't buy green bananas, if you know what I mean," he added with a wink.

"Oh, Harold." His wife rolled her eyes but giggled, as if his little joke was the funniest thing she'd ever heard.

"But we've had time together, and ain't that about the best thing ever?"

Oh, it was. Jazz agreed quickly and walked away, torn by his declaration of love and the stupid agent queries.

She'd have given anything to have more time with her mother. Her grandmother. Two faith-filled women who had loved to sing the praises of Jesus and God, and what had it gotten them?

Not one blessed thing. No pun intended.

Their deaths had left a twelve-year-old girl with nothing to call her own and not one person to love her or care for her. No one to set a good example for her, not until she got sent to Hannah's Hope as an incorrigible and met Thea and Kelsey.

Mrs. Effel loved you. Cared for you. She cared for all her girls at Hannah's Hope.

Jazz knew that. The middle-aged housemother had been the best thing that happened to all three girls. She'd encouraged their bond of friendship and the strength of faith.

Jazz clung to the beauty of friendship. As for faith?

She had kicked that to the curb a long time ago. Right where it belonged.

CHAPTER EIGHT

Thea sought Elaina when she arrived at the hospital. "How's Shannon doing? Any concerns?"

Elaina motioned for Thea to walk with her. "Doing better, coughing a lot, short of breath. I think forty-eight hours will help alleviate that."

"Has the social worker been brought on board?"

"No clue," Elaina told her. "I just got in myself, so I'm not sure. What about your county social services?"

"They've been alerted about her status. I'll talk to them," Thea said. Elaina's pager went off. She paused to check the code as Thea entered Shannon's room.

Shannon had been sleeping, but she stirred when Thea walked in. She grimaced, coughed, then opened her eyes. When she spotted Thea, she smiled.

Oh, that smile.

Thea's heart tumbled as she moved forward. "Hey, sweet thing. How are we doing?"

"You came back."

Thea smoothed a hand across Shannon's hair and nodded. "I sure did. Had to see how our girl was doing. I heard you have a nasty cough right now."

Shannon winced. "I don't like coughing," she whispered, then coughed, gripping her incision.

"Coughs are tough right after surgery," Thea told her. She took a seat on the edge of the bed and held the girl's hand. "Do you know what happened to you? Has anyone explained it?"

"I got sick."

"You sure did." Thea gave Shannon's hand a light squeeze. "A little tiny thing inside you got infected and it made your whole body sick, so the doctors took it out. And now you'll get better, but it takes a little while. So we have to be patient even when we don't want to be patient."

"Where's Gee Gee?"

Thea paused to think. "Your great-grandma?" she asked.

Shannon nodded.

"Well, she's in another kind of hospital because Gee Gee is sick, too."

"I know." Shannon's expression clouded. "I kept trying to get her better, but I didn't really know what to do."

Oh, bless her little heart. The thought of this child caring for her great-grandmother and trying to make a difference gripped Thea. She knew that struggle well. Then she smiled, approving. "That was very nice of you. Were you doing schoolwork at home, Shannon?"

"No." Her face drooped as she fingered the cotton-edged blanket. "I wanted to go to school, but Gee Gee wouldn't let me. So I stayed there and tried to help her. I miss school," she told Thea. "A lot."

She'd missed second grade. That meant she'd be repeating the year because by the time she was healthy enough to return, the school year would be almost over. If she came back to Wishing Bridge, she could start the fall session with Kelsey. Kelsey would look out for her. She'd shepherd the girl through the missed classes with kindness and care. But what if she didn't come back to Wishing Bridge?

A coughing spell hit Shannon then. Thea helped her into a more upright position until it eased. "Enough talking," she told her, smiling.

"I'm going to read you some stories. Right after you open this little package. Okay?" When Shannon opened her mouth to talk, Thea put a finger to her lips. "Just nod."

Shannon nodded and took the pink-and-silver foil-wrapped package with eager hands. She made short work of the wrapping paper, then lifted the lid of the thick ivory-cardboard box. "Oh." Her eyes went wide when she spotted the soft lamb nestled in tissue paper. "A Luvvy Lamb."

"I thought she might be fun to snuggle."

"He."

Thea pretended surprise. "The lamb's a boy?"

Shannie nodded. "I think he is. Okay?"

It was absolutely all right. "Yes, of course. And you snuggle him while I read these. All right?"

Shannon nodded and coughed, but not as long and hard this time. With the ultrasoft lamb tucked between her chest and neck, Shannon snuggled into the cotton coverlet. Thea read her four stories, adventures of children solving mysteries, playing make-believe, and slaying dragons, because the slaying of dragons was always great fun.

Shannon fell asleep before Thea finished the fourth story.

Eyes closed, her lashes lay dark against pale, thin cheeks. Thea took the quiet moment to check the little girl over. She appeared malnourished. Her skin had none of the normal glow of a healthy child. Instead of being smooth and elastic, Shannon's skin felt dry and loose over her petite frame.

Thea tucked the covers around her and stood.

The thought of Shannon going to a strange environment bothered her. It shouldn't. There were lots of nice foster families in the system. And some not-so-nice ones. She'd had her share of those. Partially her fault. Partially theirs.

But to send a compromised child into the unknown with few assurances was a valid concern. Shannon had already fallen through the cracks once. Thea couldn't risk having that happen again.

She had no legal standing with this child. No one did, except the aged great-grandmother.

Go see her.

She would, Thea decided. In a lucid moment, Gee Gee might be able to offer some insight. If she couldn't, there was no harm in trying. She'd been placed in a memory care unit in Warsaw, a quarter hour away from Wishing Bridge. Thea would make it a point to touch base with her first thing in the morning.

The pediatric social worker was gone for the day, so Thea left her a message.

It was almost seven when she got back to her car. It would take her nearly an hour to get back to Wishing Bridge. The busy university campus surrounding the hospital complex offered multiple food options, and the only thing she'd eaten that day was the megadelicious muffin Max had brought by. She turned toward the College Town complex, a "street of shops"–style neighborhood filled with options, but didn't pull in.

She was hungry, but not hungry enough to want to eat alone. Maggie had spoiled her with home-cooked meals and conversation. She headed for the expressway as a call from Jazz came in. "What's your ETA?"

"Eight fifteen."

"Perfect!" said Jazz. "Maggie made stew, and there are rolls to go with it. Don't waste your money stopping, okay? I should get home from the diner about the same time you get back."

"You don't eat after seven o'clock, Jazz."

"I'm breaking that rule tonight. It's nicer to eat together."

Emotion clogged Thea's throat, mostly because she was bone-weary, but also hungry, and so blessed to be surrounded by people who cared about her. Was this why she wasn't hurrying to put in applications in Philly or Pittsburgh or Baltimore? Because she had people here who cared about her? Her well-being?

Umm . . . note to self. That's not exactly a bad thing. The internal reminder sounded slightly cryptic. *Most folks like being cared for or cared about. It's considered normal.*

Thea knew that. She'd lived the absence of care for a long time. She'd hardened herself to need little help, so depending on the kindness of others went against the grain, even though she knew it shouldn't. Not here. Not now. "Stew sounds amazing."

"Oops, order up. See ya."

Thea got stuck on the expressway for long minutes as a newly established construction site bottlenecked traffic. By the time she got back to Maggie and Jeb's, it was nearing eight thirty. Jazz pulled in just ahead of her. She parked Kelsey's car and walked back down the drive to greet Thea. "Long days lately."

"Agreed. Hey, about the apartment?" Thea glanced toward the house. "How are we—?"

"Done," Jazz said. "I talked to Maggie before I left for work," she went on. "She's fine with it as long as we consider their place our home away from home."

Maggie's voice joined in from the porch. "I figured you girls might be getting crowded in that one room, and Jill told me what nice apartments they are!" Her voice took an upswing as she approached them. "She stopped by for some baby time earlier and said that handsome young doctor is going to lease out the second floor with those kids."

Ethan was leasing the bigger apartment?

"And you and Jazz on the third floor, how convenient is that? You walk down the stairs for work and right back up when you're done. And Hayley and I can mosey your way as the weather softens."

"And I can run over here and hang out before my shifts at the diner," added Jazz.

Thea focused on one thing. Ethan was moving those lost children into the second-story apartment. He was bringing them into an inviting, cozy setting. Anyone who thought a change of environment couldn't help mood disorders had never lived in dark circumstances. Thea knew how darkness could swallow a child whole. A clean, normal home wasn't just good—it was a huge step up.

"We'll have to dig up some furniture," Thea noted.

"Give a woman a reason to shop and you've got a happy girl on your hands," Jazz assured her. "The very thought of living in an attic has me happier than my forty-two dollars in tips tonight."

"Jacinda." Maggie put a hand on Jazz's arm. "I don't think I've ever seen Vern and Liki so happy." Vern and his wife, Vasiliki, had owned the roadside diner for over twenty years. "You know some folks come in and eat just to see you. You put some busy back into their slower season."

"Well, they've done me a great turn by giving me something to do," Jazz answered. "So it works both ways, Maggie. Both of them good."

"What would your New York friends think if they saw you now?" Maggie asked. "The ones who call you all the time?"

"Friends? Or sharks?" Thea quipped, and Jazz agreed.

"They're not really what you'd call friends, Maggie." Jazz let Maggie precede her through the door. "They're agents and corporate execs who want me to come back to work. My agent would die if she saw me waiting tables, and I am not exaggerating. She went through triple bypass surgery a year back and managed to make people crazy even from her hospital room . . . until the doctors commandeered her phone."

"Don't them folks take time off?" Jeb wondered from his recliner in the living room.

"There's always a deal going down in the city."

"You could find yourselves a cute cop to fall in love with," said Kelsey as she entered the kitchen. "Hayley's asleep, and I'm turning in. She likes her middle-of-the-night feeding, and morning comes real early after interrupted sleep. I vote you both stay and we grow old together here, commiserating over the price of gas and watching kids play soccer and put on recitals. But that's just me."

"I like the hot cop idea," mused Jazz as her stew cooled. "Affairs of the heart can be a game changer." She winked at Maggie, and Maggie laughed.

"I'd have never been here in Wishing Bridge if it weren't for falling in love with Jeb down in the big city, so I hear you loud and clear. But I do love this town. No denying that."

So did Thea.

That might have been the biggest surprise ever. But loving something and acquiring the wherewithal to stay were two different things. She'd tire of the same old, same old of small-town life after a while. Wouldn't she?

She hadn't yet, but that was because she and Ethan had hit the ground running and hadn't slowed down since. Was this the norm for a rural practice? And she couldn't even get started on the insurance issues some folks faced. She'd be giving away her services left and right. In Pittsburgh the financial realities of medicine had been a far step removed from her end of the office. The front desk handled the people. Billing handled money. Her role was to see patients in a somewhat assembly-line fashion.

It was different here.

She was getting to know people. Their lives. Their situations. More than once she'd given permission for patients to put off their payment for a month or two.

It wouldn't be considered smart business, but she couldn't do anything less and live with herself. She'd thought she was suited for a big-city setting, a large office with limited knowledge of such things. Then she could make quick decisions as needed, with no thought to someone's grocery budget or shoe allowance. Being forced to think about the big picture raised her awareness. That thought used to scare her. Not anymore.

"Stop thinking," advised Jazz. "I'm pretty sure your brain is running in circles right now."

"Guilty as charged."

"So let's apply the brakes, enjoy this food, and hope for sun, because I am that tired of gray skies and rain. But I will never get tired of Maggie's cooking."

Jazz eating at eight forty-five, breaking a hard rule in modeling. Jazz waiting tables. Pouring coffee for folks. Clearing their dishes.

What were they doing?

A momentary panic seized Thea. This was off-script behavior, and Thea never went into anything without a plan. Plans kept her sane. Plans kept her focused and in control. They helped her feel strong. Spending months in the clutches of a human-trafficking ring hadn't just changed her physically. It had hardened her. Was she a control freak?

Yes, as needed, and maybe that was the best thing about this town, because she didn't need as much control. But that might be the scariest thing, too.

Her phone dinged. Thea pulled it out and saw a text from the hospital PA, a picture of Shannon, sleeping peacefully, cradling the soft lamb.

The panic melted away.

She'd saved a child's life last week, and it didn't matter that Shannie wasn't from some vital big-city practice. She was on her way to being a healthy child because someone had cared enough to call for help. And Thea had been there to provide it.

~

Thea got to Shannon's room Saturday morning just in time to see staff helping her into a wheelchair for discharge. She pulled the doctor aside. "You're discharging my patient?"

"Technically our patient," he told her, and the way he said it almost got him smacked. "And before you hit me, releasing her is our call, but the protocol puts the county in charge, and they didn't see fit to get in touch. That's not my bad. Your office would have gotten a standard notice on Monday when you reopened for business."

"Where is she going?"

"Check with her. Judith Millner." He pointed to a stout older woman with a slightly unpleasant air about her.

Thea might be biased. She knew that. When your life had been peppered with social workers and good and bad foster placements, experiences tended to skew your worldview.

Currently, she was prepared to dislike this woman on the spot, and that wasn't her usual reaction. She needed to put on her happy face and stow the negativity. She crossed the hall from the nurse's station to Shannon's door. "Mrs. Millner?"

"Yes?"

"Hi." Thea extended her hand.

The social worker didn't take it.

Germophobe? Or a jerk? Thea wasn't sure which and found both annoying. "I'm Thea Anastas, Shannon's nurse practitioner from Wishing Bridge."

Judith Millner stood perfectly still, waiting. Not speaking.

"You're here to transport my patient, correct?"

"Wyoming County has no special-needs foster-care placements available at this time, and we're stepping in by their request. If you have a problem with that, take it up with them. As you can see, it's a Saturday and I'm busy."

Stay calm. Stay cool. Stay—

"Oddly, it's a Saturday in Wishing Bridge, too, and I think we're all busy, Mrs. Millner."

"Ms."

Oy vey. "Ms." Thea corrected herself with a smile, though it almost killed her to do it. "I'm going to accompany my patient to the foster home. Can you please text me the address?"

Ms. Millner's eyes narrowed, perhaps questioning Thea's right to do it, but Thea was the practitioner of record. Ms. Millner pulled out a phone, took Thea's number, then texted her the address.

"Wonderful. My GPS will get me right there." She smiled as if the grumpy woman's attitude wasn't an irritation, then turned to her primary interest. Shannon. "Hey, sweet thing."

Shannon looked scared. One arm clutched the Luvvy Lamb and the other reached for Thea. "I'm scared, Miss Thea. They want to take me someplace I don't know, and I'm really, really scared." She whispered the words so softly that Thea had to bend to hear them.

"Which is why I'm coming along to meet your rehab family."

"What's that?" Shannon asked.

The social worker sniffed, impatient, but Thea stooped down by Shannon's side. "It's a special house filled with nice people. They help kids who are sick or who've been sick to get better. And then you get to move on to a place closer to home."

"Gee Gee's house?"

Thea had gone to see Dotty Willoughby. There was no semblance of clarity. "Not Gee Gee's. I'll know more in a few days."

Shannon clung to Thea's hand. She held tight, and the heartbroken expression pulled Thea straight out of her comfort zone. "I don't want to go to this place, Miss Thea. Please don't make me."

"Enough." The social worker made a slashing motion across her neck and, while Thea hated to admit it, the woman was right. Getting Shannon upset would be counterproductive.

"I'll make sure you're settled and give the foster mother our information in Wishing Bridge. Your job is to get better so you can come back to us. Okay?"

Tears slipped down Shannon's cheeks.

She didn't look at Thea as the nursing assistant wheeled her out the door, and she didn't look back as they rolled her onto the animal-festooned elevator.

Shoulders stooped, the child refused to make eye contact, and when they separated on the ground floor—Thea to the parking garage, Shannon to an official Monroe County car—Shannon quietly accepted her fate, chin down.

Helpless and hopeless.

Thea's hands shook as she opened her car door.

Memories surged back, bad ones followed by horrid ones, and she had to go through some therapeutic breathing techniques to prevent herself from hyperventilating.

Calm yourself. That sweet child isn't being sold into human trafficking. She's going to a home geared for healing.

But Thea intended to ascertain that this home, and the people running it, understood that Shannon had a champion in her corner. Someone willing to run interference in case anything happened to her.

She had to be back in Wishing Bridge in three hours, but she was going to make sure Shannon and her new caregivers knew that Thea Anastas said what she meant and meant what she said. On her watch, there would never be a child left behind or left on their own.

She pulled into the driveway of a modest home on the city's east side, marched to the door, and tapped sharply on the glass, ready to speak her piece.

"Coming!" a perky voice called from within, then a small woman opened the door. She had a birdlike quickness and an infectious smile. "You're Dr. Anastas?"

"Nurse practitioner," she corrected, and when she extended her hand the older woman grasped it in a hearty shake.

"A pleasure. Come in, come in, that wind is still cold, isn't it? But once the heat hits, it sets in full tilt and you know what happens next!" Animated eyes above a winning smile gazed into hers. A small pewter cross hung around her neck, and her busy movements seemed both focused and joyous, a winning combination. "We'll start whining about heat and humidity, because dissatisfaction is human nature, more's the pity. Sister Genevieve is settling our patient right over here." She motioned toward a cheerful living room with short, bright curtains, worn but comfy-looking furniture, and a decent-sized play area. "I'm Sister Elizabeth. Sister Gen and I have been doing this for years, taking in little ones to help them back on their feet when family's unavailable to do it." The smile she aimed at Shannon—so open and kind— reminded Thea of Joan Effel in Philly.

The sisters didn't mind that she stayed a while, and when Sister Genevieve retrieved a toddler from a nap in an adjacent room, Shannon's eyes lit up. "Does he live here, too?" She slipped out of the chair to come closer. "What's his name?"

"Antonio Miguel, and isn't he the handsomest thing ever?" chirped Sister Elizabeth. "We call him Tonio, and he's here with us for a few weeks. He's had a rough winter, all told, but we're hoping his next surgery will be one of the last."

"He has to have an operation?" Shannon looked up, worried. "I don't like operations."

"Well, he's already had two, and he's little enough that he might not even remember them when he's bigger."

"For real?"

"Mmhmm." Sister Genevieve set the toddler down and grinned when he dashed for the toy area. "You can play with him if you'd like, Shannon. That would save my tired joints. They don't do those ups and downs so well anymore."

"Sure I will."

A giver. Shannon was a giver. And she liked normalcy. What child wouldn't?

The setting and the pair of kindly sisters put Thea's mind at rest. Shannon was in good hands, which meant Thea could focus her energy on working with the county to find a home for her. And not just any home.

A place filled with the love Thea had missed in home after home as a child. There was no way she was about to let Shannon go without that. Not if she could help it. But how to find the right placement was another thing altogether.

~

Jill Jackson loaned Thea a queen-sized bed and dresser.

Jazz had a bed delivered.

Maggie loaned them the extra couch she had in the dining room, along with the end table.

Jazz bought two comfy wingback recliners in cream because cream goes with everything.

Maggie loaned them dishes.

Jazz drove to the Galleria Mall and bought pots and pans and linens.

Jazz was staying.

Thea wasn't.

The apartment arrangements drove home the sharp contrast between their relative statuses. And maybe the difference in bank accounts, too. Thea wasn't hurting for money, but she wasn't swimming in cash, either. She stopped by Walmart for a few things on her way back to Wishing Bridge and was amazed at how much Jazz, Kelsey, and Hale had gotten done while she was in Rochester. She walked into the apartment and went straight to the most important part of moving. "I brought two bags of peanut butter cups——"

"Full-size or miniatures?" asked Kelsey.

"Miniatures. In the Easter foil colors because I'm a sucker for pastels." Thea stretched out the answer, as if hesitant. "Is that bad?"

Kelsey grabbed two. "It is the opposite of bad. These are the best. It's all about ratio," she explained as she unwrapped the first little peanut butter cup. "These have the perfect balance of chocolate to peanut butter. The big ones are good," she acknowledged with a nod. "Just not as good."

"How's Shannon?" Jazz asked.

"They released her today. She's in a really sweet foster-care home run by two nuns who help sick children. But that means we've got to find a solution back here or risk losing her into the system. Except I have no idea how to do that and it's the weekend, so I have to table it until Monday. But if any of you have an idea, I'm willing to listen." She hooked her jacket on the rack just inside the door. "How can I help here?"

"Make beds. There's a laundry area just off the kitchen stairs, so I washed the new sheets and blankets. The last load should be done."

"Another flight of stairs!" Thea made a mock joyful face. "Yay!"

"You will never have to worry about being out of shape here, that's for certain," noted Kelsey.

Thea headed back down the stairs. She ran into Ethan and Max on the way. They were lugging a headboard into the second-floor apartment. Ethan didn't banter. He didn't make a lame "fancy meeting you here" kind of joke. He went straight to the point. "You saw Shannon this morning?"

Max set his end of the headboard down. So did Ethan.

"I went with her to a foster setting today, a rehab spot on the east side. I'll connect with our county on Monday and see what we can get in place for her."

"Allegany County might have openings," suggested Max. "That's closer than Rochester."

"Or we could try one of the Buffalo suburbs," added Ethan. "It's not close, but she has no family here to make Wyoming County a priority."

Except that it was a priority to Thea. Because shouldn't a community look after its own? "Well, she's not an Erie or Allegany child," she told them both, and she might not have been diplomatic when she said it. "She's a Wyoming County girl, from Wishing Bridge, and I'm going to be real disappointed if no one steps up and offers this child a home. That seems wrong, like it goes against the concept of this sweet town."

"Well, then." Max's smile eased the tense moment while Ethan looked pretty uncertain about how to handle Thea's strong opinion. "Let's find her a place here."

"That easy?" Ethan lifted his end of the headboard again.

"Didn't say 'easy,'" Max noted as they moved on so that Thea could get downstairs. "But doable, I expect."

~

By that night, everything was moved in and the place looked like home.

It wasn't home. Not for Thea. She never allowed anything to matter enough to be called home. She did her schoolwork and then her job to the best of her ability, but there had never been anything she'd call "home."

Looking around the cozy attic digs, a shot of fear gripped her. For the first time in her life she was in a place that felt like it *could* be home.

Admitting that made her vulnerable, and after living at the hands of cruel men for nearly four long months, Thea had vowed that she would never be vulnerable again. And she'd meant it. But now, here, a different emotion took hold of her. An emotion that made hope and home seem a little more possible each day.

CHAPTER NINE

Ethan pulled up to the big pink house midday on Sunday. Jenny Harper had kept the kids for a few hours on Saturday while he and Max moved things into the apartment. Hale Jackson and his brother, Ben, had come by to help as well, and between them they had the furniture in place in under two hours. The guys had even helped make beds and cover pillows, which meant Ethan owed them a steak dinner before he and the kids left town.

Now was the moment of truth. He'd taken the kids out to Sunday breakfast after a short church service on Route 19, then they'd gone grocery shopping. He parked the car, climbed out, and lifted a couple of bags. "Mara, can you grab some things, please? And Keegan, can you bring the bread and rolls inside?"

"And the oatmeal, because I'm this strong!" Keegan cocked his elbow to show off his muscles. "I can carry a-a-a lot!"

He grabbed the bread bag in one hand and the box of brown-sugar-and-cinnamon oatmeal in the other.

"Why are we taking food to your work?" asked Mara. She picked up two bags reluctantly. "I thought this was our food. And why do you have to work on a Sunday?"

"Follow me."

Keegan hiked right along.

Mara dragged her steps with elongated passive-aggressive deliberation.

Ethan let it go. He unlocked the side door. "Keep following."

"Huh?" Keegan looked at the stairs, intrigued.

Mara rolled her eyes.

Ethan unlocked the upstairs door and pushed it open. The door's movement flooded the stairwell with natural light.

"Hey!" Keegan hurried up the last few stairs. "What is this place? Hey!" He spun around, grinning, taking it in.

His reaction was adorable and typical and enough to ease the chronic tightness around Ethan's heart. He turned to watch Mara.

Mara came up the last two steps, into the light. She looked around and frowned, confused, then studied the rooms again before she set the two bags on the nearby table. "What is this?"

"Our new apartment. Like it?"

Her gaze darted from him to the apartment, then back to him. She swallowed hard and brought one hand to her throat. "We get to live here?" A spark of hope ignited her normally dull voice.

"Yes."

She moved into the living area. Max had been able to purchase three beds at the estate sale, but Ethan had ordered a sofa, chair, and some living-room tables from a Rochester rental site. The effect was simple, inviting, and comfortable. "Want to see the bedrooms?"

Mara had crossed the room to the rounded turret corner. She reached out to finger the sheer curtains Jill Jackson had hung there, then swallowed. "We get to stay?"

She whispered the words, and Ethan had to fight the growing constriction in his own throat. "Yes."

"I've got all my best puppy friends in my room!" Keegan slid to a stop by the second bedroom. "When there's tr-tr-trouble, we'll be there on the double!" He power-punched the air, then immediately went in search of food.

Mara turned.

She smiled. At her brother. At his antics. Then she gazed around the rooms once more. "Can we move in today?"

"Yup."

Her smile grew, then became tentative, as if she didn't trust herself to get too excited. "This is very pretty, Uncle Ethan."

Big words for her. "I thought so, too. It's bright."

She nodded.

"I forgot how much I like a cheerful home. A place filled with light."

She lifted her gaze to his with a flicker of understanding. He didn't fool himself that a new apartment was a panacea. She'd suffered a grave loss, and her tough nature didn't embrace change readily. But if an environmental change could help her transition, he was only sorry he hadn't been smart enough to figure that out sooner. "Do you want to see your room?"

Eyes wide, she followed him across the dining area. He paused by the first door. "Your room. Keegan's room. And my room." He pointed to the right.

"You won't have to sleep on the couch anymore?"

He shook his head. "No, but that wasn't a bad deal. I've slept on a lot of couches in my time."

She paused, weighing that, then stepped into her room. She didn't say anything at first. She fingered the eyelet bedspread Jill had picked out, and the pretty pink, green, and yellow patchwork pillows. A plain white bookcase from Jill's new shop was tucked against the wall, with a half dozen books in it and room for more. So many more. "I know you like to read, and a bookcase is a great thing to have."

She looked awed. As if she couldn't believe what she was seeing.

"You like it."

"I do." She nodded, then tears filled her eyes, tears he hadn't expected and wasn't prepared for.

"Hey." He put an arm around her in an awkward hug. Keegan grabbed hugs all the time. Mara shrank away from contact, which made him reluctant to offer it. Not because the rebuff hurt him. He just didn't want to cause her any more angst than she already carried. "I didn't mean to make you cry."

More tears followed. Quiet tears. The serious ones, the ones that meant something. He squatted and hugged her, and this time she let him. They stayed like that for a few minutes, until Ethan was pretty sure his knees would never forgive him.

Then she stepped away. "I'm all right."

Was she?

He raised his brows at her and stayed quiet.

"It's a real pretty room, Uncle Ethan. And a beautiful house." She drew a deep breath that sounded like a sigh, but this time it wasn't. It was just a breath. "Thank you for getting it for us."

"You're welcome."

He felt stupid. He felt dumb and uninspired, because what had he been thinking, crowding them all into that basement apartment?

"Can we go get our stuff now?"

"Right after we put these groceries away."

"I can get more," shouted Keegan.

"I can, too."

"Go for it." The two kids clambered up and down as if they liked climbing stairs. They brought in the remaining groceries. When they were done, he locked the door and took them back to the basement apartment.

For the very last time.

CHAPTER TEN

Thea's Monday conversation with Martha Spector, the Wyoming County social worker, painted a thin picture of local services. There were no immediate placements available in the area, but they did have two emergency placement possibilities—one in Java Center and one in Bliss, both a solid drive from Wishing Bridge.

"They're very nice homes with kind, loving families," the woman explained. "I would have no problem placing this child in either setting. Now if the great-grandmother cedes guardianship to someone, we have leeway to approve. As long as she's cognizant enough to comprehend what she's doing."

Thea couldn't lie. "I wish she were, but she's not. I've been to see her twice, hoping to have her sign off, but she was caught in some form of delirium both times. In her right mind, I'm sure she wants the best for Shannon, but she's not aware enough to substantiate that."

"The only other thing would be a relative, even if somewhat distant. Steprelatives are approvable as well, if it's in the child's best interests."

"I'm pretty sure there are none," said Thea. She didn't try to curb the disappointment in her voice.

"That leaves our options as they were. Bliss and Java Center."

Thea thanked Martha and ended the call. The afternoon flew by. Sick patients, elderly mobility issues, and well-baby checkups, a mixed bag of specialties. But her last patient was her favorite by far. She walked into exam room three, sniffed the pot Maggie had set on the counter, then peeked inside and smiled. "Cinnamon steak."

"Yes!" Maggie beamed. "You gals always loved it, and it warms up so nice in the microwave that I thought I'd bring it by. My guess is," she went on, ticking off her fingers, "you're not taking time to eat, and Jazz feels guilty eating. If there's good food around, the temptation to eat it becomes an easier choice."

Maggie and Jeb had lost a daughter to complications caused by an eating disorder the previous year. Maggie understood the delicate psyche of mental health and food far too well.

"We'll love it." Thea checked Maggie over, and when she was done, she hugged her. "You're doing great. The lab results all look good, your heart seems happy, and you've been a stellar patient at physical therapy."

"And glad it's over," declared Maggie. "How's little Shannon doing? Is she getting on okay? I have been prayin' for that child seven ways to Sunday, and I'm embarrassed that Jeb and I overlooked her situation this past year. That shouldn't have happened, not with me and Jeb being stepfamily to her grandmother."

Family to her grandmother?

Thea took a seat on the stool and met Maggie's gaze. "First, you had a rough year, so cut yourself some slack. Second . . ." She lifted a brow. "Are you and Jeb actually related to Shannon?"

"In one of those roundabout not-really ways," Maggie explained. "Jeb's stepcousin was Shannon's grandmother, the one who originally took her in. So not blood related, but in the family group, you know?"

"Yes, of course." Thea's pulse jumped, because the thought of Maggie being related to Shannon, even obscurely, opened a window of possible opportunity. But Maggie had a sad history with two children she'd taken in long ago. Would it be fair to pose the question to her?

"Might just as well ask as sit there wonderin' whatever it is you're wonderin', Theadora. Worst I can say is no," Maggie said. Then she sat on the edge of the examination table, watching Thea and waiting.

Thea couldn't bring herself to do it. Not without some thought. She had no right to put Maggie in a funk in order to help Shannon. Maggie wasn't just her patient. She was her friend. "It's nothing, Maggie. You know medicine these days, we're always puzzling out one problem or another."

"Hmm." Maggie appeared unimpressed with Thea's answer. "I expect you'll tell me in good time. So what about Shannon? Is she coming home soon? I'd like to go visit."

"Once she's released from rehab with the sisters she could end up as close as Bliss or Java Center."

Maggie frowned instantly. "Shannon Carter doesn't belong in Bliss or Java Center, as nice as they are. She belongs here. In Wishing Bridge. The Carters and the Willoughbys are all from Wishing Bridge or Perry. This is her home, Thea."

"Except there aren't any homes open in Wishing Bridge right now," Thea explained. "The other side of the county is the best we can do. And there are no Carters or Willoughbys to take her in, so the county is at a loss."

Thea had discovered two things about Maggie Tompkins. She said what she meant and didn't waste words. That made her the kind of friend you could count on in all kinds of situations.

And she didn't take no for an answer. Ever.

"Jeb and I happen to have a vacancy at our place."

"Maggie, I—"

"Are you worried about my physical health? Because you just told me I'm doing great, and seventy isn't exactly death's door these days. Or is it my mental health, because of what happened the last time we took in some kids?"

Nailed. Thea winced. "Both."

"Well, I have it on the sound opinion of my doctor and nurse practitioner that I'm doing just fine as of five minutes ago. So lay that worry to rest, young lady. And"—she folded her arms in a very Maggie-like stance—"the original situation had three children involved. This is different, Thea, and if Jeb and I are the only thing even close to family that this sweet child has left, then we should step up and take her in, at least for the time being. Her great-grandma and Jeb were friends a long time back. She was older, but she had a kind heart for others. It's a shame to see her so down and out now."

Did Thea dare offer this suggestion to the social services department in Warsaw?

"Seems a shame to let that nice, clean, empty bedroom at our place just sit and get dusty again now that it's been so well used. Kelsey's on hand to help after school, and I expect that child's going to need some tender lovin' care after her ordeal."

"She will," Thea admitted. "And Maggie, if I wasn't working long hours every day, I'd take that little girl in myself, but I need to go through screening first. For family, the approval is much quicker."

"You see yourself in that neglected young one."

She couldn't deny it. "Yes. And Shannon's history makes her more vulnerable if she gets put in the wrong place, with the wrong people. She wants and needs someone to love her, and that can make a child coercible. I don't want anything else to go wrong for her."

"I couldn't agree more." Maggie stepped down and put her hands on her hips. "What do we do to make this happen? The very idea makes me feel good enough to kick up my heels, Thea."

What could Thea say? She hugged Maggie, then drew back. "If it gets to be too much, you let me know, okay? I'll step in."

"Well, not if you're gone, you won't," noted Maggie practically. "But Kelsey and Hale will be here. And Jacinda. And Jill Jackson's got a heart for youngsters, so I won't be suffering for help when you've moved on."

Thea considered herself tough. She'd learned to harden her heart and man her defenses early on, but the thought of leaving Maggie and Jeb with this new responsibility and being nowhere near to help seemed wrong. "I'm not going anywhere for a while." She made the reminder as she finished Maggie's electronic chart.

"Which only gives me more time to tempt you to stay," Maggie declared, grinning. "Enjoy that beef. It's always been one of Jeb's favorites."

"For good reason," Thea agreed.

"And mind, if you don't make that call down to social services, I'll do it myself," Maggie told her, and Thea knew she meant it. "Half a relative's better than no relative at all, and I'm not looking for payment, so the county will save itself a nice bit of change."

"I'll call," Thea promised. "Then I'll let you know what the social worker says."

"Good."

Thea placed the call as soon as Maggie left, and when Martha heard the relationship, she hummed softly. "That seems like a stretch, doesn't it?"

"Not to hear Maggie tell it," said Thea. "They're stepcousins, but there's an old family friendship as well. And if we make this arrangement it keeps Shannon here, in Wishing Bridge, at no cost to the county, with people who knew her family. I'd call that a win all around."

"Let me run it by the director," she told Thea. "I'll get back to you." Five minutes later the phone rang, and when Thea answered, the social worker gave a resounding okay.

"I'll stop by the Tompkins house to have them fill out papers asserting their relationship and check the house out. The fact that little Shannon has no one else puts the nod in their favor."

Relief flooded Thea. "This is wonderful, Martha. They will be thrilled and I'll be on hand to help out."

"There was a time when we wouldn't have approved older folks taking in a child, but that's long past," Martha told her. "These days if we can get a stable grandparent involved in a child's life, it can be a lifesaver. So thank you, Thea. Not many practitioners would have gone this far to secure a child's future. Your devotion is notable."

Thea couldn't imagine doing anything less, which seemed at odds with her past mind-set. "Let me know when we can bring her home, and I'll be the one to pick her up from the sisters."

"Will do."

She called Maggie with the news. "The county is willing to have Shannon come stay with you guys. Martha Spector from social services is going to call you and set up an appointment to fill out paperwork and see the house. You're sure you're okay with this, Maggie?"

"More than okay now that the old ticker's in top form again," Maggie assured her. "But I'd like to run up to the mall and get some little-girl stuff for the room. Make it more friendly-like. Do you have time to come along on Saturday?"

"A shopping trip with you? I'd love it. How does nine thirty sound? That way we can be at the mall when they open, check things out, and grab lunch."

"Well, I haven't had a girls' day out in a long time, so yes, that's fine, and we can be all set. When do you think she'll be cleared to come home?"

"Possibly by Monday, so we better get some serious shopping done on Saturday," Thea said with a laugh. "And thank you again for supper. I can't wait to get upstairs and heat it up."

"There's plenty for leftovers, too," Maggie said, and by the weight of the pot, she was right. "See you soon!"

The skies had cleared for a short ninety minutes midday, but the rain returned in earnest when Thea stepped out the office door. Head down, she rounded the porch, headed up the stairs, and met Ethan and the kids leaving just as a clap of thunder shook the air. "You guys have to go out?"

"Uncle Eefen burned the pasta," said Keegan. "It smells really, really bad."

"Oh, I've done that way too often," noted Thea as a flash of lightning brightened the stairwell from below. "But hey, Maggie brought me a big pot of her cinnamon steak, plenty for a crowd." She indicated the pot she was carrying, then her stairway. "Why don't you share this with me upstairs? You won't get soaked, there's a ton of food here, and Jazz texted that she grabbed a salad at the diner so I should count her out for supper."

"It smells really good," said Keegan. "And I'm really, really hungry."

"It does smell good." Mara looked from Thea to her uncle. "Can we try it, Uncle Ethan?"

Thea bit back her surprise.

Mara was being polite to her uncle. Ethan noticed it, too, because he agreed quickly. "Why not? Thank you, Thea." He reached out and drew the door open for her. She led the way up the stairs, and when the kids got inside, they exchanged grins. Mara moved toward the front windows and the turret as if drawn by the storm's antics. "This is so cool!"

"It's like living in a treetop!" said Keegan. And when the next clap of thunder followed a very convincing flash of lightning, they shrieked, then giggled.

"Can we watch the storm from the windows?" Mara asked. "Please?"

"Yes, and I'll make it better." Thea switched off the overhead light. The thick cloud cover had darkened the evening. With the inside lights off, the lightning show outside seemed intensified.

"Coolest house ever." Mara breathed the words as she and her brother knelt side by side, watching the storm.

Ethan stayed in the kitchen with Thea. She wished it didn't seem so natural, having him there. But it did.

"Plates?"

"Upper left."

He put plates on the table while she put on a pot of water for rice. Then he guessed the right drawer for silverware and added that. "New plates, new silverware, new pans." He thrust his chin toward the stove. "Earmarks of staying."

"Mostly Jazz's stuff, but who knew I was going to come north and fall in love with a sleepy little town? Not me." She measured out long-grain rice. "It gets under your skin, doesn't it?" One look at his face and she laughed. "Well, okay. Under my skin."

"It's mighty pretty skin, Thea."

She swallowed hard, eyes down. "Thank you."

He moved closer. Close enough that his soft voice wouldn't carry to the front room. "Do compliments embarrass you?"

"Not professional ones."

He reached out. Touched her hair softly. "The personal stuff."

"Not if we keep that off limits." This time she met his gaze and took a step back. "Only a foolish person risks their livelihood by dating the boss."

"I've forgotten dating." He deadpanned a look toward the kids, and she laughed.

"And that's okay when you're busy putting first things first." The kids jumped when a bright crackle of lightning split the darkness, followed by a resounding crash of thunder. "Look at their faces," she whispered, smiling. "I've never seen them so happy. Have you?"

She looked up at him then.

He looked down, and there it was again. That flash. A sizzle that had nothing to do with the storm outside and maybe something to do with a storm within.

"So will they hate me when I take them away?" His expression turned contemplative as he posed the question. "If they fall in love with this place? With the new apartment?"

"Healing takes time."

He leaned against the counter and folded his arms. "You had some healing of your own to do, I expect."

She'd been about to put the rice into the water.

She stopped. She stared down into the water for a few short seconds and just breathed in and out. Then she answered him, but she didn't turn around. "I expect that's true of most of us."

"Was it bad?"

Why was he asking this? No one brought up her past, ever. Not even Kelsey and Jazz. They'd made it a forbidden topic years ago, and she'd deliberately left it that way.

"I'm only asking because you have an affinity for kids in trouble. Not just Mara and Shannon, but when you handle tough kids or situations in the practice, it's as if you have an innate understanding of what's going on in their heads. It's a huge plus when you're working with kids, Thea." He shifted his arms slightly. "I'm just sorry for whatever you had to go through that made you so in tune with this stuff."

Days. And nights. Faceless people. Old men. Young men. The scents. The sounds. Darkness surrounding her, not just from lack of light. From men with no sense of moral goodness. Until Sonny had stumbled on her one night.

God help me. Help me now, right now, because there's a reason I don't bring this up. You know that. You've always known that. Make him stop asking, make him be quiet, make him—

The next bolt of lightning was followed almost immediately by a resounding crash of thunder that made both kids scream.

Ethan moved their way quickly. "Hey, that was close, wasn't it?"

"So close!" Keegan looked half-scared and half-thrilled at the thought.

Mara went straight to thrilled, and Thea turned her focus back to the rice.

Rice was easy. It could be trusted if timed correctly. Life, relationships, men, romance . . . those were another story.

She'd pushed that off the radar a few years ago. How does one explain to a man what she had gone through as a child? How would a normal man respond to that? Or get it out of his head if they fell in love? Got married?

She knew enough about psychology to know most people wouldn't be able to table those images, so why muddy the waters with no good end in sight? Why open herself up to the hurt? Because there would be hurt. That was guaranteed.

"That smells so good, Thea." Keegan arched his elfin brows in expectation. "I was really hungry before Uncle Eefen burned the pasta. I'm mostly even more hungry now."

"Five minutes," she told him, then motioned him over. "Can you put napkins on the table?"

"Just like they do on TV!" He scrambled her way. "Did you hear that, guys? We're gonna eat at the table!"

"Called out by a four-year-old." Ethan came back to the kitchen. He didn't bring up her past again, but when she glanced up, he looked back, assessing.

What does he see? she wondered.

The damaged woman she saw in the mirror each day? Or just the simple woman she strived to be, direct and hardworking?

"I like your hair that way."

She was reaching for a bowl on an upper shelf, a bowl for the rice. Such a simple task. And then he was behind her, reaching higher to grasp the bowl for her.

He smelled wonderful.

He shouldn't. He should smell like burnt food and antiseptic cleaners, that odd, familiar scent of medical offices and hospitals, but there was none of that. Just soap, and some kind of aftershave, and man. Whatever that was.

"Here you go. I'm guessing Jazz put the bowls up there."

"You guessed correctly." She took the bowl from him and smiled her thanks. "I usually grab a chair but thought that might not be the smartest thing with kids around to see me. Chair. Hot stove. Climbing."

"Especially not when you have taller help close by." He sent her a teasing look, but this wasn't a Hallmark movie or some feel-good story. It was life. Her life. Plain and simple. And she'd become resigned to all the constraints of that long ago.

"How'd the call with social services go today?"

While the rice finished, she explained what had happened that afternoon. When she was done, she added, "I had to deal with social services a lot in Pittsburgh, and nothing like this would have ever happened."

"Is that because you pushed harder here? Or because the agency was more flexible?"

She stirred the spiced beef, considering. "Maybe both. Does it matter, in the end?" she wondered. "It was just nice to have it all work out, and no one got angry or riled up. I've never thought about working anywhere but a big city, but being here has shown me alternatives. A great university hospital less than an hour away, and a community that cares about each other. And their town."

"You're in danger of becoming a small-town girl," he told her, making a face. "Next comes the picket fence and the two-story colonial."

"Not on this girl's bucket list," she replied smoothly, because how does one have a normal adult relationship when their entire sexual identity has been abnormal for so long?

"You didn't think you'd like small towns, either," he reminded her as he brought the pot of simmering beef to the table. "That changed over a few months. Maybe you're not as set in your ways as you'd like the world to believe, Thea."

She was in some ways, but he didn't need to know that.

"That smells so good." Mara crossed the room to them.

"Hey, Mara. Are you free Saturday?" Thea asked.

Ethan transferred the rice into the bowl. "I've got morning hours, and Hale was going to take the kids to the fish hatchery."

"But I can go to see the fish a different time," Mara told her.

"I need your opinion on some stuff," Thea told her. "There's a sick little girl coming to live at the Tompkins house, and they want to brighten the room up. She's seven years old . . ."

"Like me."

"Exactly like you, and I've never done a room for a seven-year-old girl before. Do you think you could help Maggie and me? Go shopping with us and pick things out?"

Mara's expression softened. "I would love to go shopping. I haven't gone shopping—"

Her eyes went wide, then narrow. She sighed.

"So this would be good for both of us," Thea told her. "Because I haven't been shopping in a long time, either. A little retail therapy might be just what the doctor ordered."

Mara knit her brow, and Ethan slung an easy arm around her shoulders. "No therapists involved, although I'm still going to contact the one in Warsaw. Retail therapy is just another name for shopping, honey."

"Oh. Well." Mara tipped a smile up at Thea. "That might be my favorite kind. Can I go?" she asked Ethan, then corrected herself. "May I go, I mean."

"Yes. And Thea, thank you for thinking of this." He angled her a look that Mara couldn't see, and when Mara crossed back to the window for another round of storms, he frowned. "Why don't I think of these things? How bad am I for these kids, Thea? And how crazy was my sister for leaving them with me?"

Men and shopping . . .

Men and room décor . . .

Men and—

"Ethan. Are you going to beat yourself up for not shopping? Because that'll get old real quick," she told him. "And I expect your sister either thought you were pretty darned wonderful . . ."

He made a disbelieving face, and she smiled.

"Or she was absolutely, positively out of choices and desperate, so you got the short straw. Hey, guys." She winked at him as she set the bowl of rice on the table. "Food's ready. And if you want, you can face the windows to watch the storm. Okay?"

"Yes!" Keegan's enthusiasm commandeered his whole being as he slid across the hardwood floor to the small dining table.

"This is fun, Thea." Mara slid out a chair to face the storm. She didn't look happy, but she didn't look stressed, either, a welcome change. "I didn't know watching a storm could be like this."

"Pretty cool," Thea agreed. "There aren't many thunderstorms in California, but once you get to the Midwest and points east, they're a regular thing. A sign of spring and a symbol of summer."

"Well, they're like the coolest things ever," declared Keegan. "So maybe I just want to stay here forever, Uncle Eefen, and have cool storms. I might like that a lot." Wide-eyed, Keegan gazed up at Ethan with all the sincerity of youth on his side, kind of cementing Ethan's concern that now the kids might like Wishing Bridge too much.

Thea didn't look for Ethan's reaction.

He had goals. Goals he'd worked hard for. Goals he'd already put on hold once. She understood that.

But she understood children, too. They were a gift from God no matter which way you stumbled on them, and deserving of sacrificial love.

"Let's say grace," she offered as they all took a seat at the table.

"I will, but I don't th-th-think Mara likes to do it anymore." Keegan threw his sister under the bus with a dose of preschool honesty. "She doesn't th-think God really loves anybody, because if he did they wouldn't just go around and die, right?"

Thea didn't rush her answer. Mara looked embarrassed, while concern deepened Ethan's expression. Once they'd settled in and clasped hands, Thea said a simple grace, then she lightly squeezed Mara's hand. "You know what?"

Mara shook her head as Ethan helped Keegan with his food.

"I think God loves all of us," she said softly. "We're human. And that means we're not perfect. Things happen. We get sick. We get hurt. And sometimes people have accidents and we lose them down here, but I believe they're waiting for us in heaven."

"Like for real?" Keegan made a funny face at her as if she were kidding.

"Like so totally for real."

"Why do you think something like that?" Mara's lips turned down in a now-familiar fashion, but she helped herself to rice. "Everybody knows it's not one bit true."

"I think it is, and I'm a pretty smart woman, if I do say so myself." She poured Keegan some water and kept her voice light. "When Jesus was dying on that cross, he promised a thief that he'd be with him that day in paradise. The thief asked for forgiveness. Right there, on a cross, he asked God to forgive him for what he'd done, and Jesus welcomed him into heaven. And if Jesus says it?" Thea swept them a knowing look. "I believe it. So there you go."

"He really said that?" Mara made a skeptical face.

"It's in the Bible, so yes. The sinner asked for forgiveness, and Jesus told him his sins were forgiven. And that they would be together in paradise."

"Do you think my mom and dad are in heaven?" she pressed. "Like it's really there and so are they?"

Ethan paused with his fork halfway to his mouth.

Thea didn't hesitate. "I do. But I also believe that while they would have never chosen this fate if they'd been asked, sometimes things happen unexpectedly. Good things and horrible things, like losing someone we love. There's another thing I know, too, after working with kids and families for years." She smiled at Mara and Keegan. "Your parents would want you to move on with your lives. To reach out and be happy.

Grab joy. Grab peace. Grab hope and do your best to be the best person you can be. Every day."

"My mom used to say things like that." Mara had a forkful of beef in her hand, but she didn't move it toward her mouth. "Just like that, Thea."

"Then we'd probably be friends if we'd ever met," Thea told her. "For now, you and I can be friends. And Keegan, too." She smiled at the little fellow, and he dimpled instantly.

"And Uncle Eefen, too, because he wants to be friends. Like maybe my bestest friend ever, right?"

Ethan reached up and rubbed his left shoulder, but he smiled at Keegan, then Mara. "I'll be a bestest friend for as long as I can, because being around you two makes me happy."

"It does?" Mara didn't sound skeptical. She sounded astounded, and for good reason, since she'd made it not one bit fun for the last nine months.

"Yes." Ethan faced her. He smiled, but it was a serious smile. "Because you're part of the family. Part of my beautiful sister and your dad. Your mom made me feel very special when she said you guys could live with me if anything ever happened to them. That's like the biggest job a parent can do, to figure out who should raise their children."

"Well, I'd still rather have my own daddy," Keegan told them honestly. Then he sighed. "But I love you too, Uncle Eefen, so that's okay. Right?"

"It's absolutely okay," Ethan told him.

Mara gazed at her meal. She'd eaten about half of what she'd taken, and it wasn't that much to begin with. "I think I'm full."

"Well, that would be a shame because Maggie sent cake." The last thing she wanted was for Mara to use food and trauma and lack of appetite as a means of exercising control. She knew that slippery slope from watching Jazz maneuver it. "Next time, maybe."

"I want cake!" Keegan bounced in his chair. "What kind did she make?"

"White cake with chocolate icing."

"I love that one!" Keegan's whole face lit up. "It's like a favorite one of all!"

"Awesome, dude." Ethan high-fived him. "Maggie will be happy to hear that."

Mara hesitated, then lifted her fork. "I might be able to eat a little more."

"Great." Thea smiled easily, but inside she fist-pumped a victory.

They'd touched on some hot-button topics the past few minutes, and Mara could have chosen to fall apart.

She didn't.

And when she wolfed down a sizable piece of cake a half hour later, that was one of the best indicators Thea'd seen since meeting her a few months before. Food . . . being normal . . . ranked higher than self-punishment. And that was a big step in the right direction.

CHAPTER ELEVEN

Ethan closed up the office at noon on Saturday with no work or kids waiting for him. He walked across the porch a free man, a rarity since losing Alexis and Peter. He'd been either working or parenting since then, so the thought of a few hours on his own presented itself like a gift.

Spring baseball...

A bag of chips or a monster-sized bowl of popcorn...

And his feet up while Hale and Kelsey had Keegan, and Thea and Maggie shopped with Mara.

He rounded the corner of the porch and stopped cold.

"Hey, Ethan."

Eva. Here. Now. There wasn't time to shield the surprise or the negative reaction.

"Glad to see me. Like always. Must run in the family." Arms folded, she locked eyes with him in challenge, exactly what he didn't need now or ever. He'd had his share of challenges lately, hadn't he?

"Let's go straight to surprised, Eva. What's up?" She'd taken a seat on the railing. She was dressed down, like so many young people did these days. Ragged jeans. A slouchy sweater. And her hands, hands that hadn't done much work in the past, looked dry and worn. "How'd you get here?"

She hooked a thumb.

"Please tell me you didn't hitchhike your way across the country."

"Part of the way. A few buses. And some dishwashing stints to cover expenses."

That explained the hands.

She looked sad. Belligerent. As if she wanted to take on the world. But didn't one have to stick with something—*anything*—to make a difference? He stood there, floundering for words, feeling wounded that his anticipated afternoon of freedom had just been scrapped. "Come on upstairs. I was going to watch the game."

"Where are the kids? I came to see them." She'd never visited Alexis in California. Well, wait. Once or twice. Passing through to head north up I-5. He'd never wondered about that. Was it normal, to never visit your sister?

"Good." He wasn't sure if it was good or the worst idea possible, but family was family. "They're with friends right now."

"That's nice. That they've made friends." She followed him around the corner and glanced left and right as he unlocked the ground-level door. "You work and live in the same building?"

"Convenient, right?"

"Or crazy restrictive. Your choice."

Oh, Eva.

He unlocked the upstairs door and headed inside. She followed him, then tugged her hoodie more closely around her.

"Cold?" He tweaked the thermostat. "I turned it down because it was warm yesterday, a welcome change. Spring's a little slow around here."

She studied the space, then him. Then the apartment again. And that was when he realized she didn't have a bag. A suitcase. Nothing he saw. "Where's your luggage, sis?"

"It got lifted just outside Chicago. I-90 has its share of weird people, you know?"

"Someone took your luggage?"

"My bad for using the restroom at a stop and not unloading it. At least I had my purse with me."

She'd really done it. She'd thumbed her way across the country. The good thing was that no one had killed her. The bad thing was that she'd actually done it. And seemed to think it was all right, and of course it wasn't, and he had two impressionable children who would hear her stories and not understand the wealth of danger involved. "I'd have sent you bus fare."

She made a face. "Have you ever ridden one of those things for that long?"

Sure he had. Because that's what he could afford when he was her age. "I used to take the bus all the time in undergrad and med school. It was cheap and it got me from place to place. I studied. Or I napped." He shrugged because he'd done what he needed to do. "It's a heck of a lot safer than traveling cross-country at the mercy of strangers."

"Well, it got me here with no money out of my pocket."

"But you have no clothes, no shoes, no belongings," he reminded her. "The cost of a ticket probably doesn't outweigh the loss, Eva."

"Well, that's the difference between you and me," she told him, as if he hadn't already figured that out. "You err on the side of caution. I just err."

Succinct and correct. Stop assessing and judging and go to the practicality of the situation. "You hungry?"

She nodded quickly. Too quickly. He opened the fridge and withdrew a container of lo mein from earlier that week. "I made the kids baked chicken with this on the side. It's from a little Chinese place right here in town, and it's really good."

"Forks?"

"Right there." He pointed to the drawer behind her.

She pulled out a fork and didn't ask about heating the food. She just ate it right there at the counter, as if she hadn't eaten in a while. And he let her eat while he reconfigured his day, his afternoon . . . his life?

Possibly. He unwrapped a pack of popcorn and tossed it into the microwave, but he didn't hit the popcorn button. He'd made that mistake the first time, and the apartment had reeked of burnt corn for half the day. He set a lesser time and pushed start, then turned.

"Have you talked to Dad lately?" he asked.

The fork paused, then she shook her head, eyes down. "I haven't, no."

"At all?" he pressed, because that was a little weird, wasn't it?

"Nope." She didn't look up. She didn't sound sad about it, either. More like accepting, as if she expected to be ignored.

Their father hadn't been warm and fuzzy even before life had turned upside down on him. He was a brilliant man, an engineer with a major aviation manufacturer, but if he had a gentle side, it had eroded a long time ago. "It's tough when we're all grieving a loss."

She sent him a sharp look. "I barely knew Alexis. You guys lived on the coast, I lived a thousand miles away in New Mexico with Mom and a mess of fairly weird people she took up with near our place in Santa Fe. I don't recall anyone coming to visit us. Ever. If you get my drift."

Oh, he got it. He'd been almost grown when everything fell apart after Jarod died. But he didn't pretend to understand the convoluted workings of the adult decisions that had gone on around him. He still didn't understand them, and he hadn't been a kid in a long time. "People change after tragedies. Dad's lost two kids now. Jarod and Alexis. Let's cut him some slack."

She looked like she wanted to argue, then thought better of it. "But what about you, Ethan?" She studied him from her place along the counter. "You've lost your sister. Your little brother. And your mother. How are you not stark raving mad?"

Oddly, her question made him feel mad. Not crazy—he hoped—just downright angry, because why should all these things happen to one family? "Eva, listen. I've got two kids to raise now. I can't go down bad-memory lane and dredge up all the awful in my life, because their lives are what matter now. So when they get back, I'm putting the lid on this talk. They've got enough to deal with. Let's not add more."

She frowned, then lifted one shoulder. "Makes sense. You got room for me to stay here awhile? Until I get on my feet?"

He wanted to say no.

He wanted to wind back the clock and come around the corner of that big, wide porch and find it empty, but that wasn't an option. He jutted his chin toward the couch. "Comfy couch right there. And food. But no freeloading, Eva. You need to get a job, you need to become self-sufficient. And there's a community college not far from here. If you want to go back to school, I'll help you fill out the financial aid forms."

"Too constricting." She made a classic Eva frown-face.

"And yet possibly vital to maintaining an existence as we mature," he told her. "Education and jobs aren't the enemy."

"You are your father's son." It was a quiet observation, as if gazing from outside, as if having rules was a bad thing. It wasn't, and he didn't want that devil-may-care persona to mess with Keegan and Mara. Especially Mara, now that he'd finally seen a glimmer of hope.

"I'm an adult," he told her, "and now a dad. We take things like work and paychecks and bills seriously because there is no other option."

"Sure there is." She faced him square. "I lived it. With Mom. And no one came running to set your wealth of good examples, did they?"

And there it was, the lament.

The "poor little me" thing got old after a while, because yeah, she'd had a crazy life with their mother, but it wasn't like theirs had been a piece of cake, either. And blaming him and Alexis wasn't going to do anyone any good. They'd been older . . . but they had still been kids.

"I wish things had gone better for you. For all of us," he told her. "But that's the thing about the past, Eva. It's over. Done. I don't look back, I look ahead, and that might be some good advice for you, too. If we get stuck in the past it's real hard to make progress in the present."

"It's all about progress with you and Dad. Neither one of you can simply stand still and enjoy the moment."

He pulled the popcorn out of the microwave, unscrewed the lid on a bottle of iced tea, and raised them both, the popcorn and the tea. "That's my current plan, actually. This"—he indicated the snacks with his eyes—"and spring training, Yankees versus Orioles. The season starts soon. I'm practicing my fan movements. You're more than welcome to join me." He crossed to the chair, sat down, and propped his feet on the rented coffee table.

Then he turned the game on.

She didn't budge.

She stood there, behind him, unmoving.

They didn't know each other. Not really. They'd spent no time together growing up. She was born after Jarod died, and then his parents had divorced and his mother had taken Eva back to her hometown in New Mexico. His mother had rarely called and never wrote. It was as if she had stepped out of their lives once Jarod was gone, leaving his father to see Ethan and Alexis through high school and college.

Then his mother died, and Eva appeared on his father's doorstep at age fourteen.

More drama.

More sadness.

Another kid let down by family, which is why he couldn't mess up with Keegan and Mara. He'd seen what could happen. It wasn't pretty. He needed to do this right.

"I'm going to take a walk and see the town."

He didn't want her to go walking alone. He didn't want her to shoplift something from Jill Jackson's new store or flirt with some married guy. His father had been quick to cite Eva's high school indiscretions, but she was a grown-up now. Ethan couldn't exactly say no.

"It's a great town, Eva. Filled with nice people. You'll love it." He motioned to the closet. "I've got a heavier jacket in there. Grab it. The wind is cold today."

She hesitated, then crossed to the closet and retrieved the jacket. "Thanks. I won't be gone long."

"I know." When she raised an eyebrow, he thrust his chin toward the window. "Small town. Doesn't take much time to see it."

"Ah." She tugged the zipper up and slipped out the door. She left her purse behind. He waited until he saw her walking up Maplewood Avenue, then quietly checked the purse. He wasn't aware of any drug use in her past, but he wasn't about to take chances with the kids.

She'd shoplifted in California. She'd had several run-ins with police when she was younger, but then she'd straightened up somewhat. She had managed to graduate from high school only to ditch community college when she deemed it too hard, but then his father discovered she'd been having a relationship with a married professor. He'd thrown her out and she'd headed up to the Pacific Northwest in search of herself or some such nonsense.

What was she doing here now? Looking for direction? Or a free ride?

He had no idea, and he wasn't sure how to handle it, either. She was his sister. He should be kind. But her bad choices didn't bode well for two impressionable children, and they had to come first.

He turned the game off.

The urge to watch it faded as he weighed his options. And when he heard Mara's voice coming up the stairs, he tucked Eva's purse up on a shelf in the closet. It held nothing more dangerous than a small bottle of ibuprofen—which he checked the contents of—and a small pocketknife.

Pocketknives and children weren't a good mix. But with the surprise of Eva waiting outside his door, he wasn't really sure what would be a good mix right now.

CHAPTER TWELVE

Mara came through the door and hurried to Ethan's side. "Is it all right if I help Maggie get the room ready for this little girl? She's coming home to their house on Monday, and we have to have everything all set for her. Just so," she added in a Maggie-like tone. Then she paused and drew a deep breath as Thea came through the door. "It smells funny in here."

"Popcorn." He motioned to the bowl.

She shook her head. "Popcorn doesn't smell funny. It smells really good. No, like . . ." She sniffed again, thinking, then made a face. "Like perfume funny."

Thea paused at the door. She glanced around, as if expecting some-one to be there, then shot him a look of over-the-top chagrin, as if they'd walked in on him and a date.

At some point he'd ponder why he hadn't had a date in nearly eigh-teen months, but not now. "Your Aunt Eva came into town a couple of hours ago. She's taking a walk right now, but she'll be back."

"Aunt Eva?" Mara frowned. "The one who came to the funeral with all the funny-colored hair?"

She'd done exactly that, pulling attention onto herself instead of Alexis and Peter and their orphaned kids. "That's the one."

"We don't know her." Mara searched his face for guidance, and it was tough, because he didn't really know Eva all that well, either.

"Then this is a chance to get to know her," he said lightly. "What's in the bags? Did you do some shopping, too?"

Mara shook her head. "This is for Thea's house, upstairs, but we do have to go shopping, Uncle Ethan."

"For?"

"Easter clothes."

"Easter clothes." He repeated the words with a hint of question.

"For church on Easter Sunday," she explained. "I didn't even think of it 'til we went to the stores, but they've got Easter dresses and shoes and all the things we need because Keegan's not the same size he was last year, and I'm not the same size, either. And Mom and Dad always got us new clothes for Easter."

"When is Easter?" He looked to Thea for help, and she didn't make fun of him for not knowing. He'd taken the kids to church some weekends, and he tried to listen to their prayers nightly because Alexis had done that, but he'd been spotty.

"Two weeks from tomorrow," Thea told him. "Next Sunday is Palm Sunday, heralding Jesus's triumphant ride into Jerusalem."

"And then Easter. Of course. I actually aced an undergrad course on early Christianity. No lectures about the irony in that, please."

Thea splayed her hands. "I'll refrain."

"Appreciated. So"—he shifted his attention back to Mara—"we need to go dress shopping?"

Mara nodded, watching him.

How hard could it be?

"And stuff for Keegan, too. Like a little suit or something."

Keegan had worn one to the funeral, probably the one his mother had bought him for last Easter.

"Can Thea come? Do you have time to come, Thea?" Mara turned her way, looking hopeful. Such a contrast to the sullen, angry child he'd brought to Wishing Bridge. The difference was startling.

"Well, we need to get a dress for Shannon, too, so yes, I'd love to come, but we have to do it when Warsaw Medical is on call. Ethan and I can't be in Rochester or Buffalo together if one of us is on call."

"Which means Wednesday or Thursday evening," said Ethan.

Mara waited.

Thea pulled out her phone and tapped it. "Let's shoot for Wednesday. If something comes up we'll still have Thursday. Okay?"

"Will Shannon be able to come?" Mara asked, and Thea hesitated.

"We'll see. I would think so, but she might be too tired."

"And do I get to meet her on Monday?" Mara pressed. "I want to show her the new room when it's all done."

"After Ethan picks you up at Mrs. Harper's, okay? As long as your homework's all done. If that's all right with Ethan?"

Mara redirected her attention to him with a hopeful look.

"It's fine. I want to see Shannon myself," he told them. "Can you clear it with Maggie?"

"Will do. Kid"—Thea pointed upstairs—"let's stow this stuff and get that room done. I'm on call tonight, and we're running short on time."

"Okay!" Mara hurried up the adjacent stairs to put the bags away, then came right back down. "Done!"

Enthusiasm. Smiles. Not full tilt, but a marked improvement. Would Eva's negativity drive them back to square one?

He feared it might, but he couldn't just turn his back on her, either. Did that make him kind? Or stupid?

"I'll bring her back in an hour," Thea promised. She noogied Mara's head lightly. "She's a great shopper, Ethan. Doesn't get bogged down and doesn't whine. She's a keeper."

Head tilted, Mara grinned up at Thea. She leaned in slightly, almost inviting a hug. She drew back at the last minute and hurried toward the stairs. "Gotta go!"

"We do." Thea gave him a short wave and a commiserative look. About Eva? About shopping for dresses? About—

Stop whining, his conscience berated him. *How about looking in the mirror at all the good things you have, that you've done, that you've seen? Get out of the funk, man. You're wasting time. Wasting life. Maybe it's you that needs the therapy. Ever thought of that?*

Not until now, no, but the mental smackdown provided a wake-up call. If only everything didn't seem so tight. So heavy on his shoulders. Heavy enough that sometimes it hurt just to take a breath.

Maybe Mara will take better to counseling if you go together? What about that?

Why hadn't he considered that before? Like during that long, drawn-out autumn following their loss? They were less than two months away from the one-year anniversary, and he was still treading water, as if life was on hold until he moved to Chicago. That was his mistake. Not theirs.

The door buzzer interrupted his thoughts. He hit the intercom and Keegan's voice rang through. "We got to see so many fishies!" Pure joy raised the little fellow's voice.

Ethan hit the release button. The lower door opened with a bang, total Keegan, and when he burst through the apartment doorway with unbridled enthusiasm, Ethan caught him, swung him up, and hugged him. "You had fun."

"So much fun!" Eyes wide, Keegan pointed back at Hale. "We saw like a million little bitty fishies, and some medium ones, and the lady said they'll let them go when they're bigger, because you know why?"

"Tell me."

Keegan leaned in as if sharing a big secret. "Because the big fishies will eat the little ones. Eeek!" He made a gruesome face and slapped his hands across his mouth as if in mortal danger. "So they let them l-l-live there a little longer . . ." He struggled to form so many Ls in a row. "Then they let them go. It's like they're adopting them just like you're adopting us. Just like that!"

Another thing he'd let fall by the wayside, waiting for the new job. Official adoption meant organizing time and legalities and protocol, and he'd been shoving it off. Not because he didn't want to do it but because laws varied from state to state, and it didn't make sense to start the legal process in New York, then move to Illinois midstream. But maybe not jumping on that increased Mara's feelings of loss and abandonment. "That's cool, Keegs. You hungry?"

"Miss Kelsey brought me fruit snacks, and then she gave me a juice box and then a cookie. And her baby threw up all over her coat and smelled yucky, so she had to go back to Maggie's house. When's supper?"

"He's a boy." Hale grinned and shoved his hands into his pockets. "Bottomless pit."

"Is Hayley all right?" Ethan asked.

"She's fine, just ate too fast and burped up a sizable amount. Pretty normal. I'm heading over to Maggie's. Oh, she sent these." He set a tin of cookies on the table. "She said it was a housewarming gift."

Supper. Cake. Cookies. A single dad should never take a friend like Maggie for granted. "I'll call her and thank her."

"She'd like that. Dude." Hale bumped knuckles with Keegan. "See you soon, okay?"

"Okay! And th-th-thank you!"

Hale laughed. "You're welcome." Hale headed down the stairs at a quick clip. He'd become a good friend. Max had become a good friend, too, and when Ethan had worked downstate, he couldn't really say he'd had good friends. The true friend type that would swing by and take a kid to see little fish or go shopping or anything like that.

He got Keegan settled with a color-by-number book, called Maggie to thank her for the cookies, and pondered frozen chicken casserole or PB&J for supper.

The sandwich option won just as Keegan scurried to the bathroom and the downstairs bell rang.

"Eva?"

"Yes."

He hit the buzzer. "Come on up."

"I'll need a key if I'm staying awhile," she announced as she came through the door. "Ringing the bell is a royal pain."

"I prefer the term 'slightly inconvenient necessity.' We can share my key for the moment. The landlord is careful about handing them out." It sounded lame, but smart landlords knew better than to pepper the community with property keys.

"What if I lose it and we only have one?"

"The landlord has one. He's a retired state trooper. A great guy. You'll meet him if you stay around."

"Want help with supper?" She eyed the empty kitchen with a hungry expression.

He shook his head. "Sandwiches. Keeping it easy."

Keegan appeared just then. He stared at Eva, then slipped over to Ethan's side, silent and shy.

"Hey, Keegan." Eva squatted down. "I'm Aunt Eva. Your mom's little sister. I came to visit you and Mara."

Keegan narrowed his gaze. He studied her, still quiet.

"How old are you, buddy?"

"I fink my real aunt would know how old I am." He frowned deliberately. "I know how old you are, silly."

"You do?" She posed the question in a voice that suggested he didn't actually know her age.

Keegan nodded but didn't let a sliver of daylight show between him and Ethan. "You're twenty-two years old. Right?"

Eva looked surprised. "How'd you know that?"

"I am very smart," Keegan assured her. "But I th-th-think Uncle Eefen told me when we were looking at pictures."

Ethan motioned to a built-in bookcase. He'd put pictures there to remind the kids of their parents. Their grandparents. The whole family on both sides. It seemed like the right thing to do.

"That is pretty smart," Eva told him. Then she looked at Ethan. "Have Peter's parents acknowledged you as the kids' guardian? Or are they still threatening court action?"

Peter's parents had expected the children to come to them. They made that clear when the will was read. Their promised fight hadn't occurred, and Ethan hoped it wouldn't. He shook his head at her and dropped his gaze to Keegan.

"Ah. Sorry." She made a face and actually looked contrite. "I have to sharpen my kid-friendly intelligence skills."

"Crucial strategy around here now. Do you still have a cell phone, Eva?"

She pulled out a pricey device. "No matter what else happens, this bill gets paid."

Total millennial mind-set. Phone first. Forget safety. Dismiss work. Shrug off self-discipline. But don't be without a smartphone. "Mara's helping a friend for a little while. She'll be back soon."

"Perfect. I'll be here. Hey, is there an ice-cream store open in this town? I could work there. I'm great at scooping cones and creating sundaes."

Ethan held back his opinion of that particular resume skill. "They open for the season soon. The kids love stopping there. It's on Franklin, right around the corner off Main Street. Next to the municipal parking lot."

"That's about the size of a postage stamp. When you said small town, you meant small town." Dismay wrinkled her nose. "I can't imagine what folks do to keep themselves busy here."

"Work. School. Sports. Church."

She lifted her brows at Keegan. "Sounds like a great time, doesn't it, buddy?"

He shrank closer to Ethan's leg, and Ethan hadn't thought that was possible. "I get to play soccer now. It's real fun. But sometimes I get kicked," the little guy admitted.

"Bummer."

Keegan frowned. "Can I have my sandwich now?" He peered up at Ethan as if begging a respite. "Like right now? P-please?"

"Sure. Want one, Eva?" Ethan crossed to the kitchen counter.

"Where's my purse?"

"Top of the closet. Out of reach of little hands."

"You go through it?"

He didn't look up from his supper task. "Sure did. An ounce of prevention . . ." He smoothed peanut butter across the bread, then marshmallow crème. Keegan didn't like jam.

"Did you remove anything?"

"No." He set the top piece of bread on the sandwich and faced her. "But we can't leave dangerous things around where the kids might find them."

She crossed to the counter where a small wooden rack held carving knives and steak knives. "Like this isn't an attraction for them?"

"Kids need to learn how to use kitchen knives. But I didn't want them snooping and finding something intriguing. They're curious, Eva. Don't make it more than it is."

She studied him, then made a face of regret. "Sorry. I know I do that. I'm trying to get better about it. It's childish."

"And that's a refreshingly mature statement," he told her, and smiled when she smiled first. "Since I'm a work in progress, too, we can improve ourselves together."

The glimmer of hope blinked out when Mara came through the door just then. She saw Eva and stopped dead, staring. Then she burst into tears. Heartbroken tears. Desperate tears.

She didn't turn to Ethan.

She turned to Thea and buried her head into Thea's jacket, sobbing.

"Hey, little one. Hey." Thea crouched down and held her. She raised a questioning look to Ethan, then Eva, then Ethan again.

He shook his head because he had no idea why the sight of Eva— And then he knew.

With bone-crushing insight, he realized exactly what happened. Eva hadn't come to Wishing Bridge with rainbow hair. She'd gotten rid of the spiked pixie cut. She'd lost the attention-drawing spectral hues and let her hair go back to its natural ash-blond. With the longer hair and the normal appearance, she'd come to Wishing Bridge looking a lot like her older sister had at that age. Looking like Alexis.

"Mara." He reached out, and Thea guided Mara into his arms. "It's all right, baby. It's all right."

"It's not." The words burst from her, despairing and angry. "It's not all right, it will never, ever, ever be all right, because they're gone! They're gone and all I've got is you and Keegan, and I just want my mommy and my daddy so much. I just want them. Not anyone else, not you, not her, and not anyone! Why don't you understand me?"

She pulled away, darted off to her room, and slammed the door hard. Twice.

Keegan had been reaching for his sandwich.

He stopped, crossed to the couch, and just sat there, head down, staring at nothing, looking as helpless as Ethan felt.

Eva swore softly.

Ethan raised a hand of caution. "No swearing."

"You're letting her get away with that?" Eva asked. She looked incredulous, as if she had expected a very different greeting from the one she had received.

"You surprised her, Eva."

Eva bristled while Thea stood just inside the door, probably not daring to move.

"So I inspired the over-the-top reaction? Great." Eva rolled her eyes. "Funny how the commercials make raising kids look like fun. Clearly propaganda."

"You look like Alexis now."

Eva paused, mouth open.

"The last time Mara saw you was the funeral. You had crazy hair and makeup and eyebrow piercings. Today she walked in and I think the first thing she thought was what she's been wishing and praying for since last June. That her mother had come walking in the door."

Eva brought her hand to her throat. "I never thought of that when I went natural. I just figured it was time to start playing by grown-up rules. Oh, man." She twisted the small gold chain that hung around her neck. "I didn't mean to upset her, Ethan. Honest, I didn't. I never thought about such a thing triggering that kind of reaction."

"Welcome to my world." He drew a deep breath and faced Thea. "Thank you for today. I'll go talk to her once she's calmed down. She had a great time going out with you girls."

"As did we." Thea shifted her attention to Eva and offered a hand. "Thea Anastas. I live upstairs, and I'm the nurse practitioner at Hillside Medical. Nice to meet you."

"Eva Brandenburg. Out of work, derelict, irresponsible younger sister."

Ethan wasn't sure if she meant to be funny or gain sympathy, but Thea didn't opt for either. She went straight for the heart. "You've picked a great town to turn over a new leaf, Eva. Welcome to Wishing Bridge." She turned back toward Ethan. "I'm on call until noon tomorrow, but give a shout if you need me. And Jazz will be home soon. A movie night with hot dogs and Jazz might be a better alternative for the kids. Just until Mara's emotions settle down."

It was a great suggestion. He didn't want to hurt Eva's feelings, but Mara's reaction had skyrocketed to critical in the blink of an eye. How was Mara going to get used to having Eva around if every time she looked at her she saw her mother's face?

"Time, Ethan." Thea spoke quietly from the door. "Prayer and time work wonders. And life goes on."

He understood the time thing. He hated it, because he'd gone through it when Jarod died. When his mother moved to New Mexico, leaving two children behind, then her death. And then losing Alexis . . .

He knew it.

But he didn't have to like it.

CHAPTER THIRTEEN

Thea pulled into Maggie's driveway late Monday afternoon. She put the car in park and let Shannon look around. "I'm going to live *here*?" Shannon faced Thea. "In town?"

"Yes."

"I've never lived in town." Shannon peered left, then right. She climbed out of the car and crossed to the sidewalk, studying the vintage neighborhood rising just east of Main Street. "Are there people in all these houses?"

"There are."

She smiled. Not a scared, fearful smile, but a gentle, genuine look of peace. "I've always wanted to live where there's people, Miss Thea."

"Just Thea, sweetheart. That's fine. And we bought you some new clothes, but you'll need more, so we'll go shopping together. All right?"

"I've always wanted to go shopping, too," Shannon admitted, as if going shopping was a sought-after goal. "But where's Gee Gee? Is she inside?"

Thea shook her head as she clasped Shannon's hand. "She's in a special place where they can make sure she takes her medicine. The old house had gotten kind of worn out." She didn't go into detail about the leaking roof and the cold, squalid existence. "This way Gee Gee's safe and warm. And you will be, too. We'll go visit her once you're settled here. She's only about fifteen minutes away."

Shannon gazed up at the Tompkins house just as Maggie and Jeb came out the front door to greet her. "Is this Miss Shannon?" asked Maggie. Her sprightly voice brought light to the moment.

Shannon looked from one to the other. "Yes."

"I'm Maggie, and this is Jeb," Maggie told her as she came down the stairs looking more spry than she'd been a few months back. She reached out a hand and touched Shannon's shoulder. "Thea was staying with us for a while, but now she's got her own place and we've got an extra room that might be just perfect for a seven-year-old girl."

"Except I'll be eight in June." Shannon frowned slightly. "Will it be all right for an eight-year-old girl, too?"

"I think it will," said Jeb in a kind voice. "But let's go in and you can let us know what needs changing. I'm a handy one with changing things, and I like to keep busy."

Shannon studied him, then snapped her fingers in a very convincing manner. "I saw you!"

"Do tell." Jeb smiled down at her, looking most interested.

"In Nana's pictures, there was a picture of you and my Nana and Papa and Gee Gee."

"Your Gee Gee and I were old friends, and we're related in a kind of fashion, if you know what I mean."

"I have no idea what you mean, and that's for certain, but I like the way you talk, Mr. Jeb." She put a hand into his, and Thea was pretty sure she grabbed his hand *and* his heart in that moment. "I sure do like it a lot."

"Let's go in and get you settled, hmm?" Maggie led the way.

When they got upstairs, Shannon walked into the room, eyes wide, mouth open. "This is for me?"

"Your room, dear. Yes. And if we need to change anything, you let us know."

"Oh, there's nothing to change, is there?" She gazed up at Maggie, surprised. "It is so perfectly perfect just like this." She touched the edge of the pink, yellow, and white comforter. "And pink and yellow are my favorite favorites. How did you know?"

"You told Thea. And she told us. And we all went shopping together."

"You excited about goin' back to school, honey?" asked Jeb.

Worry drew Shannon's expression down. "Well, I'm excited about school, I love school so much, but I don't have any clothes to wear to school. Unless . . ." She peeked up at Thea. "Did maybe someone get my clothes from Gee Gee's house? Because we could do that."

"You'd outgrown them!" Thea didn't mention that the clothing had been left on purpose. She kept her voice easy and motioned toward the dresser and closet. "I hope it's okay that we bought a bunch of things to get you started. Pants. Shirts. Dresses. Leggings. But we have to go shoe shopping together. And for an Easter dress."

"I've never had an Easter dress in my entire life," breathed Shannon, as if the thought amazed her. She yawned then, and Thea took the hint.

"How about we let you explore the people and the town and the clothes tomorrow." The doorbell chimed and Thea motioned Shannon downstairs. "That's probably Dr. Brandenburg and his two kids. He wants to see how you're doing now. He came to the hospital right after your surgery, but you were sick that day. You might not remember him."

Shannon made a face. "I mostly just remember you and Miss Elaina and Luvvy Lamb. They were so nice to me!"

"The hospital staff was incredible," Thea agreed. "Come on, pretty girl. Let's go meet some new folks." She led the way downstairs as Ethan ushered the kids in.

"Maggie!" Keegan hurried toward Maggie and claimed a hug. "Thanks for the cookies, they're my *almost* bests! They made me smile a lot!"

"Well, good." Maggie hugged him back while Thea drew Shannon forward.

"Shannon, this is Mara. Mara helped us pick out the things for your room."

"Oh, thank you!" Shannon seemed to take no notice of Mara's sour face. She hugged her quickly and quite thoroughly. "It is the prettiest room I've ever seen, like in my entire life."

Mara shrugged back toward Ethan, uncomfortable. "It's okay."

"I've got cupcakes in the kitchen," announced Maggie. "I know it's suppertime, but we wanted to celebrate Shannon's arrival."

"I can show them!" In typical fashion, Keegan hurried to the swinging door and pushed it open. "Chocolate and white! My best ones!"

Shannon grabbed Mara's hand as if they were already friends. "I love cupcakes. Don't you?"

Mara didn't seem to know how to react to Shannon's enthusiasm. She hesitated before she acknowledged her. "They're good. And Maggie makes really good ones."

"Then this is like a dream come true because my Gee Gee's stove was broken for a long, long time . . ." She kept Mara's hand in hers as they moved forward. "So we never had anything like cupcakes. Or even bread or stuff unless Old Sophie stopped by if she came to town. We got hungry a lot," she said, as if going hungry was the norm and not some horrid thing that should never happen to anyone.

Maggie drew a quiet breath. She folded her arms as the girls disappeared into the kitchen. "She won't have to worry about food anymore, old man." She looked up at Jeb. "Mark my words."

"Or warm shoes and mittens," he added.

"Being with you will be good for her," noted Ethan in a soft voice.

"Good for us, you mean." Maggie set him straight with a determined expression. "She'll bring us out of our shell whether we want it or not, I expect."

"She's a live wire, for sure, and seein' her eyes light right up makes me smile," admitted Jeb. "I think I'm goin' to have one of them cupcakes myself and listen to them chatter. Does an old body good to listen to youngsters, now don't it?" He moved into the kitchen with a happy expression.

"Maggie, can you bring Shannon down to the office and let me have a look at her tomorrow?" Ethan asked. "About twelve thirty?"

"Happy to do it, and they're calling for sunshine tomorrow and a warming trend. My old bones and my daffodils will both welcome the change," she declared. "Thea, are you set on Wednesday night shopping for the Easter clothes?"

"Yes. If that's okay?"

"I've got a church meeting that night, so if you don't mind taking Shannon on your own, it's fine."

"We'll have Mara and Keegan along, so we can make it fun for all of them as long as she's not too tired. But from the looks of things, she's doing all right."

"The county's coming by tomorrow morning to see that she's settled. Jazz will be here to watch the baby while I talk with them."

"Wonderful." It *was* wonderful. Surprising, but good. No one would have expected a few months ago for Jazz to step in as backup babysitter. And to have Maggie take in an orphaned child after her anguished history with two orphans long ago . . .

Was it irony? Coincidence? Or something more that put them all in this place, at this time?

"I could go for one of those cupcakes myself," Ethan said.

"Then let's join the party," Maggie told him. "Nothing like fresh cake to go with a good cup of coffee. Or tea," she added, smiling at Thea.

"Coffee," Thea told her. "Tea's for cold, dark winter nights. With the sun hanging out later, I want to take advantage of every minute of daylight I can get. If that means caffeinating myself at five thirty, I'm all right with that."

Keegan was running the kitchen conversation, and as topics leaped from soccer to lightsabers to trucks that looked like dinosaurs, Thea watched the girls.

Shannon seemed delighted with Keegan's prattling. Was that because she'd been alone so long? Or did she have a true affinity for smaller children?

Mara kept herself slightly apart. Not angry. Not huffy. But distant, as if she'd set up a personal barrier, a concept Thea understood quite well. But every now and again she glanced at Shannon as if drawn, as if the other girl's reactions meant something.

After cupcakes and milk, Ethan started to hustle the kids out the side door. When Keegan fussed, Ethan pointed to the clock. "Soccer practice, remember?"

"I forgot! Let's go!" He paused at the door, swung around, and waved up to Maggie. "Th-th-thank you so much for the cupcakes, Maggie! They were my first favorites!"

"Which one?" she called back as he pushed through the door.

"All of 'em!" He grinned assurance to her through the screen, then hurried to the car.

Mara stood up and faced Maggie. "Thank you for the cupcakes and milk."

If Maggie recognized the lack of joy in Mara's voice, she let it slide. "You are so welcome, my dear, and if you wouldn't mind coming by now and again to play with Shannon, that would be a marvelous thing." Maggie bent to Mara's level. "I expect she could use someone more her age to hang out with, and you're totally up on how things go these days while I am hopelessly old-fashioned. What do you think?"

Mara looked at Shannon, then Maggie. She hesitated, and Thea was pretty sure she was about to refuse the invite, but then she lifted one shoulder. "I can come over. Sure."

"Perfect!" Maggie left it at that, but she sent Thea and Ethan a satisfied look that Mara didn't see. "Once the weather breaks it's a short walk from here to the ice-cream shop, and what better way to become good friends than over a nice walk for ice cream?"

Mara frowned. "You'd let us walk there? Like alone?"

"Well, you're both nearly eight years old, so yes. Of course. How does one learn independence if never allowed to be independent? One of the joys of living in town. Everything is in walking distance."

"And you live close to the trails," noted Mara. "Uncle Ethan takes us on the trails sometimes."

"For the trails you need a grown-up," said Maggie. "But there are enough adults around to make that happen. Thanks for coming over, Mara."

"Yes, thank you." Shannon licked a bit of frosting from her finger and smiled. "And thanks for helping with my pretty room." She yawned again, longer this time. "I love it."

"Okay." Mara didn't linger, but when she descended the steps leading from the kitchen to the side door, she paused and glanced back up at Shannon.

She seemed puzzled.

Then she furrowed her brow and walked out the door, chin down.

Hayley fussed from the front room.

"You have a baby?" Shannon's eyes went wide. "A real one?"

"Just as real as you and me," Maggie told her. "Wash up your hands and I'll introduce you to Hayley. Her mom will be here later. There's parent-teacher meetings tonight," she said to Thea. "We won't see Kelsey until seven o'clock, and Miss Hayley will be good and hungry before then. Jeb will warm a bottle and we can sit in the front room and feed that baby, all cozy-like. How does that sound, honey?" She faced Shannon, and when Shannon smiled and nodded, the kindness in Maggie's expression pushed a lump to Thea's throat.

She'd seen Shannon's meager existence. The rodent droppings, the banging shutters, the cold, wet room, the rags for clothes.

I'll make a difference, one girl at a time.

That's what Mrs. Effel used to say, back in Philly, and it was part of what pushed Thea into family practice.

"A little patience, a little prayer, a warm bed, and some good food. I keep my formulas pretty simple. Because they work." Joan Effel had repeated her reasoning often enough.

Simple formulas. Simple choices. A simple life.

Thea thought she'd be bored in a small town. She was absolutely, positively the opposite of bored, and probably far too busy to be considered healthy, but she loved it.

She'd considered small towns confining. Too many busybodies, and didn't everybody die famous in a small town? She didn't want fame. She preferred a dose of anonymity. And yet, she didn't want to be invisible now. Not anymore. Why was that?

"Hey, Thea!" Jill Jackson was sweeping the sidewalk in front of Jackson's General Store. She called out as Thea braked for the single stoplight. "Nice night, isn't it?"

Oh, it was. The warm front, the disappearing puddles, the soft southern breeze. "Beautiful. I'm coming over to try your new coffee bar tomorrow. Everyone's raving about it."

"See you then!" Jill smiled as the light turned green. "And Addie Miller's Amish butter cookies are the best to go with it."

Coffee and cookies.

Parents pushing strollers, ambling down the street.

No crowds. No rush. No honking horns from angry motorists, frustrated by a thirty-second delay.

Peace stole over her. A calm that came from within, a serenity born of seeing Shannon settled in a good, clean home. Seeing her smile. Knowing she could have died in that hovel, but she didn't because one person picked up a phone to make a difference.

Did Old Sophie make the call that saved the child's life?

Maybe.

But as Thea parked her car by the walk-up apartment entrance, she was just glad someone had done it. The accidents of timing or God's perfect timing?

She couldn't say, but answering Kelsey's call for help in December, newly unemployed, then having this job fall into her lap . . . there was more than coincidence at work here, and whatever it was . . .

Thea liked it.

CHAPTER FOURTEEN

Nature had granted Jazz a stunning day.

She breathed in the scent of pine tinged with the crush of old leaves and pungent needles as she cruised through the forest preserve Wednesday morning. She'd sneaked into Central Park a few times over the years, chasing the sun's rays, dodging paparazzi. Even at the height of summer, those rays were often blocked by street after street of skyscrapers. She risked it because once in a while she wanted to run an easy pace in a natural setting.

She felt normal here. Not busy enough, but normal in other ways, so maybe the trade-off would be enough? Eventually?

Winter ice and snow had kept her to the more southern trails until now, but the sun's higher arc made the north trails accessible. She passed an old maple-syrup-maker's cabin on a downslope, and when she turned east, a street opened up before her. It wasn't a standard rural street like the village sported. This was a different kind of neighborhood, nestled into the lush, forested hillside. Each house sat on its own generous plot, part of the neighborhood but not *of* the neighborhood. She wasn't sure where the street curved or ended, but she had the day off, Maggie was watching Hayley, and Jeb had taken Shannon to visit her great-grandmother at the memory care unit. She veered out of the forest, onto the street, and strode off at a brisk pace.

Who lived here? Rochester-area executives? NFL players from Buffalo?

The pretentious development certainly wasn't home to the everyday working-class folks from Wishing Bridge.

Harrowsmith Woods Circle.

Now the development meant something. Her financial advisor had hooked her up with a local Realtor the week before, who then sent several possibilities for Jazz's consideration, including 31 Harrowsmith Woods Circle.

She took the curve to the right and nearly ran into a woman standing dead center in the road. "What are you doing here?" Arms folded, the woman's stance and demeanor threw down a challenge. "This is a gated community. If you don't live here, you don't belong here."

Count to ten, Jazz.

Count to—

She kept jogging in place, unwilling to minimize the cardio function of her run. "Someone must have forgotten to gate the woods. Oops." She deliberately didn't remove her sunglasses. The stout woman reminded her of a wardrobe dresser she'd had to work with far too often, a powerful, square-shaped woman who found fault with everything. The similarity in attitude and body type pushed a fair share of old buttons.

"Which means you came through private property to get here. You don't belong here, you don't live here, and I'm asking you politely to leave before I call the local sheriff."

Hale and Garrett Jackson had become her friends months before, so the threat of them being called out wasn't exactly worrisome. But the woman's stern demeanor hit a nerve. "Actually, I'm looking for real estate here, and this development came highly recommended. I understand that ivory-and-brick home on the hill has been listed recently."

The woman looked at the house in question, then brought her attention back to Jazz, as if the last thing she expected was a leggy black woman to buy into their hidden enclave.

"I'm Jacinda." Jazz stuck out her hand in greeting, pretty sure the woman wouldn't take it. "How about that? We could be neighbors soon."

"There is nothing for sale in this neighborhood, as you can plainly see." But the woman looked nervous, and when Jazz replied, the woman looked more worried still.

"Oh, sugar, everything's for sale." Jazz tipped her glasses down and smiled as she moved around the woman and kept right on running. "For the right price."

She didn't look back to check the reaction. She didn't need to. She cut through a landscaped opening alongside the tall, broad wrought-iron gates and looped back toward town. Within seconds, the opulent community was obscured by the thick forest.

She'd ask Maggie about it. No street sign labeled the turnoff to the private road. That simple omission helped mark its anonymity.

As she reentered the forest preserve a quarter hour later, she realized she'd come farther north than she'd thought. That meant the posh homes weren't part of Wishing Bridge. They were within the Wyoming County border, but a good distance from town.

Her finance guy wanted to talk more about her short- and long-term goals. She'd consciously changed her life, but she didn't want to grow old and be broke, so prudent investment now was crucial.

She'd call him later. Seek his advice.

And she might buy one of those uppity houses just to make that woman squirm. No one got to treat her like that. Not now. Not ever. Sometimes meeting folks like that on their own turf was the only way to level the playing field.

But then you'd have to live near her. The mental reminder was enough to make Jazz reconsider the whole thing. *Why do that when you enjoy being in town? Being among the people? Girlfriend, do not put yourself in a situation that might undo all the good you've done just because a mean-spirited middle-aged woman called you out. Puh-lease.*

The voice was right.

Sticking herself into the middle of self-serving, pompous people wasn't on the current agenda.

But she couldn't deny that a part of her wanted that woman to see not only that Jacinda Monroe could afford to live in their posh neighborhood, but that she'd fit in just fine. And make them sit up and take notice, too.

She wound through the last two miles of her run at a slower pace, then walked along the village streets to cool down.

The noon fire whistle blew loud and long. Right about now the local country station would be playing the national anthem, a salute to men and women in uniform. Straight ahead, a worker in a truck's cherry picker affixed American flags to the village light poles, another sign of the seasonal change.

She didn't need pretense.

She didn't want posh surroundings. Been there, done that. Overrated. And yet she wasn't afraid of a great buy if it came her way, and the Realtor had called that house a great buy.

Seddy Jacobs, the new director of Friends Free Library, was about to cross Main Street, but she paused when she spotted Jazz coming her way. "Jazz, I've got that new series in at the library. The one we talked about."

"For real?"

Seddy laughed. "Ask and you shall receive. We had enough money in the budget to grab a few more books, and you seemed really interested in them."

She was, but she could have bought the series online with a click of a button and not missed the nearly hundred dollar cost. In Wishing Bridge, a hundred dollars was nothing to be taken lightly. "Seddy, thank you. I can't wait to read them."

"I'll have them in the system within a day or two. We've got kid tours coming through to learn about libraries. The historical aspects, good old Ben Franklin, and how people work together to help one another, so the next few days are busy. But it's good to see kids in libraries. I want to see them with their noses in a book. Not a smartphone."

Not being around kids often, Jazz hadn't considered that, but it made sense. Everybody's face was downturned these days, scouring their devices.

Was that good? Bad? Nothing much?

She didn't know, and maybe didn't need to care, but she'd escaped into reading a lot as a child. It would be a shame for kids to grow up not realizing what a wonderful foray into fantasy that could be. "Library tours are a great idea. I'll stop by in a few days."

"Wonderful." Seddy crossed just as Jeb turned up Wyoming Hill Road with Shannon. He pulled into the driveway and shut the engine off.

"Hey, sweet thing." She drew close to Jeb's car and smiled at Shannon, but the girl's normally happy countenance looked sad.

Jazz looked to Jeb for guidance. He grimaced slightly and shook his head as he climbed out of the car, which meant the visit with Gee Gee hadn't gone well.

Jazz opened the back door of the car and squatted to Shannon's level. "Can we talk, girlfriend?"

Shannon looked puzzled.

"With you going back to school on Friday," Jazz continued, "I was thinking a trip to the zoo tomorrow morning would be fun."

"A zoo?" Shannon seemed to ponder the question. "You mean a place with animals?"

"Exactly. They've got a great one in Buffalo, and the weather's supposed to be nice tomorrow. How about you and I take a ride there and have lunch together, too?"

"A real zoo?"

"Quite real, I'm told."

"I would like that a lot. I've never been to a zoo before. I saw one on TV when I was little—"

When she was little, as if seven years old was all that big. "Let's call it a date. You and me and the zoo."

"Thanks, Jazz!" She hugged Jazz then, a sweet hug, the kind you didn't know you needed until you got it.

"You're welcome. Now I'm going to grab a shower here since I'm helping with the baby today, then I'm coming down to the kitchen for lunch, okay? Maybe we could eat together."

"Okay. Maggie told me she's going to make fried-bologna sandwiches. With ketchup."

"Delicious!"

Jeb laughed at her, then hefted a bag of groceries from the opposite side of the car. "Old-timers love that sort of thing, but I expect fried bologna fell out of fashion in New York a while back."

"And yet there's a Brooklyn restaurant that specializes in fried-bologna sandwiches. Great food on a tight dollar, notable for the Big Apple."

"For certain?" Jeb looked surprised and almost impressed as they climbed the front steps. "Well, then, that big city's got more sense than I've given it credit for, because fried bologna is some good eats. Not that I expect you've tried it," he added with a wink. He swung the door wide with his free hand to let the ladies precede him.

She laughed because he understood the dynamics of her history. "I haven't, but I'm willing to try one today."

"I've got some nice mustard to go along with it," he told her as he slung his flannel shirt on a free hook. "Kids might go for ketchup, and that's fine, but when the bread's good, a nice ripe mustard can only make fried bologna better."

And a half an hour later, when Jazz took a bite of her first fried-bologna sandwich ever, she had to agree.

It was mighty fine eats.

CHAPTER FIFTEEN

Shopping with three kids.

The itch beneath Ethan's collar turned into an anxiety rash and crept upward as he turned toward the expressway entrance.

"Are you getting an Easter dress, too?" Shannon asked Mara. She'd folded her thin hands tightly in her lap. She seemed to be a mix of happy and nervous. "I don't remember ever going shopping before, so I'm not sure what to do. Like not even a little bit sure."

Mara looked at her as if wondering what planet she'd sprung from. "You've never gone shopping?"

"Well, maybe when I was little." Shannon shrugged. "But it doesn't count if you don't remember it, right? My Gee Gee didn't drive, and my Nana went to heaven, so maybe Nana took me and maybe she didn't. But I'm going to the zoo tomorrow, and that makes this perfectly special. Shopping and the zoo!"

"Zoos smell." Mara curled her lip and wrinkled her nose in distaste.

"Do they?" Shannon grinned with excitement. "Well, that will be something to know now!"

"Animals poop a lot," offered Keegan. "And then people clean it up. I would not want that job," he added firmly.

"We had coyote poop and bear poop in our yard," Shannon told them. Keegan looked amazed. Mara looked disbelieving.

"I bet you didn't."

"We did," Shannon assured her. "Old Sophie told me what to look out for, and she showed it to me. Because animals lived in the woods. And so did we."

"I would love that so much!" Keegan pretended a soldier's stance in his booster seat. "I would be like a pioneer man and put on a furry hat and shoot that bear! And the coyote, too, maybe. And maybe a turkey! My teacher says that people didn't used to go to the grocery store and buy food, that they had to go hunting all the time and that's why nobody got really fat. Mostly."

Thea leaned toward Ethan, close enough that the fresh scent of her perfume made him take a second breath. Just because it smelled that good. "I expect that lost a little in the translation, but it's absolutely hysterical in the retelling."

"His reaction is funny. But Mara . . ." He whispered the words as Keegan and Shannon talked. "I don't want her to be mean to Shannon."

"We'll nip it as needed. Here." She handed him an unwrapped chocolate-covered cherry. "My very first patient today pronounced these as your favorites, and Jill had some in the new store."

"You bought me chocolate, Thea?" He pulled up at the stop sign just before the expressway entrance and took a moment to look her way, then didn't want to stop looking her way. She was so beautiful.

Not beautiful like Jazz.

But beautiful in a way that made the future seem brighter. Better. More achievable. Which was silly because his future was five states away.

"A kindness in times of trouble." She smiled at him then, and he had to remind himself to drive because he'd honestly rather just sit there and look at her. Talk to her. And that was a far cry from their initial standoffish relationship. "Or just a kindness in any old time."

He couldn't remember the last time someone had done something like this for him, something just to be nice. And then Max came to mind and all his work on the new offices, even though Ethan had originally shrugged him off. And Hale, helping arrange babysitting for the kids during Christmas week when Ethan had messed up his schedule and forgotten to find an interim babysitter.

He headed down the expressway ramp, wondering why he hadn't really noticed these kindnesses before, and why he noticed now.

By the time they got to the mall, Mara's snippy attitude had erased all thoughts of kind acts from his head because keeping her in check would require his undivided attention, and wasn't that grossly unfair to Keegan?

"Let the excitement begin," said Thea. She helped Keegan out of his door while the girls scrambled out Ethan's side.

Thea led them to one of the big department stores. "We can begin here. Keegan, you're first."

Mara sniffed on purpose, but Shannon took his hand. "You're going to be so very handsome!"

"I know." He grinned up at her, looking about as adorable as a kid could get while Thea scoured the racks for size fives.

Ethan held up two suits, one in light blue, one in steel gray. "What do you think, buddy?"

Keegan pointed to the blue one, then one with a sweater vest sporting a puppy. "Can I try this one, too?"

"Sure can. And while we're here, let's grab a few pairs of pants for you. You've gotten bigger."

"So big!" Keegan couldn't have looked prouder. "I'm going to be this big, like my daddy." He stretched his right arm up as far as it would go. "Big and tall and so strong."

Mara shot him a death stare, but Keegan was too busy to notice.

Thea noticed, though. She didn't say a word, just stooped to Mara's level and met her gaze, eye to eye, then held it.

And Mara backed down. Without a word, without a fight, without a struggle.

Later, when they were alone, he'd have to ask Thea how she had done that, because it sure looked like a Vulcan mind-meld to him.

The vested suit with the embroidered puppy won the right to come home with them for Easter, and when he added three pairs of pants, four pairs of shorts, and four T-shirts to the mix, Ethan was pretty proud of himself.

Shannon stared at the pile of clothing in his arms and swallowed hard. "You can buy all those things today? Wow." She patted Keegan on the head. "That's so cool, little buddy."

"He's not your buddy." Mara made the pronouncement in a steely, cold voice.

"Mara." Ethan waited until she grudgingly looked his way. "Don't."

She huffed, folded her arms, and dragged her toes as they moved to the girls' area. Shannon stopped midstep, awed by the sea of pastel lace and layers. "There's so much stuff here. Like for everyone."

"It's pretty impressive," agreed Thea, and when they picked out several dresses to try on, Ethan couldn't get over Shannon's look of grateful amazement, while Mara thumbed through the display, looking bored.

"What would you like to try on, Mara?" Thea tucked Shannon's choices on a rack near the fitting rooms. "We can share a room if you'd like. Or I can bounce from one to the other."

"I'm not a baby, I can dress myself, and none of these are exactly what I like." She scowled at the dresses, then acted like she was doing the dress a favor by flicking a finger at it. "This one is almost pretty."

Thea pulled it out in her size. "Any others make the cut?"

"That one." She pointed to a ruffled blue floral that Shannon had picked out as well. "And maybe this one, too." Thea added a layered dress in some pink material that looked like a ballerina could wear it.

"That gives us some nice options." Thea ushered them into the fitting rooms. Each girl modeled her choices for Ethan and Keegan. Ethan thought Keegan would get bored, but he seemed excited for the girls. Both of them. And when Shannon came out wearing the blue floral, Keegan smacked a hand to his forehead. "I th-th-think th-that is the prettiest one of all, Shannie. It's so really, really beautiful."

Shannon's eyes lit up. "You think so?"

"I think so a lot!" He grinned up at her as Mara came out in the rose-toned dress. "And that's so pretty, too, Mara. I love it!"

"As pretty as that one?" Mara asked smoothly, and Keegan shook his head.

"No, that one is the prettiest, but this one is the almost prettiest."

"I want that one." Mara pointed to the blue floral. "Keegan loves it and he's my brother, not yours, and I should get that dress."

Shannon looked from her to Thea and Ethan, uncertain.

"You can both get that dress," Thea reasoned as she took another size eight off the rack. "There's nothing wrong with having the same dress."

"Except I said I wanted it first, and I don't want her dressed like me." Mara frowned at Ethan, then Thea. "I think I should get to have my own dress without someone copying me. I don't get to have a father or a mother for this Easter or forever, but at least I should get my own stupid dress!"

She burst into tears, tears that flowed onto the pink fluffy dress below.

Keegan shrank back against the chair he'd been sitting in.

Shannon's eyes widened, then she reached out a hand to Mara's arm. "I don't mind if you have the dress, Mara. It will be beautiful on you. Please don't cry."

"Don't touch me."

"Okay." Shannon backed off, but she didn't look hurt or angry. She looked utterly sympathetic. "I'm going to take it off now so you can have it."

"I'll have that one." Mara pointed to the one on the hanger. "Nobody's touched that one."

Ethan wanted to shake her. He wanted to remind her that she wasn't the only one who'd suffered the loss of her parents, that she was hurting another person's feelings, and that—

Thea picked up the blue floral dress from the rack and faced Mara dead on. "Of course they've touched this one. It's probably been tried on by dozens of people. Absolute strangers instead of nice, new friends. There you go." She tucked the dress aside with Keegan's new clothes, then redirected her attention to Shannon. "Hey, sweet thing, while I like the blue *very much*," Thea said, intentionally stressing the words, "I think this one"—she held up a ruffled dress that alternated shades of pink, green, and yellow throughout the skirt—"with all the spring colors would be great with your eyes and hair. Want to give it a try?"

Shannon nodded but shot Mara a sympathetic glance. "Sure. It's a real pretty dress, too. They're all pretty, I think."

The stark difference between the two girls shone like a floodlight in the night sky. Shannon, grateful for anything. Mara, angry at everything.

Thea helped Shannon into the dress.

It was darling. Ethan said so, but Keegan wisely stayed quiet. He'd learned his lesson, that honesty and dresses didn't always go hand in hand.

Ethan and Mara picked out some spring outfits while Thea selected two other dresses with Shannon. And then sneakers and shoes and socks.

He didn't want to take Mara for ice cream.

She'd been a brat. She'd been mean. She'd managed to revert straight back to her angry self since seeing Eva a few days before, and nothing Ethan said or did seemed to matter.

"Ignore her," Thea whispered as the three kids moved ahead of them through the mall. Ethan had stowed their purchases in the back of the SUV so they could walk unencumbered.

"Pretty hard to do when she's nasty."

"Well, don't ignore all her bad behaviors, but I'd let it go for tonight. Let the others set the example for how to have a good time. Instead of being the negative leader, she'll be the odd man out. Two against one."

He'd never have thought of that, but he recognized the wisdom of it as soon as she said the words. He reached for her hand and took hold. "I don't know how you know all this stuff, but you're amazing, Thea. Around kids. Around the office." He paused and dropped his gaze to hers. To their joined hands, and then her face. Her mouth. He let his gaze linger there before drawing it back to her eyes, her pretty hazel eyes. "And around me."

~

Thea's heart stopped.

Never mind the physiological impossibility of such a statement, Thea knew when a heart was pumping and when it wasn't. Hers paused the moment Ethan took her hand and held her gaze.

Then it started beating again, way too fast and far too erratic. She tried to speak, to shush him, to warn him off, but he just smiled. A real smile, not one of those tired ones she'd grown accustomed to seeing since December. Then he lifted her hand to his mouth for a kiss. A soft kiss, true. But when he squeezed her hand lightly, the message behind it was clear.

And yet their lives were distinctly muddied despite the current arrangement. She eased her hand away. "Two roads diverged upon a path," she said, quoting Robert Frost. "Your road is scripted. You'll be gone by summer, and the prospect of a broken heart holds little appeal."

"Chicago's a big city with scores of opportunities," he reminded her, but he wasn't pushing. Just . . . saying. "If you survived winter here, you can survive winter in the Midwest."

"It's not the season," she told him as they drew closer to the kids. "It's the geography. And now the people."

He stared at her as realization broadsided him. "You've decided to stay."

"It's made the list of possibilities," she admitted. "No one is more surprised than me because I'd have laughed at the idea of working in a small town. I'm not laughing now." Thea aimed a smile toward the three kids. "I'm enjoying it. The town. The job. And that precious little girl." She jutted her chin toward Shannon. "There's something about it that feels right, like it could be home. That's a concept I never put much stock in. Until I came to help Kelsey. You look surprised."

"Possibly astounded."

Still gazing ahead, she smiled. "I'm taking it a little at a time, but it's under consideration."

"You've got friends here. That helps."

"Do you have friends, Ethan?"

He avoided the question by waving the kids toward the restaurant on their left. "Food and ice cream, my treat."

"I'm having the best sundae ever!" Keegan hurried to the door, ready to be seated by the teenage hostess. "I'm so 'cited!"

Shannon wrung her hands lightly, unsure what to do, and Mara grumped along, every single step of the way.

Right there was reason enough for him to stay. Thea saw it and wasn't sure why he didn't. Those beautiful kids, needing structure and warmth and love and normalcy.

Mara and Keegan could be lost in a big school. They'd be set afloat once more, because there was nothing lightweight about research-hospital schedules.

And if that's what he wanted so desperately, why couldn't he apply here? To Golisano Children's Hospital in Rochester or Buffalo? Both had great programs and marvelous opportunities.

Not your call to make.

It wasn't, of course. Not her call. Not her business.

"Can we just have ice cream? Like for supper?" Keegan blinked the sweetest look up at Ethan, and Thea figured he was about to cave, when she cleared her throat.

"How about . . . no." She ruffled Keegan's hair. "But you can split a kid's meal so we get a minimum of protein into you under the guise of good parenting, and then ice cream. That's what we call a compromise, my friend." She smiled at the boy, and when he grinned back at her, her heart played havoc with her head.

Keegan was falling in love with her, and she was pretty much doing the same thing with him. And Mara—

Mara needed something focused in her life. A new normal, an everyday existence. An unscarred woman would find it easy to fall in love with Ethan. With those children. Follow a scripted road. But she bore scars. Deep ones. And it didn't seem fair to bring that to the romance table.

Then Shannon touched her arm. When she looked down, Shannon pointed to the menu. "I can't read this. I'm sorry."

For once Mara stayed quiet as Thea read aloud the list of meals.

Shannon eyed the choices, then made a face. "I don't know what to do," she whispered to Thea. "I like all these so much. How do you pick just one?"

Her predicament took Thea back in time. She understood having nothing. She recognized the emotions. She smiled at Shannon and said, "Pick one this time. And you can have something different the next time we go to a restaurant, okay? Jazz wants us to come visit the diner, and Vern will make you a real special burger, just the way you like it."

Eyes wide, Shannon gripped Thea's hand. "I think this is a really, really special night, don't you?"

Thea ignored Mara's huff and leaned down to plant a kiss on Shannon's forehead. "I sure do. Best night ever."

And when Ethan smiled at her and Shannon ordered chicken strips in a soft, clear voice, Thea was pretty sure she was right.

CHAPTER SIXTEEN

Eva appeared content to live in pajama pants and a T-shirt all weekend, Mara pretty much hid in her room except for a trip to the grocery store with him and Keegan, and Faye walked in and quit Monday at 8:37 a.m., all of which made Ethan's research appointment look crazy attractive. The thought of immersing himself in work, more work, and nothing but work yawned like an escape hatch on the *Millennium Falcon*.

"I can't handle the uncertainty around here anymore," Faye told him. She gripped her purse strap with one hand and her desk supplies with another. "No one knows what's coming or going, and I don't want to live with a cloud hanging over my head. I'm joining an internist's practice in Mount Morris where at least they have a plan. I'm tired of living on pins and needles."

In a purposeful move, she hadn't closed Ethan's office door. And when she stormed out as the first few patients were walking in, Ethan wasn't sure which fire to extinguish first. The similar concern on Laura's and Sheila's faces? Or the surprise of those Monday-morning patients?

He faced Sheila and Laura first. "Am I that clueless?" he asked softly so patients wouldn't overhear. "Do we need to make decisions or hunt for answers now? I'll apologize if I've been remiss in all this."

"It *is* hard to make life plans when you don't know if you'll have a job in two and a half months," admitted Sheila. "I've been the office manager for a dozen years, and I'd hate to go elsewhere. It's not like any of this is your fault, but we've got bills to pay and kids to look after, and I've got a grandbaby on the way midsummer. It's important to know your job will still be there, day to day."

"Becky has told me she's got the practice up for sale . . . and in the good Lord's hands," added Laura. "Now that's fine, but if no one *sees* the listing, then Sheila and I need to look elsewhere." She leaned closer. "We'll have to start looking soon, Ethan. We can't afford to be without paychecks, and once Paul died, no one had a strategy. And life needs a plan."

"I understand."

And he did, he got it, but why was it his worry?

This town is getting to you. You can pretend it's not, but you're wrong. You like it here. Admit it. And you don't want to let these nice people down. Is it possible you've grown a heart somewhere along the way?

Not likely. He went patient by patient through the morning, another busy day that only drove home what the loss of the practice would mean to this town. The community. Like Maggie had once told him, a town needed a doctor. And a doctor was generally in need of a town.

He'd meant to grab a quick sandwich upstairs, but an emergency pushed him through lunch, and the coffee didn't taste right today. He sipped it, then tossed it, the metallic aftertaste not worth the caffeine.

He was tired. So tired. He, who never got tired, who'd worked constantly to attain his goals with a strong, forward-focused attitude, was plain dog-tired lately.

You've had a lot going on this past year. Emotional stress causes fatigue. Stop worrying so much.

He heeded the mental chiding. He understood the "whole body" concept, how the mental and emotional could affect the physical. He'd thought himself immune.

Clearly he was wrong.

He sat down to update some patient notes late in the afternoon.

His left arm ached. He lifted his elbow to take strain off the nerve, rotated the shoulder, and kept typing.

The pain came again, deeper this time. Into his jaw. His chest. His shoulder.

Heart attack.

Impossible. Thirty-four-year-old men didn't have heart attacks. But when the pressure in his chest increased, he picked up the interoffice phone and hit Thea's code. She answered quickly. "Thea here."

It took long seconds to work the words around the growing pain. "My office. Now."

He sounded funny.

But did he? Or was it his hearing?

Thea raced into his office. Her expression tightened. She went into full work mode, but the hand she laid across his forehead was gentle and caring. "Flushed and sweating. What's going on?"

"Chest." He put his right hand on his chest, then moved it to his shoulder as another wave of pain blossomed. "Shoulder." He drew a breath, but not too deep. Deep breaths hurt. Right now everything on his left upper half felt like a woodworker's vise had him in its grasp.

She grabbed her phone. "We need an ambulance at Hillside Medical on Maplewood Avenue for a possible myocardial infarction." She tucked the phone beneath her chin and pulled baby aspirin from his top desk drawer, a bottle kept for emergencies. He'd never considered *he* might be the emergency. "Chew these, Ethan." She turned slightly and raised her voice. "Sheila, Ethan's office. Stat."

Sheila hurried around the corner and paused. The shock on her face said he must look pretty bad.

"The ambulance will be pulling in any minute for Dr. Brandenburg." Thea's voice stayed calm.

He liked that. He liked it a lot. That she didn't panic or go ballistic. She stayed matter-of-fact and in charge, and he'd grown to appreciate that over the last few months. He'd have to tell her when he felt better.

"Bring them in here, cancel the last few patients, and get Maggie and the Prayer Warriors on the job."

She slipped a nitroglycerin tablet under his tongue once he'd swallowed the baby aspirin.

He wanted to tell her he didn't really believe in all that prayer stuff, or the whole "wishing" thing the town embraced, but then he remembered they'd already had that conversation. And she still called on them. That was nice, wasn't it?

His chest seized.

Pain radiated from a high center.

The peal of the ambulance siren came closer.

Was he going to die? Was his heart giving out? It couldn't be, he had things to do. Responsibilities. Two kids counting on him.

Thea knelt in front of him and took his hands in hers, looking concerned. "You panic and I'll smack you. Got it?"

He almost smiled. He would if he could. But he couldn't, so he was saved the smackdown.

"We've got this. Give the medicine a few minutes to dilate the vessels, and let your heart chill out. Under no circumstances are you allowed to go nuts on us or fall apart. Okay?"

It wasn't okay.

The practice was shorthanded. They had patients to see. He had children counting on him, and he was already tired. No way could he handle one thing more. Especially something life threatening. And yet, here he was. "Okay."

"We've got this." She stood and moved aside as Lita and Brian rolled a gurney through the door. "You're in good hands."

"Thea." He reached out his right hand. He wanted her to take it. To hold it. But before she could, Lita and Brian had him on the gurney, trussing him up like a holiday turkey.

Then she was there again, on his right, bent low.

"Stop worrying." She laid a cool hand against his cheek, his brow. She didn't look worried. She looked beautiful. And concerned. But she kept her eyes on his as she gently touched his right hand. "Focus on getting better and being a good patient."

He frowned because he was probably not an ideal patient. Ever. "Trust us, Ethan."

He wanted to. He wanted to be able to trust others to get things done. Take care of things. But with so much needing attention, needing help—

"Let's roll," said Lita. They guided the gurney through the office, out the door, and down the access ramp.

Trust us . . .

Thea's hand, cool and soft. Her voice, calm and steady. But he saw the worry in her eyes. Because he was that sick? Or because she had feelings for him?

He hoped it was the latter, but he feared it might be the former. In which case—

"I do believe the lady told you to stop fretting." Lita was placing sensors on his chest to forward an ECG to the ER. "If you don't, I'll blow you in to Thea, Doc. And you know I will."

Tough girl, Lita.

He managed a wan smile. "I'll stop."

"Thea will meet us at the hospital. You rest. Let me do my job," she told him. This time she used a softer voice.

He laid back, closed his eyes, and took a deep breath. It didn't hurt as much as it had a few minutes before.

He rested.

~

"Pray, guys." Thea fought the threatening thickness in her throat an hour later as she talked with Maggie, Kelsey, and Jazz on speakerphone.

"The angioplasty showed major blockage on the right. They're inserting a drug-eluting stent to open things up and prevent scar tissue formation, but he needs our prayers."

"How can such a healthy young man have a heart attack?" chirped Maggie. Worry hiked her voice. "Isn't that unusual?"

"They figure he might have been ignoring symptoms for months," Thea answered. "Maybe longer. But they're acting quickly to keep heart-muscle damage to a minimum."

"Tell him we've got the Prayer Warriors on board," ordered Maggie.

"Do you need me to call Sheila and Laura?" asked Jazz. "I'm happy to help, Thea."

"I just spoke with them," she replied. "I'm going to run the practice on my own while Ethan recovers. If we can find an interim to come on board, that would be great, but if not, I'll manage. We'll modify the schedule accordingly."

"And folks will understand," Maggie promised. "They might bark now and again, but when there's real trouble afoot, they join forces."

"Jazz, can you help with the kids? Eva's there, plus she's called their grandfather in California, but Mara's giving her a hard time. Ethan's sickness isn't going to improve the situation."

"Happy to," Jazz replied. "Stop worrying about us, we've got this. Keep an eye on Ethan and we'll cover things here. And keep us posted, okay?"

"I will."

Thea pocketed the phone, angry with herself.

How had two medical professionals missed this?

She knew how. They'd chalked up his symptoms to grief, the change of location, change of circumstance, and influx of children, never looking for an organic cause.

"We'll be tucking him into the CICU when he comes out of recovery."

"Can I see him?"

"Briefly. He'll be in ICU for a while, so let visitors know he's pretty much off limits except to immediate family."

"And his NP."

The surgeon smiled. "Well, of course."

She waited until they came for her.

"Five minutes."

"Got it." She moved into the cubicle. Lines and machines and beeps and whirs were usually old hat.

Not that evening.

That night they were the difference between life and death for someone she cared about.

She took one of his hands in both of hers and prayed quietly.

He didn't wake up.

That was all right. He was in good medical hands and God's hands. Right now, she couldn't think of anything better.

∼

Ethan felt Thea's hand against his cheek, against his forehead. He thought he heard her voice, but when he strained to make sure, everything hurt. Inside and out, pain commanded his focus.

He stopped straining, but just before he fell asleep, two hands—*her* hands—touched his.

She'd gotten him here. Gotten him help. She'd stayed calm and cool and collected the whole while.

And now her hands held his in a gesture he didn't understand. But he liked it. A lot.

Calm washed over him.

He slept.

∼

"Is he going to die?" Arms folded, Mara faced Thea an hour later, belligerent. "People need their hearts, so having it messed up isn't good. Right?"

Eva stood silent, and there was no mistaking the worry on her face.

"I don't want Uncle Eefen to die." Keegan dashed to Thea, arms open. She picked him up and took a seat on the couch with him in her arms. "I just want him to be here. Wif us. Like always." He darted a doubtful look at Eva. "When is he coming home?"

Thea snugged him close. "Soon. They fixed the part that wasn't working, and now he has to heal. He'll be back here in a few days. But no jumping on him, okay? We've got to give him time to get better."

"I won't even jump once," said Keegan. "I'll be so careful. I promise."

"Are you sure he's coming back?" Mara hadn't moved. She stood absolutely still. She ignored Eva and kept her gaze trained on Thea. "Because I don't want people telling us stuff that's not true."

"I'm certain." Thea faced Mara. "The doctors jumped right in to make things right. They know he needs you. And you need him."

"Who's going to watch us?" Mara sent Eva a dark look, as though daring her to speak.

Eva took the challenge pretty well. "I will," she told them. "When you're not with Mrs. Harper," she added. "Ethan wants your routine to stay normal."

"Normal?" Mara's hands clenched tighter. "Nothing is normal, nothing is good, and I don't want you watching us ever! You're weird and you think you can fool me because you kind of look like Mom, but you can't fool me at all." She faced Eva directly. "My mom said you didn't have any common sense and that you monkey around a lot. Me and Keegan don't need someone who monkeys around. We need . . . we need . . ." She choked on the words, tears streaming, because they all knew what she wanted. What she needed. She wanted her parents back and the inconvenience of death wiped from her young life.

"We're all praying for Uncle Ethan." Thea reached out a hand. "The patients, the town, the people from the churches, and all the folks who work with him. It's almost Easter, Mara, and this is a time when we pray extra hard for God to help us be good people. To take care of one another. I think we're blessed to have your aunt here, ready to help."

"What if God never answers prayers? Because my mommy told me how to pray and she'd pray with me. Now she's gone, and no one listens to my prayers. Not now. Not then. Not ever. Do you think my mom and dad prayed to leave us all alone? I bet they didn't. I just bet they didn't!"

Seeing the girl's pain, witnessing her anguish, seared Thea's heart. This was another mountain to climb when the child's faith had already been soundly shaken. What could Thea say? "I don't have answers, darling."

Mara sniffed loudly as if she had expected that reply. "No one does, because there *are* no answers. There's no stupid stuff out there that helps us, it's just all made up. Dumb, dumb, dumb."

Jazz came to the door just then, and Thea had never been so glad to see anyone in her life.

"Hey." Jazz walked in and hooked her thumb toward the door. "I know it's later than usual, but I heard it was homework time. Mara, would you like to work here or in our apartment?"

"Homework is stupid."

"That seems to be the theme, sweetie." Jazz held out an arm. "I find it best to keep busy when everything goes wrong." She opened the door a little wider. "Let's head up and get this out of the way. All right? We don't want to give your uncle something else to worry about, do we?"

Mara didn't agree, but she didn't put up a fuss, either.

Keegan laid his head against Thea's chest and popped his thumb into his mouth. "I'm scared, Th-thea."

So was she. Not because she doubted the cardiologist's ability but because she wondered how much one family could take. "Me, too."

"You are? For real?" He sat up and met her gaze. "Do grown-ups get scared of stuff?"

They sure did, but he didn't need to understand to what degree. "Sometimes. But I know God's going to watch over me no matter what happens."

"Like sending Uncle Eefen for us when we needed somebody to love us."

Keegan's innocent trust offered a glimmer of hope. "Just like that."

"Then I'm going to ask him to take care of Uncle Eefen. Because I l-l-love him so much." She cuddled the boy while Eva busied herself with dishes, and when Keegan dozed off, a feeling of sweet affection didn't steal over her.

It rushed up from within, as if she was cradling her own child. Her own son.

He wasn't, of course, but if these kids needed some old-fashioned motherly love, she'd do what she could. Her heart would break when they left. That was a given. Her fault for letting this patched-together family grab a piece of it.

But for now, it worked, and in a day-to-day world, that was all right.

CHAPTER SEVENTEEN

Thea saw the text from Max once she had tucked Keegan into bed. Heading to hospital first thing in morning. Praying. Pestering. Hanging out for duration. Promise. Tell Eva I'll take her along if she wants.

Max, the unsung hero. The kindly guardian. A gentle giant who always went the distance. I'll tell her. Thank you. Thank you. Thank you.

He sent back a thumbs-up emoji.

And that was it.

No fanfare, no belaboring. Just quietly doing the right thing.

"Max is a real Saint Joseph type," noted Maggie when she stopped by with brownies later. "Knows his job, does his job, not looking for glory. My Jeb's like that. Me, I say too much, squawk too much, but I get the job done. Just not as quietly as I could."

"Me, too."

"Well, there's quiet and there's too quiet." Maggie set the brownie tray on Ethan's countertop. "And my man edges toward the latter too often, but every now and then there are things that need saying. That means someone's got to do it."

"You brought these for us?" Eva had grabbed a shower while Mara was upstairs. She emerged looking younger without her makeup . . . less hardened.

"I thought you and the kids might enjoy them."

"Love them is more like it." Eva sampled one. "Oh my gosh, these are decadent."

"Dark chocolate chips make the difference," said Maggie. "You don't hardly see them, but you taste them."

"I'll say. Thank you, Maggie. Thank you so much." Eva looked genuinely touched that Maggie had thought of them.

"Eva, Max just texted."

"The ex-cop landlord."

"Yes." A number of better descriptions ran through Thea's head, but that one worked. "He'll pick you up in the morning to go to the hospital if you'd like. I'll run the practice, then come in later."

"Can't I just take Ethan's car?"

"I never thought to grab his keys. Sorry."

"He must have an extra set."

"You'd think so, but I couldn't find them. We'll get the keys tomorrow so you can have the car while he recovers. Sorry I didn't think of it sooner."

Discomfort drew Eva's mouth down. "I'm not accustomed to riding with cops, retired or otherwise. Someone must have a car I can borrow."

"Max is a good man," said Maggie. "He doesn't trust easily, so if you need to earn that trust, do it. If you're thinking of staying, that is."

"Why would I stay if Ethan's not staying? It's not like there are opportunities here." Eva frowned at the thought, a sure way to spike Maggie's ire. The locals didn't take kindly to having their sweet town disparaged.

"There are opportunities everywhere, young lady." Maggie's expression matched her tart tone. "All depends on if you're willing to look for them. If you're waiting for life to hand them to you, you've got a long wait coming. Thea"—Maggie turned toward Thea as she reached for the door—"I've got to get home, but keep me posted, all right? And I'll keep the prayer groups apprised."

"I will."

Jazz and Mara came down the stairs as Maggie said goodbye. Maggie reached out and hugged Mara. "I'd like it real well if you'd come over and play with Shannon. Now that she's back in school, it would be nice for her to have playmates come by."

"Playmates?" Mara hiked her brows with a sarcastic expression. "Um, hello, pre-K."

"Mara." Thea bent to her level. "Do not disrespect your elders. Ever. Got it?"

"Got it." But she made a face to show she didn't care.

"Oh, child," said Maggie, and she accented the words with a big, drawn-out sigh. "You may be telling the good Lord about your heap of trouble, but if you don't soften your ways, that mountain is only going to get higher and harder to climb. A little gentling would be in good order."

Mara escaped into the apartment.

Eva exchanged looks with the other women. "Her mother would be appalled by this behavior, just so you know. I appalled Alexis on a regular basis." She made a face of regret as she followed Mara with her eyes. "How I wish I had a second chance to be the good person she wanted me to be. To show her that I wasn't just a jerk."

"Just show yourself," Maggie said gently. "We can't change the past, but we have the future in our hands. Ours and the good Lord's. We change what we can and work around the rest."

"Sounds simple, so why is it so hard?"

Maggie didn't mince words. "It takes effort, child. Every single day. And if you let a day slip without the effort, the next day is harder. It takes practice to make being good easy, but that devil isn't about to make being bad or selfish hard to reach. He makes that even easier, and being human, we slip and fall. The fall is normal. Getting back up? Well"—she tugged her shawl more firmly around her shoulders—"that's up to us."

She headed down the stairs.

"Can I have a brownie?" Mara called out, and Eva hurried back inside the apartment.

"Not if you wake up your brother. Yes, one brownie."

Mara began to fuss, and Eva held up one finger. "One. Then brush your teeth and go to bed."

She turned back to Jazz and Thea. "Thank you both. Can I call on you if anything goes wrong overnight?"

"We're right there." Jazz pointed up.

"Don't forget her prayers," advised Thea softly. "Even if she's mad at God and everyone else, her mom made that a nightly thing. She'll miss it if you let it pass. Even if you just pray by yourself."

"I'll cover it. I'm rusty, but I understand the concept."

"Rusty prayers are often the best," said Thea. "That whole squeaky-wheel thing we all hear about."

"Then mine should come through extra loud."

"There you go."

Jazz faced Thea when they got upstairs. "You've had quite the day, my friend."

"You're not kidding." Thea braced her elbows on the counter and leaned her chin on her hands. "And in the midst of it all, a Mount Airy practice affiliated with Temple has invited me to interview."

"Back in Philly."

She nodded. "I sent that application so long ago I just assumed they weren't interested. Now they are."

"Except how can you go there when there's no one here?" whispered Jazz. "Oh, sweetie, I am so sorry. The timing couldn't be worse, but it's an amazing opportunity. Just what you wanted. Back in the thick of things. Helping kids, helping families."

Like you're not doing that here? her conscience chided. *Because I'm pretty sure you are, cupcake.*

She was.

She'd helped folks, a lot of them. And she actually knew their names.

The truth of that hit hard, because it was much more difficult to get to know individuals when the revolving door of patient care included so many people, so many choices.

She went to bed conflicted, and when she dozed off, images of Ethan and city lights and children vied for her attention. In between the kaleidoscope of thoughts, she snatched some broken sleep. When she got up, she didn't dare examine the tired face in the mirror too closely.

She'd relax and sleep once Ethan was doing better. Once she had time to process the events of the last twenty-four hours.

Until then, coffee . . . strong and hot . . . would do.

~

Ethan would never put the words "hospital" and "rest" in the same sentence again.

The two did not exist simultaneously, at least not in the cardiac ICU.

He was nervous.

No, wait, scratch that. He was downright scared and yet he knew he was in great hands. He understood the skill of the local cardiologists and the great care he was receiving.

Thea was praying for him. The whole town was praying for him from the sound of it, like the opening scene from *It's a Wonderful Life*, and he was picturing the movie's second-class angel when Max walked in the door.

Max wasn't an angel. But he had proven himself a good friend to Ethan and the town, numerous times over. "Max."

"Just wanted you to know everything's all right back home. Thea's got the practice in hand. She wanted to be here but figured you couldn't both play hooky."

That removed one worry from Ethan's mind. He didn't want to let people down. Ever. "Good girl."

"Amazing," corrected Max. "We could use a go-getter like her in town. That girl's got New York energy and down-home common sense, a rare combination."

"And she's beautiful."

"Well, there's that." Max gave him a funny kind of smile. "You're drugged, aren't you?"

"Just some stuff to make me forget the pain."

"The thought that I could use that to my advantage is paramount right now, but I'll be a good friend and let it lie. Ah. Eva."

Eva slipped into the room. She took one look at Ethan and started crying.

"Hey. Stop that. They've got me woozy, kid." Ethan motioned her over with a hand. "Car keys. In that drawer. Can you take that stuff home for me?"

"Yes, of course. I was afraid you didn't want me to use your car. Afraid I might wreck it or something."

He had to pause to find air. Then, "I let you watch the kids but don't trust you with a car?"

She made a face and swiped a tissue across her eyes. "Silly, right?"

"Agreed. So. You." He peered up at her as waves of sleepiness hit him. "Be brave. Be strong. Take advice from the big guy if he offers it," he added, yawning. "I'll get through this. And then . . ."

He fell asleep before he got past "then."

∿

Ethan heard his name. He dragged his eyes open. The cardiologist was smiling. At her right stood his father, Kevin Brandenburg. His father was most assuredly not smiling, but that wasn't anything new.

"Hey, Doc." He tried for a smile and missed the mark, then looked toward his father. "Dad. You came."

"Wouldn't have felt right not to."

That was Dad. Ethan had learned a long time ago to take what Kevin offered. "Thanks."

"Ethan, good news," said the doctor. "All of your other cardiac veins and arteries are normal. This was the only one affected by abnormal plaque buildup. At first I thought we might have a familial leaning toward heart disease, based on your brother's malformations, but there was simply a bad turn."

"You thought this could be related to what killed his brother all those years ago? Because that was a congenital thing, how could Ethan have it and be this healthy?" His father sounded almost angry that the cardiologist said it, but that was par for the course. He'd been angry for as long as Ethan could remember.

"Inherited problems can vary by degrees depending on the genetic makeup," she told him. "And there is an adult form of Pompe disease, so we wanted to know exactly what we were dealing with. Genetics isn't my specialty."

"Then maybe you should stick to what you know," Kevin said brusquely. "Ethan couldn't have the same thing, because he grew up. Became a doctor. Jarod didn't make it to kindergarten. It doesn't take a genius to figure out that one has nothing to do with the other."

Ethan wanted to shush him. Or interrupt him, but he had no strength to do it.

The cardiologist kept her cool, and Ethan reminded himself to thank her when he could think again. "That's what we discovered. This particular artery allowed sludge to back up in minute amounts over time. The medicated stent will keep it open and running more freely. The rest of the heart looks and measures fine, and that's the kind of news I like to deliver." She directed a look of sympathy and understanding toward Ethan. "We're going to let you rest for now, and the nurses will be looking after you. Try not to set off any codes, all right?" She smiled. "I could use a nap."

He nodded.

She exited the cubicle and motioned for his father to follow. He did, not looking too pleased, but that wasn't anything new, either. He'd lost a lot over the years. His son. His marriage. Then his daughter and son-in-law.

Ethan couldn't begrudge him his unhappiness. He understood the taxation of grief too well.

But there were children involved. Two hurting children. Shouldn't their health and well-being take precedence?

In a flash of dozy insight, realization struck him. It made some things clearer and muddied others. In his parents' grief over losing Jarod, and maybe their guilt about being the source of the boy's flawed genes, they'd never recovered enough to put their kids first again. Not for him. Not for Alexis. And he was darned sure it hadn't happened for Eva.

Were humans that fragile? Or did they just not care enough? The bubbly young nurse strode in, drew the curtain, and stood next to him, arms folded. "The doctor told me to get in here and tell you to put a cork on worrying or she'd medicate you enough to make you stop."

He managed a weak smile.

"That's better. She said if family stuff was going to work you into a tizzy, she'd post 'No Visitors' and mean it. Except for the cute doc that brought you in."

They meant Thea. He managed another almost smile.

"Better," the nurse declared. "You know the drill, Doctor. Rest now rather than repent later." She dimmed the lights slightly.

Machines hummed and beeped around him. He knew they'd be in to check him regularly. They'd take care of him, allowing his body a chance to heal.

They thought Thea was nice. And cute.

Correct on both counts.

And that was his last coherent thought before sleep claimed him again.

CHAPTER EIGHTEEN

"It was the best of times, it was the worst of times . . ."

Ethan stared at his very sorry-looking reflection in the mirror a week later, and was pretty sure corpses looked better than he did. Before and after embalming.

He breathed in, still aware of every movement but not as bad as the week before.

"Hey, Ethan. Thea's here," Eva called.

He came out of his room reluctantly. He didn't want her to see him weak, but he'd asked her for a daily consult and she'd agreed. After an argument. The argument had been the first time he'd felt like himself since the heart attack.

"Not looking too perky this morning." She crossed the room and checked him over. The kids had gone off to school, and he was facing another day of not too much. "While I'm sure the inactivity is going to drive you crazy, no running marathons for a bit, okay? And you shouldn't even have to get up this early for updates, but you're the boss."

He was pretty sure he wasn't the boss, but he motioned her to a chair. "You let me think I'm the boss."

"Excellent point," she said with a smile. Eva brewed coffee while Thea went through the patient list and her findings with Ethan. She was thorough. Quick. To the point. Like everything she did.

"Any problems of note?" he asked.

Her look soured. "A snake."

"A what?"

"In the basement." She growled, and it was a really convincing growl. "A circuit got tripped. Sheila went down to flip it back on and was greeted by a snake."

"Like a poisonous one?" Eva moved closer. "There's copperheads around here, right?"

"Not in a hundred years," Thea assured her. "A garter snake. Perfectly harmless but disconcerting nonetheless. I've put Max on it."

"How did it get in?"

Thea let her eyes wander the big, gracious home. "My guess is that old basements offer rare opportunities, but as long as it stays there and we stay here, I can deal. If there's no visual contact between me and Mr. Snake, we're golden. I can handle rodents. I cannot handle snakes. Ever."

He read fear in her eyes. Thea, who carried off her fearless demeanor like a pro, was afraid of the snake. "Did Max dispatch it?"

"Couldn't find it. He's setting traps today. I don't know what that means, and I don't need to know what that means, because it will only keep me up nights envisioning it. Let's just say I'm ignoring the situation. I will never go into that basement again, and it's a good thing the laundry room is on the first floor or I'd be using the local Laundromat."

The urge to protect her washed over him. "If he doesn't get it, I will. Like soon. When I'm strong enough to do something again."

"I will hold you to that, my friend." She stood and smiled at him. "The way I see it, there are two options. Either Mr. Snakey slithered in while Max was popping out windows and doors, leaving gaping openings. Or"—she scrunched up her face—"it used a smaller opening, much harder to find and impossible to control, so more might come in. My hope is for the first option because one sneaky snake is tolerable from a distance. A colony of them?" She shivered, and it wasn't a fake shiver. "Reason to run and hide, right there."

He texted Max when she left two minutes later.

He didn't like seeing her unnerved.

He wasn't exactly a big fan of seeing her bossy, either, but he'd gotten used to that. Liked it, even, that she made decisions and stuck with them.

But seeing her scared was something else again.

He stared at the walls when Eva drove to the grocery store in Warsaw.

He would never take surgery and recovery casually again. Doctors that treated them as same old, same old should have their licenses yanked or at least have to go through a very boring, very long class on empathy building, because there was nothing casual about this.

It wasn't the pain that got him. He could handle pain.

The inactivity was making him crazy, but he'd been yearning for a chance to dive into updated genetic research since last year. Weeks of quiet days offered an opportunity to brush up on current studies and findings. Today's technologies moved at an impossible pace. A year away from the research wasn't just an impediment. It could be a game stopper.

He heard Eva come back. She peeked in, saw him working, and didn't interrupt.

He wasn't sure when he dozed off, but the ringing doorbell woke him midafternoon. He didn't try to hurry out of the recliner. The term "hurry" had left his vocabulary the previous week. By the time he stood, he'd received a text from his father. I'm downstairs. Buzz me in.

He crossed the room and hit the button to release the lower lock. Kevin climbed the stairs like a man half his age. The man wasn't afraid to keep himself in shape, although being in shape didn't soften his temperament. "Hey, Dad."

"Not dressed yet?" Kevin eyed Ethan's sweatpants and thermal pullover. "You don't want to get used to lazing around. It could be your downfall."

He'd never lazed around. Ever. His father had always expected major league effort on a minor league dime. "I'll avoid the downfall, but thanks for the advice. Did you stop by so you can see the kids before you head to the airport? They should be here in an hour or so."

Kevin shook his head as he brewed a cup of coffee. At no point did he offer to make one for his recuperating son. "I got an earlier flight at no added expense, pure bonus. I'll see the kids the next time I come east. Or you can bring them back where they belong and save me the cost of a ticket. Nothing cheap about coming east from California."

"My work's not in California."

"It could be," scoffed his dad. "Especially if you're thinking of staying in a nickel-and-dime town like this."

"Well, I'm not thinking that," he replied, then wondered why he felt bad saying it. Because his father had impugned the town with his comment? Or because the little town was growing on him? "Eva will be back soon." He picked up the note she'd left on the counter. "She went by the pharmacy to get my prescription."

"Watch the pain pills," said Kevin. "They'll get you. Your uncle had a problem with addiction, that's why you never got to know him. I wasn't going to have him around my house. My kids."

He'd met his uncle Brett when he was young, but not later. Now he knew why. "I'm down to ibuprofen. No major addiction problem there."

"Good. Well." He slugged his coffee with a glance at the clock. "I'm heading out. Glad you're doing better. Keep me up to date."

"I will. And Dad?"

Kevin didn't hug him. He could count on the fingers of one hand the number of times his father had hugged him, and skip a finger or two. Was it different before Jarod died? He honestly couldn't remember.

"Yeah?"

"Thanks for coming." It had taken effort and money to come across the country and miss a week of work.

"They owed me time." He shrugged. Did that mean if he hadn't had vacation time, he wouldn't have come? That was probably the case. "Take care of yourself, okay? We've done our share of gravedigging. I'd be okay not to see another one for a while."

So would Ethan, but he wasn't sure that was in his hands. "I'll try. According to the doctors, I'm probably going to be the healthiest I've been in a decade, so that works out all right. Especially with two kids to raise."

"I didn't tell Peter's family that you were sick, but Mara did. They called me a few days ago. They're pretty worried, and I expect you'll get a call once you're feeling better. At least they're giving you time before they launch an attack." He frowned and took a long slug of his coffee. "I said it was a dip in the road, nothing more. They were just getting used to the idea of the kids being out of state. Knowing you were at death's door would have set the sharks circling, though what a pair of sixty-five-year-olds want with a couple of kids is beyond me."

It *would* be beyond him, because Ethan was pretty sure his dad hadn't wanted kids in the first place but did what was expected in their small central California town. The state might be liberal, but Perryville clung to its Western conservative roots. You grew up, got married, had a family. And maybe Kevin would have been a better dad if Jarod hadn't suffered so much. Watching your child shrivel and die had to be the most helpless feeling in the world. "They love the kids. I wish we were closer to them. But Alexis and Peter designated me, knowing I was across the country. I'm assuming there was a reason for that." He crossed the room as Kevin opened the door. "Have a safe trip, Dad."

"Will do. Take care." No hug. No handshake. Not even a gentle knuckle-bump to his shoulder. Just the cool, hard façade he'd known for decades.

He'd no sooner left than Eva came up the stairs with a metal tin in one hand, the kind Maggie used for cookies, and the slim prescription bag in the other. "Did I just see Dad pulling away?"

"He got an earlier flight."

"And no goodbyes?" She set the cookies on the counter. "Did you tell him the kids would be here soon?"

He wasn't about to lie. "And that you were due back. Yes. I think he was worried about getting through security on time."

She made a face of disbelief, then handed him the prescription bag. "Nothing new or different about that, I guess."

"Eva, I'm sorry." He was, too. He'd been working in a downstate New York practice to hone his skills while doing research on the side, and Alexis and Peter had been building a new life as a married couple in the southern end of California while she was in high school. Ethan didn't pretend that living with their father was exactly a cakewalk.

"Sorry he didn't stay to say goodbye."

"No biggie." She shrugged, but he knew it was. What kind of father did that? "It's better that way."

"Hey, it's not." Ethan closed the distance between them and hugged her gently. Very gently, because his chest wasn't overly fond of hugs at the moment. "It's never all right to treat kids casually."

"Ethan, I—"

"It's not," he insisted, drawing back. "Listen to your big brother. I care about you, and I owe you big-time for jumping into the fray here. You've been a huge help, Eva. I couldn't have done this without you."

Her face softened. "You mean that?"

"Every word. But don't get sappy on me. I've got new journal papers to get caught up on. And speaking of journals and medicine and genetics, I'm paying for you to have genetic testing done to see if you're carrying any of the family flaws."

"Maybe I don't want to know," she told him.

"I hear you. But you should know if you're a carrier. I got tested about five years back. I'm a carrier. If you ever decide to have kids, it's good information to have. You didn't know Jarod," he added.

"I saw pictures. It wasn't pretty."

"He was such a great kid," Ethan told her. "Good-natured and sweet. It was incredibly hard to see him suffer. Alexis and I grew up feeling guilty for being normal. To be able to run and play and make choices. But Jarod never seemed to resent us. Through it all, you'd never meet a happier, more resilient kid. I used to think what I'd be like if that all happened to me, and I knew I'd fall short." He worked his jaw, thinking. "Jarod never did. He'd cry sometimes, when the pain got bad, but mostly he just stuck his chin in the air and planted a smile on his face."

"Like Keegan."

"Yes." Ethan hadn't realized that until she said it, because the two boys looked nothing alike, but Eva was right. They shared that same engaging, anxious-to-please nature. A giver, Thea had said.

Jarod and Keegan were both givers. The thought made him smile. Alexis had paid for genetic screening on both kids when they were small. She knew she was a carrier, but when both showed up with clean tests, she'd called him, crying with relief. Her reaction gave him a tiny glimpse of how guilt ridden his parents must have been, knowing their genes had doomed Jarod. Ethan had entered medicine wanting the best background possible to pursue the secrets of genetic intervention and prevent damage to susceptible muscle cells. Cardiac tissue needed to be strong and elastic to function.

"I'm going to work for another hour or so until Mara gets dropped off." He'd asked the bus garage to bring her back to the apartment today, to give her time to say goodbye to her grandfather before his evening flight. "Can you let Jenny Harper know that Keegan's grandpa won't be here, so she can buffer things a little?"

"He won't care like Mara does." She said it gently, another improvement. "He doesn't remember him all that much. But Mara saw him as a link to California. A road home. Mostly because he told her that Peter's parents miss them a lot."

That sounded like the kind of thing Kevin would say. He liked to instigate, then deny responsibility. "Mara told them about my heart problem."

Eva waited.

"They were just starting to accept the terms of the will. That Alexis and Peter wanted me to raise the kids, although there's plenty of days I question that judgment, too. What were they thinking?"

"Ixnay on the pity party, okay?"

The kid-friendly term made him smile.

"No one falls into being a parent with experience," she reminded him. "They hand you the baby and wish you well. Yours came as a package deal with grief attached. I don't know much about kids or even about being a family, but I think you're doing all right, Ethan."

Mara knew Peter's parents missed her and Keegan. She spoke with them on a regular basis. He didn't monitor the calls, and she probably told them way too much. He hoped they could separate the grief from the play-by-play and read between the lines.

They'd wanted the children. They had made that abundantly clear after the funeral, but they'd been more accepting lately, and Ethan didn't realize how much he needed that acceptance until it happened.

"I think he made it almost sound feasible for them to go back."

Ethan sighed. "Playing both ends against the middle, like usual. But why mess with kids' heads?"

Eva said nothing. She didn't have to. Kevin hadn't ever worried about their emotional well-being because he was too invested in his own. Why should it be different for his grandkids?

"Shrug it off and get to work. If you make yourself crazy thinking about why parents do what they do, it'll just drag you backward. Nobody wants to go backward, do they?"

"You're pretty smart, kid."

His words deepened her smile. "Getting there, big brother. One step at a time."

~

Thea pulled the door shut, tested the lock, then rounded the wrap-around porch. She'd grabbed a sweater, but the west wind sucked the warmth straight through the loose weave as she turned the corner.

Mara was sitting on the bench there, facing the wind, staring at nothing much.

Thea didn't want to pause. She wanted to grab the kid and hustle her out of the wind and into a more congenial setting, but Mara clearly wasn't feeling the cold, and that was a worry in itself.

"Hey. What's up?"

"Nothing."

Thea sank onto the wooden porch swing and had to bite back a shriek. The cold, damp slats of wood against her butt made her suck in a sharp breath, but she concealed the reaction and pretended she wasn't chilled to the core. "And yet you don't look like a kid with nothing wrong. Why is that, do you suppose?"

Mara kept her gaze outward, hands folded. Then she slanted a look to Thea. "Did Uncle Ethan almost die?"

"No."

Disbelief drew Mara's brows down and in.

"You're asking me a question, and I'm giving you an answer, and I don't lie, so listen up." Thea held the girl's gaze frankly. "He suffered a serious heart episode, something that could have killed him, but we got to it quickly with medicine and equipment and then surgery. According to his doctors, he's probably going to outlive all of us, but they'll keep a check on his heart and circulatory system to make sure it doesn't get clogged again. So yes, it was serious but treatable, and a full recovery is expected."

"Cross your heart?"

The winsome expression didn't just cross Thea's heart. It grabbed hold and refused to let go. "Cross my heart. Why are you asking all this on the cold porch? Don't you have a cozy apartment with a gas fireplace?"

"Grandpa left."

Thea waited.

"He didn't wait to say goodbye to us. Not me or Keegan. Or Auntie, either. I waited all day in school, thinking about how I'd get home and I'd see him and talk to him about California and maybe . . ."

Silent, Thea kept waiting. And freezing.

"I want to go back so bad." Mara dropped her gaze to her lap, to her two small clasped hands. "I know there's nothing really there. Not like it was before. But I miss it so much that my heart feels like it's hurting inside, like Uncle Ethan's. And maybe no one will notice that my heart hurts this much." She lifted her eyes to Thea's. "Would anyone notice, Thea? They haven't yet."

"Oh, honey." Thea wrapped her arms around Mara, glad to give warmth as well as take it, as a chilled gust of wind bent the bare branches their way. "We've all noticed. But no one is quite sure what to do because there isn't a pill or an operation to help what's hurting your heart. There's just time and faith and moving forward. And none of that is easy when you're seven years old." She hugged Mara close and was glad the girl didn't resist. "Maggie said she was hoping you'd come over and play with Shannon, remember?"

"I don't want to."

"Because?"

"Why make friends when I just have to leave them at the end of school? I'm tired of missing people, I think. Just tired of it."

Thea believed her. She stood and tugged Mara up with her. "Come inside, let's get warm and have hot chocolate, and we'll pray for a turn in the weather that makes lemonade sound better than hot chocolate."

"That's a silly prayer."

"Best I've got at the moment," Thea said. "I think we'd all benefit by soaking some heat into our chilled bones. And there's something amazingly special about spring in the Northeast."

Mara didn't look convinced.

"Wait and see. Everything that's been sleeping and dormant for six long months comes alive. It's like rebirth flows across the land, waking up all the dozing flowers and the dull, gray trees."

"I've got homework to do."

"Come upstairs and do it with me. Jazz is working and I'd love the company."

"For real?"

"I don't lie." Thea pointed a finger at herself. "Remember?"

"I remember."

"There you go. You head up. There are apples on the table, maybe some clementines, too. Help yourself while I stop in and go over today's patients with your uncle, okay?"

"Okay."

She handed Mara the upstairs key when they got to Ethan's door. The girl hurried upstairs while Thea entered Ethan's apartment. He was sitting at the table, working, but closed the laptop when she came in. "I've stolen Mara for a little bit."

"I saw." He pointed to his phone, where the office security camera relayed motion-detected images straight through to him.

"Privacy might just as well be stricken from the dictionary," she muttered, then indicated the pictures with a frown. "I know you got sideswiped last week, but we need to get her some help, Ethan."

He pulled a card from his pocket and handed it over. "Can you take her to the first appointment on Monday? It's a busy time with Easter and all, but I didn't want to delay things any more than I already have, and this woman comes recommended by the cardiologist at the hospital. Her cousin lives in Warsaw, and she says this was the first therapist her son didn't fight her on."

"I'll take her, sure. Is Eva tied up?"

"Mara gets mad around Eva, and I thought that might make for a bad first session. Or a good one, I guess. Plenty of material to work with."

"She gave me a clue about part of her resistance today."

Ethan waited, listening.

"She doesn't see why she should be nice and friendly to anyone. Why make friends when she has to leave them? She said she's just so tired of missing people."

Ethan steepled his fingers beneath his chin. "I don't know how to fix all this, Thea." He studied his hands for a moment, then drew in a deep breath. "The whole thing makes me tired, like Mara. But it makes me mad, too, fighting mad, like I want to go one-on-one with circumstances and just prove I'm bigger, braver, and stronger than anything life sends my way."

"That's a lot of fighting, my friend. For you." She tipped her gaze to the apartment above. "And for her. Maybe the two of you need to focus more on acceptance and less on pummeling the bad guy. One builds strength. One saps it. And believe me, Ethan, I learned that lesson the hard way as a child, so seeing Mara like this breaks my heart. It brings back all kinds of memories I rarely revisit, but I also know that coming through the darkness into the light made me stronger, braver, and bolder than I ever dreamed of being. Now, part of that was old Mrs. Effel," she explained, "the tough-but-sweet woman who ran the foster home I was in, but the other part was making friends with Jazz and Kelsey. In the end, when grown-ups didn't have a clue, those two friendships kept me from dangerous thoughts. Their love and friendship literally kept me alive."

"You thought of killing yourself?" Surprise and sadness changed his expression as he stood and closed the distance between them. "Thea. Why?"

Such a good question. Back then it had been more like, "Why not?"

She didn't want to keep Mara waiting, but this wasn't the first time he'd asked about her past. She'd dodged the question before, but maybe it was time to stop dodging. For him and for her. She sucked in a long breath, then let it go. "My mother sold me to a drug ring for sex trafficking when I was twelve years old."

His face . . .

Oh, his face . . .

It couldn't have looked more sad and disbelieving and maybe even disgusted. "No one could do that, Thea. Not to anyone and certainly not to their own child."

"Well . . . she did." She kept her voice as pragmatic as she could. "I was the trade-off for a regular supply of heroin or whatever they had in stock. They had me in their 'stable' for a few months until one man couldn't bear to hear me cry. Or see me sold. He got me out of there, got me to safety and police intervention. Then he ended up taking a bullet to the head for his trouble."

"Thea." His arms closed around her. She struggled to get free, but he didn't let her go. He kept her there, snug in his arms, and she didn't want it to feel so good. So safe. So perfect. "I'm sorry, Thea." His cheek was pressed against her hair. One hand cradled her back, the other cradled her head. "So, so sorry."

"I know." She swallowed hard against the growing lump in her throat. "Me, too. They left me with multiple infections and wretched trauma, possibly ruining any chance I had for a normal relationship with a man or childbearing. I hope I've come to terms with all of that, but at least I lived through it. That wasn't the case for all the kids they trafficked."

"Thea." He stroked her cheek with his right hand. Eva and Keegan were watching a puppy show in Keegan's room, and the innocence of the music was incongruous as a backdrop for their topic. "I'm so sorry," he said again. "I wish—"

"That it never happened," she filled in when he hesitated. She drew a cleansing breath and pulled back. "A wish I share, but it did, and while I didn't come away unscathed, I came away."

He looked sorry. And sad. Sad for her. But she'd pushed herself beyond sad a long time ago. She'd gone straight to mad . . . then grabbed hold of life and held on tight. "Mara has it much better in that respect, but it's not about degrees. It's about the inner nature of the child. She needs to get beyond this anger and grasp life, but she's downright scared. So she won't let herself move on because she sees no point in moving on."

~

His temporary assignment.

Temporary homes.

Short-term commitments.

All the things he thought were best might prove to be the worst possible things he could have done.

Thea switched the subject as she stepped back. "I told the kids I'd take them to church this weekend. It's Palm Sunday. The ice-cream shop usually opens on Easter weekend, but Easter's late this year, so they're opening a week early. Is it all right with you if I take them?"

"Yes. But how about a better idea? How about we all go together? If you'd like to, that is?" He wanted her to say yes. He wanted her to think it was a great idea when he had to pretty much drag a pleasant expression onto his face taking the kids to church each week. He wanted her to know that being with her meant something to him. Mostly he longed to reach out. Protect her. Protect her the way someone should have years ago.

She'd started to turn away.

She looked back, surprised. Why? Because of what she revealed?

She brought a hand to her throat. Tough, strong Thea gazed up at him, vulnerable. Almost fragile.

She studied him quietly for a few seconds, and when she spoke, her reply eased his heart in a very different way.

"I'd love that, actually. So would they, I expect."

He didn't try to hide his quick smile. "Good. I haven't asked a pretty girl out in nearly two years, so my moves are rusty. Goes along with the rest of me right now," he added with a rueful look at his chest.

"I'm bringing Shannon. Maggie and Jeb are helping with the pre-service triumphant march into Jerusalem, but Shannon asked if she could go with me, and I said yes. You sure that won't set Mara off?"

"She's got to deal with things, one way or the other. Maybe one of these times it will be a breakthrough."

"We could use one, for sure. But Ethan, taking kids to church isn't considered a date."

She'd firmed her tone and her expression, but she couldn't fool him now. And not ever again, because she'd let him glimpse the scars. Now he simply wanted to help heal them. "That's a matter of perspective," he assured her. When her eyes widened, he knew he'd made a point. "Are you okay to do homework now, Thea? I can help her if you're not." Could she walk up those stairs and launch herself into second-grade reading after their conversation?

He expected angst. He would understand anxiety. But when she reached one hand up to his cheek, it was as if she was comforting him. Not the other way around. "I've kept her waiting too long already." She moved to the door as Eva and Keegan came out of Keegan's room. "I'll send her down when we're done. Hey, guys." She greeted the pair as they went in search of food.

But then she turned and sought his gaze. And when she shared a look with him, a look that offered more than words, his newly repaired heart began to feel something it hadn't felt in a long time. It began to feel good.

CHAPTER NINETEEN

Jazz hit the northbound forest trails regularly now that the weather was breaking. By that Saturday, evidence of spring began seeping into the trees. Bushes poked buds of tiny leaves to life. Grass turned green. Bold beds of daffodils waved happy heads across the town and, in the forest, splashes of purple, cream, and gold blanketed the hollows and swales with tiny, violet-like blooms. The transformation created a fairyland setting.

Saturday was her long run day, so she headed for the rolling trail leading to Harrowsmith Woods. She'd checked with Hale, and despite the community's adversity to people, she had every right to use the sidewalks and street for her loop. And with her money guy pushing her to diversify her investments, she wanted to make a smart choice. She might not like the rude woman who'd challenged her a few weeks before, but if investing was the goal, one rude person wasn't going to stand in her way.

She took the path's turn toward the grassy knoll edging the development, then headed for the curved walking path that wound its way through the posh neighborhood.

"Cinda!"

A small but familiar voice called her name as she curved along the first loop of houses. "Emerson?" Emerson and his dad ordered take-out food from the diner on a regular basis. If Maggie sent cookies along for Vern and Vasiliki, Jazz would tuck a pair into their to-go containers. She didn't know their story, but being a single dad couldn't be easy.

The little boy dashed across a pristinely landscaped yard. "Hey! Hi! Did you come to visit us?"

She laughed and bent low. "I didn't know you lived here, my friend. I was just out for a run, and I like coming this way now that the weather's getting nicer. How are you? Did you like the cookies I sent you yesterday?"

"We both did."

The deep voice drew her attention upward.

"Gus." She palmed the little fellow's head and stood. "I had no idea you two lived here."

"Should you have known?" The tall, fair-haired, crazy good-looking man looked puzzled but also intrigued. As if finding her running down his street amused him but made him question, too. "Addresses aren't required on to-go orders."

"A valid point." She tucked a fringe of hair back, behind her ear.

"Or . . ." He drew out the word intentionally. "You didn't think a guy named Gus would live in this neighborhood."

"That, too." Caught out, she made a funny face toward Emerson. "The old-fashioned name sounded pure country, so this could be considered atypical."

"What were your initial thoughts?" he mused. He wasn't smiling or frowning, and that was disconcerting enough. Kind of cute, too. And he asked it like a rhetorical question, not expecting a reply.

"I'm going to plead the fifth on that one," she said. "Gorgeous neighborhood. Have you lived here long?"

"Seven years."

Long enough to know the pluses and minuses of this particular market. "May I ask a question?"

He hesitated. "Am I required to answer?"

"You are not."

"Ask away."

She wasn't sure what he expected, but when she flipped the switch to real estate figures, his demeanor cooled. "How has this neighborhood been for value appreciation, and are the taxes too high to offset any increase in value?"

He looked surprised. Then a little suspicious. Because it was financial talk? Or did she sound nosy? He raised a brow. "Nothing you can't find on the Internet."

"And from my Realtor as she looks around," she replied smoothly. "I was hoping for a straightforward personal opinion from someone who lives here. My bad." She stepped back to resume her run as he frowned.

"Hold on."

She tapped her pricey technological wonder watch. "No can do. I'm helping pack food baskets at the church then helping Vern at the diner. Saturday nights are busy now that the weather's broken. Glad you liked the cookies," she told Emerson. "I'll tell Maggie."

She ran off, circling the complex, studying the layouts. Real estate investment wasn't about today's cost, except in how it related to tomorrow's appreciation. If this area was overpriced, it would be a bad idea. If it was escalating in value, that was a different story.

She'd set up a meeting with the Realtor. Purchasing real estate elsewhere would leave the property management in someone else's hands. When you grow up broke, limiting who took a piece of your lucrative pie was paramount. And her grandma had always said, "Girl, you do what you can, when you can, and do it best. Don't let anyone be runnin' your life but you and the good Lord. If you do that, no one's gonna bring you down, Cinda. I swear it."

She'd been right, but Jacinda had managed to bring her own self down. Maybe she had tried for too much control . . . or maybe just tried too much overall.

No more.

She took the curve leading back to the road. A few people were in their yards. No one was mowing. And most of them turned to watch her run. She read questions on some faces, but a few folks actually smiled and waved.

In the village, lawn mowers had started over the past week as the greening grass grew lush from the spring rains. But in this posh neighborhood, not one homeowner was mowing on a brilliant April Saturday morning.

Landscaping services.

The lightbulb moment hit as she steeled herself for the uphill grind back to the woodland trail. A broad opening through the forest's edge allowed a landscape view of the neighborhood from above, an almost Google Earth experience. The yards and gardens splayed out in such balanced perfection that they seemed surreal, like a computer-generated image of a virtual neighborhood, and just that cool and distant.

She'd talk to the Realtor on Monday, but even the thought of investing in something that needed to be perfect annoyed her.

Life wasn't about perfection. She'd tried that. It had threatened her very existence.

How much better to be in the village neighborhoods, swapping recipes and keeping an eye on other people's kids as they rode around on their Christmas bicycles.

She'd keep an open mind and talk things over with an expert. But the thought of all that intertwined perfection pressed old buttons.

Perfection was a ruinous expectation. And it wasn't a game she ever intended to play again.

~

"Hey. You guys ready? We've got to be at the park in ten minutes." Thea had picked up Shannon and swung back to grab Mara and Keegan for the annual church-sponsored Easter egg hunt on Saturday morning.

"I'm ready!" Keegan spun in a circle, then high-fived Thea before he grinned at Shannon. "Hey, Shannie! Hi! We're going to a Easter egg hunt right now!"

"Me, too," she told him. A dimple flashed in her right cheek, absolutely endearing. "I've never been to one in my whole life, but they had one on *Dora* once, and it looked like so much fun!"

"*Dora*'s for babies. So are Easter egg hunts." Mara slumped in her chair with a look of disdain. "I'm staying here."

"You're not," said Ethan as he crossed the room. He looked better. So much better. But he didn't look thrilled with the thought of a power struggle this early on a Saturday. "Good morning, Thea. Thanks for doing this. Hey, Shannon." He bent down and smiled at her. "You look like you've recovered quite nicely."

"I feel good." She dimpled up at him. "And I can't believe I get to go to an Easter egg hunt with Thea and your kids."

"We're not his kids. We're not anyone's kids. Not anymore." Mara glared at her from the chair. "Don't you know anything?"

"Mara." The warning in Ethan's tone made her slump farther into the chair, and Thea hadn't thought that was possible.

Shannon didn't look offended. She looked absolutely sympathetic as she halved the space between them. "I do know, Mara. I really do."

"We've got to get going or we'll miss it completely," Thea said. "Let's hustle, guys."

Ethan shrugged into a lightweight jacket. "Let's go."

Her heart definitely did not just shift into some kind of adolescent overdrive. Did it? Because he was coming along? "Are you sure you're up for this?"

"I've been putting my time in on those daily walk regimens and physical therapy." He shared a rueful smile, then turned. "Mara. Coming? Or staying. Eva's here."

"Let her stay," said Thea, calling the kid's bluff. "We'll take these two and have a ball." She waited while Keegan zipped his jacket. "Okay. We're out."

They started down the stairs. Thea began counting to herself. By the time she got to seven, she was afraid she'd misjudged the girl's challenge. They got through the side door and were on the sidewalk before she heard, "Wait!"

Mara burst through the lower door, shut it quickly, and came their way.

No stranger to his sister's negative antics, Keegan watched with more than a little apprehension, but Shannon waded right in. "I'm so glad you're coming. I don't know too many people yet."

Mara frowned. "Me, either."

"That's so perfect!" Shannon laughed, joyous. "We can make friends together! I used to think how much fun it would be to live in town, to see people all the time. There aren't a lot of people in the woods."

Keegan seemed enthralled by her lilting conversation. He grinned up at her and took her hand. "You talk happy."

"I do?" Shannie made a little face of surprise. "Well, how fun is that?"

"So much fun!" he told her, swinging her hand. "I like to talk happy, too! It's like the best way, right?"

"Well, I'm just so happy to have someone to talk to," Shannie admitted. "Gee Gee said a lot of things, but you couldn't exactly talk to her. And she didn't like noise because if you were noisy, she might not hear who was coming. Although no one ever came except Fat Mary now and again. And Old Sophie."

"You. Just. Called. Someone. Fat." Mara rolled the words out in an obnoxious tone. "That's not nice."

"Well, she was fat, and that was her name, so I *was* being nice. Her daughter was Skinny Mary, and she'd moved away last year with some man she met in a bar." Shannon relayed the events in the matter-of-fact style born of complete innocence. "Fat Mary and Old Sophie were the only people who came by after that. But I suppose you're right," Shannon said as if she'd just figured something out. Ethan exchanged a raised-brow look with Thea. They were approaching the festive park setting. Spring-toned balloons were fastened to just about anything that would hold them, and kids of all ages milled about. "Once Skinny Mary was gone, there was just the one Mary left. I guess I never thought of that."

"Normal people don't go around calling people names like 'skinny' and 'fat.' It's not polite." Mara had stopped, and the scolding look she gave Shannon was meant to put her in her place.

It didn't work.

Shannon gazed at her as if she were a benefactress and nodded. "I think you're right. There's so much to learn now, and Maggie says not to worry, not to fuss, I'll get it all, but it takes me a little time because this is all so absolutely lovely here. I didn't really think lovely was real until Thea brought me to Maggie's house. And now I've got lovely all the time." She breathed the happiest of sighs and grasped Thea's hand and an even bigger chunk of Thea's heart. "I'm so glad you came to check on me! I didn't like the hospital one little bit, but I love everything else."

Mara stared at her as if seeing a two-headed alien. Thea ignored the look and handed them their egg-collecting bags. "I'm glad you're finding all the lovelies in life, darling. Now girls, you're in the seven-and-eight age group and they are lining up over there. Head on over and find a spot."

Ethan stepped to the girls' side. "I'll take them while you take Keegs, all right?"

"Yes." She looked up, into his eyes, then didn't want to stop gazing into them. He didn't seem to be in a big hurry to break the connection, either. And when he glanced down, at her lips . . . and lingered there . . . she longed to lean forward. Close that distance. Just to see.

"Come on, Thea! Come on!"

Ethan smiled at her . . . then Keegan, then her again. "Duty calls."

"Yes."

She crossed to the preschool area and met Kelsey. Maggie was watching the baby, and Kelsey and Hale had volunteered to help organize the hunt. "Thea, isn't this like the cutest thing?"

Kelsey looked happy. Perfectly happy. And that was something the three girls had hoped for back at Hannah's Hope but never truly expected. "You mean the hunt?"

"The whole thing." Kelsey grasped Thea's hand and couldn't seem to stop smiling. "The town. The kids. The park, all decked out for a special day, and I'm not immune to the smell of those pancakes and syrup."

"Look who's becoming a hometown girl," Thea teased.

Kelsey bumped shoulders with her. "That's a surprise, isn't it? Back in the day, who would have thought we'd be in a town like this and actually feel like we belong? And don't pretend you're not feeling that way, this place is growing on you. On all of us. You can't fool me, Thea, so don't even try. Now if we could just convince Ethan to stay." Kelsey followed Ethan's progress with a firm expression.

That wasn't about to happen. She tried to scold Kelsey with a look, but it didn't work because Kelsey had become immune to Thea's looks long ago. "I am of the strong opinion that some things should never be forced."

"Oh, please." Clearly falling in love had tipped Kelsey into "the more, the merrier" mode. She reached for Keegan's hand. "I'll take Keegan, if it's all right, and you can cheer for the girls."

"That would be great. His sister is currently in fight mode."

Kelsey winced in sympathy. "I remember that all too well."

"Me, too." Keegan would be happy regardless, so Kelsey had given her the perfect solution, and Mara was in rare form. An extra adult with the girls wasn't a bad idea. She started toward the older kids with a quick wave. "See you in a few."

"We'll be here."

Thea crossed back to the opposite staging area. Wishing Bridge didn't just roll a thousand eggs onto a grassy knoll. They tucked them into the edge of the woods for the older kids, and beyond the playground equipment. They kept them away from leftover puddles, but other than that, the park was fair game. And when the kids were done hunting, the Knights of Columbus would serve a traditional country breakfast inside the big cedar lodge. The smell of buckwheat pancakes filled the air, mingling with the scent of warm New York maple syrup. The combination of the beautiful day and the scents added to the anticipation.

The girls gripped their bags. When the starting buzzer went off, they raced down the hill with the other second and third graders. Near the bottom, Mara's shoelace came undone. She toppled down the last few feet of the hill as the rest of the children ran ahead.

All but Shannon.

She glanced back, saw Mara's dejected figure on the ground, and raced to her. "Are you all right?"

Mara scowled. She banged her fists onto the ground and stayed right there. "I'm fine. Leave me alone."

"What?" Shannie didn't leave her alone. Astonished, she grabbed Mara's right arm and pulled her up. "With all those treats to get? Come on, come on, we're wasting time. Let's go!" She tugged Mara forward, and to Thea's surprise and amazing relief, Mara went.

"She went with her." Ethan sounded just as surprised.

"I know." Thea looked up at him. "I was expecting total meltdown."

"This is much better." He almost whispered the words, and the smile he gave her was a mix of relief and amusement. "Shannie's killing her with kindness."

"Weapon of choice," Thea agreed. "I don't think it would work for us, but from a peer? Pretty powerful stuff. Are you feeling all right?" she asked then. "The walk wasn't too much for you?"

He held her gaze for so many beats that she was pretty sure it was *her* heart that was now in need of some resuscitation. "I'm better than I've been in a long time, and I think coming over here with you and the kids is the best medicine ever."

Thea dipped her chin to hide the heat in her cheeks. Greek girls didn't blush, but she was only half Greek, and the Celtic side seemed to blush on its own. But when Ethan grazed one finger along the curve of her warm cheek, she knew he saw.

But to what end?

Reality forced her to tone down the reaction.

Focus on the kids. Not the handsome guy tugging your heartstrings. And, by the way, hearts have no strings. What a silly saying.

Shannon led Mara away from where the bulk of kids were hunting, and when they walked back up the hill five minutes later, they each had nine eggs. Not a huge haul, but way better than nothing.

"That was so much fun!" Shannon twirled her bag at the top of the hill. "We did it!" She high-fived Mara, and Mara high-fived her back. Was it habit, to meet the other girl's hand? Or camaraderie?

Either way, she did it. "And you got nine eggs apiece. Wonderful!"

"Well, Mara got eleven and I got seven, but she shared so we were even," Shannon explained. "Wasn't that like the nicest thing?"

"It was the nicest thing." Ethan wrapped an arm around Mara's shoulders and hugged her. "Well played, kid."

"That was the most fun I ever had in my entire life!" Keegan ran toward them with a bag of eggs. "And Mr. Hale said I was maybe the best h-hun-hunter he'd ever seen! Can you believe it?"

"I sure can." Thea sent Hale a smile of thanks, then tucked the kids' bags into the grocery sack she'd brought along. "Let's get breakfast with the other kids. And then we can play awhile. If you'd like to."

"Oh, yes!" Keegan jumped into the air, and the girls looked happy. They dashed into the pavilion, milling about with the dozens of other children, finding their way.

"This is deceptively normal," Ethan said as they crossed to the shelter. "Like the kind of thing childhood should be made of."

Pancakes. Syrup. Sausages. Juice pouches. And the chatter of over a hundred local children, welcoming spring. "Maybe only deceptive because we've never experienced it," she argued. "Around here, I think it's the norm. We're just jaded by experience. And maybe choices." She shrugged. "Either way, it's crazy fun, and I'm not on call, so it's *really* a weekend. I'm loving it."

Mara joined in the festivities. Not full force, like Shannon, but she didn't shrink back or avoid the kids, and when a group of second graders invited the girls to eat and then play with them, both girls accepted.

"I brought coffee." Max joined them at the top of the hill overlooking the park once breakfast was cleaned up. "I stopped by Jill's store. Fancy for you." He handed Thea the mocha latte she loved from Jill's coffee bar. "Straight for the rest of us. And a chai for Kelsey."

"Max." Kelsey accepted the to-go cup with a grateful smile. "I was thinking of this all morning, but then we were running late, and there wasn't time to stop in before the hunt. Thank you."

"Well, Jill might have inspired the idea."

Hale laughed. "Sounds like Mom."

"But inspiration without implementation is just an empty promise, so I don't mind taking some of the credit."

"Well deserved," noted Thea. She raised her cup to toast him and smiled, "A hearty thank you to all concerned. And every time I look out our attic windows and see how spring is finally moving along, I thank you again. What a delightful place to live."

Max rocked back on his heels, hands in his pockets, pleased. "I'm glad. And good to see you getting around, Doc."

"Good to be seen," said Ethan. "I'm anxious to get back to work."

Thea made a face.

"Only because I hate leaving people in the lurch," he told her. "Not because I question your capabilities."

"Luckily cold-and-flu season is winding down, and we've got a temp coming in from Travel Care for the next four weeks," Thea replied. "They sent a confirmation e-mail overnight."

"That's a relief. We can have him—"

"Her," she corrected.

"Her do the school physicals and well-baby checkups. That's pretty cut-and-dried, and I think people will do all right with that, don't you? Our version of giving her the simple stuff?"

"That could work." She sipped her coffee and kept her eyes on the kids. Ethan had offered a good suggestion, especially if she was leaving. Building a rapport with the local people, the young families, and the school-age kids wouldn't matter if she was going back to Pennsylvania. But it did matter if she was staying. Well visits helped set the stage for a great doctor-patient relationship.

The Philadelphia medical office had requested an interview. A city practice, linked to one of the top universities in the country, one of the best medical bastions in the nation, and she could be part of it, if chosen. Helping the less fortunate, the young Theas of the world. "She comes in on Tuesday, and we'll set things up."

"I'll come down, and don't fuss," he warned her, but it was with a teasing tone, as if getting his heart fixed had done more than open a plaque-clogged passageway. It seemed to have broadened his whole outlook. "I won't stay, I won't micromanage, but I'd like to be in on the meeting."

"Perfect. But now we have to break up the kids' fun, because I promised Maggie I'd have Shannon back by noon. They're going to the memory care unit for what might be the last time. Gee Gee is slipping, and Shannon wants to see her before she passes away."

"What a great kid." Hale blew out a breath. "To have endured all of that, dealt with losses, neglect, dementia, and bugs—"

"Let's not talk about the bugs," Thea scolded. "But you're right, she's a survivor. Her gentle nature lets her accept things even while she tries to change them. And she seems so resilient, in spite of it all."

"Faith of a child," said Hale, and when Ethan raised a brow, Hale didn't back down. "There's something to it, Doc. The whole trust thing. Give things over. Stay simple. I can't explain it in preacher terms, but I feel it. And after finding Kelsey buried in snow on a night when it was impossible to see my hand a foot in front of my face, I got proof, if proof was what I needed." He settled an arm around Kelsey and pulled her closer. "Shannon has an abiding faith in spite of everything. She wears that little cross her Nana gave her before she died and she'll tell anyone who'll listen what got her through. Jesus. Faith. And her Nana's words, in her ear, to stay strong and stay good no matter what happened. And that's what she did."

The kids reached them just then. Keegan almost launched himself at Ethan, but remembered at the last minute. "Oops!" He grinned up at Ethan and hugged his leg instead. "I'm so glad we came to this! Thank you, Uncle Eefen! Thank you, Th-thea!"

"It was the best, wasn't it?" Shannon beamed at Mara. "You know it was, Mara," she teased, in case Mara was about to shrug it off. "And maybe we can play tomorrow? After church?"

"Or now?" suggested Mara, and she seemed to miss the surprised looks on the grown-ups' faces. "You can come to our house. It's pretty, and there's a big yard outside."

"I will love your house," Shannon assured her, but she shook her head. "I have to go see my Gee Gee. She hasn't been feeling good for a long, long time. Maggie thinks she'll go to heaven soon—"

"You mean die?" Mara interrupted, surprised.

Sadness changed Shannon's features. She nodded. "We kind of took care of each other when my Nana died. And Gee Gee didn't mean to forget about me most times, she just can't remember anything anymore.

But I think she'll remember stuff in heaven, and then she won't be sick or sad or nervous."

Mara studied her. Then she leaned forward, just a little, and her face turned serious. "Do you think she'll be hurting? In heaven, I mean?" She breathed the words just above a whisper. "Because I don't think it would be nice to be hurting in heaven. Would it?"

Thea bent down to their level and met their gazes. "No hurting. No pain. No sorrow. There's just angels and saints and sweet souls, dancing in peace and spending time with God."

"Do you really believe that?" Mara stared at her. "I think that's something they make up so kids don't worry. Because I'm like very good at science, and I can't figure out how it works. Neither can anybody else. Because I asked."

Thea didn't elaborate. She didn't go into a theology lesson or a Sunday homily. She kept it simple, like Hale suggested. "I believe. I can't explain it, but I believe it. And that's enough for me."

Mara reached out for her hand. "But what if it's not enough?" she whispered. "What if people are always hurt? Like maybe it never gets better, even after they die?"

Thea drew her in gently. Carefully. "There is no pain after death," she whispered. "None. There is peace and quiet, totally. And time with God, Mara."

She knew Ethan wasn't a believer. He'd made that clear. But the kids' parents had taken them to church on a regular basis. They'd put Mara in Sunday school, so to them, belief was real. Faith was real.

"Thea." Kelsey spoke softly and tapped her watch. "It's time to go," she said. "Unless you want us to take Shannon back to Maggie's."

Thea kissed Mara's cheek, the first time she'd ever dared a gesture like that. "No, I'll take her. I'll be home later if you guys want to visit me upstairs," she told Mara and Keegan. "You're always welcome."

"And make popcorn?" suggested Keegan. "You make the best popcorn. Like with the most butter!"

"Shh." She put a finger to her lips. "Let's not tease your uncle about
butter, okay? But you know I've got your back, kid."

"I know." He grabbed Ethan's hand and sighed. "You bofe do."

Another corner of her heart squeezed open.

Wishing Bridge hadn't been in her plans.

But it was in her heart.

She'd deliberately embraced the obscurity of the big city. There, she
could have a positive effect but keep her distance.

No one kept their distance in Wishing Bridge, and that had half
strangled her the first few weeks she'd been here.

Now she liked being in the thick of things. Knowing folks. Caring.
In Dr. Seuss terms, she'd grown a bigger heart. Was that because her
faith was growing? Or because she was brave enough to let people in?

Shannie had grasped her hand as they left the park. Now she swung
it and pointed down Franklin Street as they passed Jill Jackson's new
store. "Maggie said the ice-cream shop will open this week and that we
can get ice-cream cones. And that I can walk there all by myself!"

The normalcy of that touched Thea. An almost-eight-year-old,
strolling two blocks through the village to get a treat. It was total
Hallmark Channel, and fairly unbelievable in this day and age of heli-
copter parents, but here, in Wishing Bridge, people looked out for one
another. Old Mrs. Lucas was just as likely to scold a boy for lobbing
snowballs too close to a house as his parents were. And shopkeepers
knew the kids, knew them by name, and that seemed to make a difference in how the kids behaved.

There were no nameless faces in Wishing Bridge. She thought she'd
hate it, but she didn't, and maybe that was the biggest surprise of all.

"Thea, thank you for getting her back now." Maggie and Jeb were
waiting on the porch when she and Shannon strolled up. Merry-looking

jonquils lined the front gardens and the walkways. Deep yellow, pale melon, and ivory, the bursts of color added cheerful brightness all around them. "We'll head right over." The look she exchanged with Thea indicated they had good reason to hurry to the Warsaw nursing home.

"I'll watch Hayley until Kelsey and Hale get back."

"She's sound asleep, monitor's on, she ate about thirty minutes ago, and you know where everything is, dearie. We'll be back after a bit."

Thea let herself into the Tompkins house through the front door. Quiet greeted her.

Quiet used to unnerve her.

Not anymore.

She used to grab extra shifts to keep busy, but here, she didn't fear time off. Time to lull. To read. To think. Mostly because when she allowed herself to relax here, it felt fine. It felt . . . normal.

Heading over to the fire hall to fill Easter baskets, then to the diner for short shift, Jazz texted. How about if I bring home a pair of Greek salads for supper?

As long as we can add nuts and dried berries, I'm in, she texted back.

Done.

The baby squawked in the living room. Thea crossed the old-fashioned braided rug and lifted little Hayley. "Hey, you," she whispered against the three-month-old's soft skin. "I think you were supposed to sleep longer, missy. But Auntie Thea's here, and it's way more fun when you're awake, so how about we see to that diaper, okay?"

Hayley didn't just smile at her.

She grinned as if Thea had just offered the very best of ideas. She grinned like they were besties or bosom buddies, kindred spirits or any wonderful friend term ever invented. Then she reached up to Thea's face. Her cheek. And her glasses.

Oops.

She had to wrangle her glasses out of Hayley's very tight grip. That made the baby cry, and she wasn't all that fond of the diaper change, either, but once done, when Thea had tucked her glasses up on top of her head, peace reigned.

For ten minutes.

She warmed a bottle, ignoring the feeding time frame. If a baby was hungry, they got fed in the Thea Anastas School of Child Care, as inexperienced as she was, and when a four-ounce bottle made Hayley happy and playful once again, Thea congratulated herself.

She bundled a blanket around the baby and took her onto the sunny front porch to watch the world pass by. It wasn't a big, busy world, like the one Thea had known, but it was beautiful. Sitting there, rocking a baby, while tiny leaves poked bits of green, red, and amber on the trees, realization swept over her.

She didn't want to leave.

She wanted to stay. Stay here, now, in this Mayberry-style town filled with sweet people (and a few old cranks).

She sighed, breathed in the clean, warm air of an April day, and made her decision. No matter what happened—no matter what Ethan chose to do—she was staying here because it felt right, and Thea had learned hard lessons about life at a far-too-young age. To have something feel this good wasn't all that common, so she was going to reach out and grab hold.

She'd cancel the Philly interview, and she'd talk to Becky about buying the practice. She wasn't sure if she could afford it on her own, but she'd find a partner, if necessary. Doc Wolinski had run the practice independently for decades, but it had grown the past few years. A partner would be good. If there wasn't anyone interested for a while, she'd wing it by herself, and the thought of having no boss absolutely delighted her.

Ethan would go. He had his dreams, his goals. No one took a research fellowship lightly. She understood that. But they were on opposite sides of a mighty serious divide, and she'd watched too many relationships fall apart over the years to not measure things with care.

Faith, hope, and love were crucial because she'd lived the lack of them, and she never wanted to risk going back to that again.

She hated letting him go. Letting those children go. But sitting on Maggie's front porch, seeing the village through a baby's eyes, made it so clear.

This was where she wanted to be. Where she needed to be. This was where she was meant to stay. And that was that.

CHAPTER TWENTY

Jazz was waiting on a table of teenage boys when Gus and Emerson Whitaker came in for their take-out order that night. She finished dropping off the teens' order before she headed their way. "You surprised me when you called. My little friend said Saturday was pizza day."

"He changed his mind after seeing you this morning," Gus admitted. He looked a little uncomfortable. Maybe more than a little. "Listen, Cinda, I didn't mean to sound curt this morning."

So the rich guy didn't mean to brush the waitress off for being in his neighborhood? Whatever.

Was she defensive?

Absolutely, and when you grew up as a person of color, sometimes a good defense was your best offense. "No harm done. It makes for perfect mileage on my long run days now that the snow is gone. I stumbled into your little enclave by accident. It's well hidden, isn't it?" She met his gaze now and didn't hide the challenge in her tone.

"Not everyone's a village person."

Not a village person.

Funny. She would have thought that about herself before she got here. Village people were simpler, weren't they? Maybe less educated, with smaller homes and less pretentious lifestyles. Not surrounded by impeccable yards and untouchable gardens. Or in her case, a high-rise apartment she had rarely seen, with two security guards posing as normal doormen.

She swallowed hard . . . real hard . . . to bite back what she wanted to say and simply nodded instead. This guy saw what he wanted to see. A black waitress, waiting on an upscale white family.

So be it. She was almost tempted to drawl her voice, then stopped herself. He could be whatever he needed to be. It was nothing to her.

She didn't need to react. She handed him the bags and waited while he inserted his card into the chip reader. Like always, he slipped a two-dollar tip across the counter. "Thanks so much." She pocketed the tip, smiled at Emerson, and was about to walk away when the little boy grabbed her in a hug.

"Thank you for being so nice to us all the time." He gazed up at her with green-flecked hazel eyes. "And for the cookies and stuff."

She ruffled his hair lightly. "Brownies today. My friend Thea made them and they're amazing. But eat supper first, okay?"

"I will!"

She walked away, wondering.

They must have a story. No mom in the picture. Food for two, adult and child. Huge, upscale house in a somewhat hidden, affluent neighborhood short minutes from the interstate linking Rochester and Buffalo.

Honey, we all have a story. Don't we?

"Miss Monroe, may I have a refill. Please?" asked one of the teen boys at the table of four.

Miss Monroe.

She smiled at him when she dropped off the drink on her way to another table. "I love your manners. Here you go. Tell your mama she should be proud."

He blushed. When she walked away, the other guys teased him until Vern cruised by their table and quieted them with a simple frown.

Gus and Emerson hadn't made it past the lure of the giant gumball machines. When a big, yellow gumball cascaded out, it landed on the floor and rolled straight across to her feet. She picked it up and put it in her pocket. "Well, that was some bad luck, my friend. Let's try again, okay?"

Gus frowned. "Can I get a few quarters? That was my last one."

"Well, a waitress always carries the odd quarter or two in her apron," she told him and slipped a coin to the boy. "There you go. Keep your hand cupped this time, okay?" She curved her hand beneath the machine's spout. "These big ones roll out fast and furious."

"Thank you!" And when a red gumball rolled straight into Emerson's cupped hand, he grinned her way. "Got it."

"Well done."

"Thank you." Gus was watching her. Not exactly studying her, but watching as if trying to figure her out.

He didn't want to know. Not really. Her reality put her in an emotional place that boggled her mind at times. Other times?

She felt amazingly normal, but she knew better.

She'd staved off the calls from New York and London so far, and she'd ignored the requests from two Paris designers. If they could see her now, they'd mock her. Scorn her for cleaning tables and giving brownies to little boys.

But she was her own person now, and all the glitz and fame and earthly glory paled to that reality. She was free to do what she wanted, eat what she wanted, and be where she wanted to be.

She couldn't predict how long it would last. She'd never allowed herself to think in terms of forever. But it was hers to grasp now.

Gus turned as he went through the door. He looked her way, one last time, musing.

She didn't return the look.

She glossed over it as she wiped down a table and greeted an elderly pair of regulars, brother and sister. Folks who got up in arms because a woman—a black woman—had the nerve to add their loop to her running route weren't worth the bother. That wouldn't stop her from going through Harrowsmith on her long run days. Not because she wanted to be in their faces. But because it made a perfect cooling loop before heading back uphill. When you ran in the hills bordering the Southern Tier of New York, the flat spots were the gravy in a very meat-and-potatoes kind of dish.

~

Thea answered the phone just past seven thirty. "Maggie, what's up? Everything all right?"

"The home just called." Worry stressed her voice. "Dotty's breaths are slowing down, and Jeb wants to be there, seeing as how he's the only person left with a connection, but I've got Shannie and the baby here."

"I'll go with him," Thea told her. "No worries."

"Thank you."

Jeb was a solid driver, but making the drive to Warsaw alone, facing death, then driving back home in the dark of night seemed wrong. She buzzed off a quick text to Jazz: Heading to Lifelong Care with Jeb to see Dotty. Put my salad in the fridge, okay? Thanks.

She picked Jeb up and drove swiftly. When they got to Dotty's room, it didn't take long to confirm the staff's assessment. Pale lips. Pale nail beds. And slow, shallow breaths.

"Jeb, take this seat." Thea drew up a chair alongside Dotty's bed.

"Don't mind if I do," he told her. He sounded tired, and Thea was glad Maggie had called.

A woman brought an extra chair. When Thea turned to thank her, she paused, surprised. "Sara Hilbert. Are you working here?" Sara Hilbert and her family were patients at Hillside Medical. They'd fallen on tough times when her husband's new business had burned to the ground in late December. Speculation about the cause of the fire had held up insurance payouts, putting the family in dire financial straits.

Sara nodded. "For the past five years, actually. I've been working nights and evenings until our little guy goes to school this fall, but I've got my RN now. I'll be looking for a daytime position soon, and it will be nice not to be gone every evening. Or fill in on overnights."

"I bet. Thank you for the chair."

"My pleasure. Can I get you guys anything? Coffee? Juice? Tea?"

"Jeb?"

Jeb waved it off. "I'm good, thanks."

"Me, too." She smiled at Sara. "But thank you."

"I'll be right outside if you need me." She slipped out, leaving the door slightly open but giving them privacy.

Jeb reached over and took Dotty's hand. He held it in his, not too tight, just enough. "Dot, I know we're about to part ways, but we want you to know that little Shannie's doing fine. Just fine. I know you'll remember her real well up in heaven. There's no lost memory there, and no sadness, either. Just peace and light and the sweet Lord Jesus leading us home, and that's all good. Here on earth, we'll be doing the same thing with your girl. Raising her. Loving her. Laughing with her. And Lord have mercy, Dot, that girl can talk, can't she? She's got an opinion on everything and the sweetest nature that probably came right down from her great-grandpa Henry." He paused, searching for words, searching for more to say, but what was there to add?

Thea began humming "Amazing Grace."

"Dotty's favorite." He sent her a tiny smile of approval. "Maggie's too, one of 'em, because she's got more than a few."

"Let's sing her home, Jeb."

And they did.

They sang softly, all the hymns they knew and a few they didn't know well, but when they joined in a third voicing of "Amazing Grace," Dotty Rose Willoughby forgot how to breathe.

Jeb couldn't finish the song. He stopped midverse and gripped the old woman's hand between his. "Gone home, Dotty. Gone home to God, right where you belong, and nothin' of this disease will follow where you're goin'. I swear."

Sara slipped back into the room. She checked for vitals and asked Thea to call the time of death.

She did.

Then she drove Jeb home.

Tomorrow they'd make plans. Set times. Firm up arrangements. For now, Maggie waited for him just inside the door, and when Jeb climbed up those broad front steps, she opened that door and took the old fellow into her arms.

Just that.

A marriage of nearly fifty years, holding strong. An image so beautiful, so filled with love, that tears of longing slipped right down Thea's cheeks, all the way home.

They were silly tears.

Who cried when inspired by gladness and goodness? Her, obviously.

She wiped her face with a paper towel once she parked, then climbed the stairs. Ethan's door opened as she hit the landing separating the staircases. He took one look at her and stepped out, concerned. "What's wrong? What's happened? Are you all right?"

The tears started all over again.

"Thea." He reached out and pulled her into his arms, holding her close. "Don't cry. Or wait, maybe you should cry, maybe it's like good therapy or something. I'm trying to make myself more sensitive," he explained softly, into her hair. "So I'm not clueless. If you're supposed to cry, go ahead and do it. Otherwise, stop. Like right now. Okay?"

His face curved into a smile against her ear, her cheek, and she pulled back. "I'm fine, just tired, I expect. And experiencing emotion, a thing I managed to block for a lot of years, so it might be a backlog. Dotty died tonight."

"Ah." Compassion softened his expression. "It's never easy to lose a patient."

"It wasn't that, it was Jeb. And Maggie. And seeing how Jeb went the distance to be with Dotty when she died. What he said, what he did . . . and then how Maggie held him when he got home. It was all so blasted perfect, and I kept thinking how marvelous it was and how completely unfair life is because I'd have given anything to have people like that in my life. To have that love and affection and devotion. So is it selfish of me to want to stay here and have that when I should be working in the city, helping kids down on their luck and families who fall through the cracks? When that was my dream and my goal for so long?"

He stared at her as realization sank in, and his face . . . his sweet, handsome face took on a look of resignation. "You're staying."

She breathed deep, then used the wadded paper towel to dry her eyes. "That's it, I guess. I don't want to leave. I love it here. It was the last thing I expected, but maybe that's how things work. How they're supposed to work."

"And I'm going."

She gave him a watery smile and couldn't do more than whisper her reply. The knot in her throat choked back her words. "You'll go your way, it's your dream, but this . . ." She took a breath. "This seems to be mine. Trust me, no one is more surprised about that than I am. Big-city Thea tucking herself into a faith-filled little town surrounded by forests and farm fields. Never in my wildest dreams would I have predicted this, but there it is."

"Thea." His eyes searched her face. He reached up one hand and cradled her cheek gently. "You're sure?"

She was, and it felt both wrong and right at the same time. "I am."

He didn't press his point. Didn't belabor it with questions. Instead he drew her into his arms and kissed her. And when he paused, it wasn't to stop and apologize for kissing her. It was to do it all over again.

"Ethan."

"Shh." He held her there, on the landing, and stroked her hair. "I've been wondering what it would be like to kiss you for way too long. Now I know."

"But—"

"I know." He pulled back and met her gaze. "You're staying. I'm going. I get that. But if it's only for this little while that our dreams intersect, I'll take it, Thea. Because I've never met a woman who could exasperate me and enthrall me as much as you've done. And I'm not sure what to do about it."

"We move on." She reached up and put her hands over his. "With so many differences between us, we realize it can't possibly work and we move on. But I'll never regret knowing you and the kids. I will regret not seeing them grow up."

"There have to be sweet little towns near Chicago," he reasoned. "Isn't it worth a look, Thea? Together?"

She wished it was, but she knew better. "I've got to follow not just my heart but my faith. And that's a nonstarter with you."

He looked surprised that it could mean so much, but to her, after all these years of trusting God, it meant everything.

Her phone buzzed a text from Maggie, thanking her.

She stepped back. "I've got to answer this."

She didn't. Not really. But how could he understand the importance she placed not just on love but on faith?

He couldn't. He'd said it outright: he didn't get the "God thing."

She did and no matter how wonderful this attraction seemed, she had to look at the big picture. She'd never allowed herself the chance to luxuriate in sweet dreams, girlish fantasies of white gowns, fancy weddings, and happily-ever-afters. She'd lost her innocence at the hands of evil men, so she wasn't even sure she could be a normal wife. What if she couldn't? What then?

But faith had set the rest of her free. It had helped her scale mountains and ford rivers, it had been her strength and mainstay. She hadn't come to Wishing Bridge expecting to fall in love with the town, or the irascible doctor, but she had. One she could have.

The other she had to let go.

She shut her apartment door softly.

She wanted to cry again but fought the urge. She had too much to be grateful for to languish in tears.

And if she did nothing more in her life than provide good medical care for a down-on-its-luck town filled with kind people, that was more than most could claim. It would be enough because she'd make it enough. When sleep refused to come that night, and she thought of Ethan downstairs, struggling with the same reality, her heart grew heavy.

Ask him to stay . . .

She shoved the thought aside.

She couldn't ask him to give up his dream. He'd already sacrificed a year, and that couldn't have been easy.

Aren't love and life about sacrifice? her conscience prodded. *Isn't that the very definition?*

Not if the sacrifice turned to resentment. She couldn't risk that. Loving a good man was hard enough for a woman with her past. Loving him and losing him would be more than she could bear, so on a risk-to-return ratio, she'd avoid the risk. Every time.

CHAPTER
TWENTY-ONE

Thea was staying.

Ethan didn't have the option to pace the apartment, because Eva was sleeping on the couch. He'd pace his room, but with furniture it was too small to do much good.

He sat on the edge of the bed, considering her words. Her reactions. That kiss.

He loved that kiss.

He yearned for the tough-as-nails woman on the other side of that kiss, because she wasn't nearly as tough as she pretended to be. Strong, yes.

But not tough. Jaded and hurt . . .

Yeah, he read that in her eyes.

But he saw the warmth and compassion, too. The straightforward manner, softened by a sweetness.

Staying.

Here.

He dropped his head into his hands.

He thought of Jarod, his little brother, and the relentless deterioration he'd endured because a miniscule blip of bad DNA had replicated incessantly, a mistake so small . . . and yet life changing and brutal.

He had the education and the focus to make a difference. He'd worked hard to make his mark in the research world while practicing downstate, and he'd succeeded. He'd reached his dream—his goal—to get a place at a top research facility that could save lives. He wasn't meant to prescribe amoxicillin eight times a day. Was he?

And yet . . . he'd made a difference here, despite his reluctance. He was a good doctor, a good practitioner, but anyone could peddle pills and suture a few wounds. Not everyone could visualize genomic sequence and identify protein indicators of cancer cells or rogue broken ends of tiny chromosomes.

He could because he'd devoted the last seven years of his life to outside study, determined to find answers to microscopic questions.

And then he had come here.

Right now he hated the town. It tempted people with pastoral beauty and small-town cuteness.

Small towns weren't cute. They were stifling. Boring. And single minded.

Except Wishing Bridge wasn't any of those things, and maybe he hated that discovery most of all.

He fell into a troubled sleep, and when his phone alarm buzzed him the next morning, he swiped the screen so hard the phone flew off the little table. He picked it up, sure it was broken.

It wasn't. The screen hadn't cracked, and the phone looked fine.

But he wasn't fine. He was getting better physically. He couldn't say the same about his thoughts and emotions, and he didn't have a clue what to do about that except pretend a calm he didn't feel. For the kids. For his work. For his life . . . when the last thing he felt was tranquil.

He'd fake it because Mara and Keegan didn't deserve his angst. They needed and deserved his love, and that's exactly what they were going to get.

Church bells rang out at eight o'clock sharp, signaling the first Mass at the Catholic church around the corner.

Eva growled from her makeshift living-room bed. She pulled the pillow over her face and let out a tortured groan. "Heaven spare me from those stupid bells every stinking Sunday morning. Don't they have a noise ordinance here? And if not, why not?"

"I love the bells, Aunt Eva," said Keegan, struggling on the floor with his pants.

Ethan had showered and was getting ready for the nine o'clock service at the Lutheran church. With Thea, Jeb, and Maggie there, and a bunch of other locals, they'd have people they knew in the pews.

He moved toward Keegan. The little guy was trying to pull pants over his pajamas, a thankless task. "Bud, you have to lose the jammies first or the pants won't fit."

"Oh, man!" Keegan grinned up at him with a look so engaging that it brightened Ethan's dark morning mood. "That's so silly! I forgot to take my jamas off!"

Mara came out of her room just then, completely ready for church. Her normal ritual had been to insist on going to church because Alexis had taken them in California . . . and then impede the process every step of the way, habitually making them late.

But not today. He smiled at her as he made a fresh cup of coffee. "You look wonderful, honey."

"Thank you." She fingered the edge of her dress lightly. "I didn't want to be late for a new church, I guess."

Big words from his angry little procrastinator. Maybe the new therapist wouldn't have as tough a job as he'd supposed. "Well, you look great. And it's nice to be close to so many churches now, isn't it? Eva, the bathroom's all yours."

"Ethan, I know what you're doing," she told him from her spot on the couch. "But I'm not into the whole church thing. It's not my gig."

Except she was living there, on his dime, and he wanted—no, make that *needed*—a great example for the kids because they'd already faced more than enough. "We're considering it a family gig these days." He jerked his head toward the bathroom. "I'll make your coffee. You're always happier once you've had coffee."

"Grrr . . ." She pretend-growled but didn't argue. When Ethan heard Thea and Jazz coming down the stairs a half hour later, he poked his head out the door.

"Give us two minutes and we'll walk with you." Was he trying to win points with Thea?

Yes.

But maybe he had other reasons for changing things up, too. The kind of reasons you just rolled with, trying to make things right that might never be right again.

"A contingent," Jazz said. She smiled at him, then Thea. "How nice."

"Very nice," added Thea. She sounded calm, but his heart and head were racing. How could she be that peaceful?

And then she gazed right into his eyes and smiled so kindly that he was pretty sure he could stand there and smile back all day.

Ready to go, Keegan slipped through the door and grabbed Jazz and Thea in a hug. "Good morning!"

"Hello, little one." Jazz grinned down at him. "I see I'm not the only one on a new adventure quest this morning. Wishing Bridge Lutheran, here we come!"

"Will you guys sit with us?" asked Mara as she stepped out the door behind Keegan. "Or maybe I can sit with Shannie."

"She'd like that." Thea took Mara's hand. "Let's go wait on the porch. It's not cold and that's such a refreshing change, isn't it?"

"I love it!" Mara held tight to Thea's hand as they went down the stairs. "And did you hear how many birds were out this morning?" Excitement laced her voice. "Like a million. At least. I couldn't even sleep it was so fun and noisy and cheerful, Thea."

"I know." Thea smiled down at her, and the profile they presented reignited that odd longing within Ethan. "You can see so many of them from the attic windows because the leaves are itsy-bitsy right now. Come up later and do some bird-watching. Okay?"

"Me, too?" begged Keegan as they reached the downstairs door. "I like birds a lot! Like this much!" He stretched his arms so wide he almost toppled down the final step.

"Yes, of course. As long as it's all right with your uncle." She tipped her gaze his way, and suddenly it didn't matter that thirteen steps separated them. That she was in the sunlit entry and he was in the shadowed doorway. It just mattered that his eyes met hers.

"It's fine," he said. "Maybe we can barbecue later. Max put his old grill in the garage, and this looks like a great day for hamburgers and hot dogs. Doesn't it?"

"I would love that so much!" Keegan spoke with his usual excitement. "My dad used to do that thing on the grill, Uncle Eefen. Like all the time! Let's do it!"

Mara's smile faded. She turned and moved through the door as if her legs had suddenly gone heavy.

"Ready, Ethan? Since you're dragging me to church at this crazy early hour?" Eva came through the door.

He hit the lock and swung the door shut. "Yeah."

She followed his gaze to Mara's profile, moving across the porch. "Alexis did holidays and church days pretty big, Ethan. I didn't live close to them, but I knew it was her thing. Then you've got the anniversary of their deaths coming up in June. I can't imagine being a kid and facing so much dark stuff. I know I'm a whiner." She touched his arm as they came to the bottom of the stairs. "But I'm going to try and do better, and my new goal is to do fun stuff with these kids as often as I can. Maybe that could be my job, Ethan." She spoke with an unexpected earnestness, and then said something even more surprising. "Maybe I could be their nanny in exchange for living with you."

Say what?

Didn't he have enough on his plate already? And now—

He didn't think. He reacted. Huge mistake. "Live with me? Like forever?" She couldn't be serious. And yet the moment he said the words, he wished he could snatch them back.

Her expression dulled like a thick curtain drawn over a sunny window. "No, of course not. That was dumb." She tugged the lower door open, thrust her hands into the pockets of a worn jacket, and walked out, chin down.

Why had he spoken like that? What was the matter with him?

She moved ahead, not with Thea and Jazz, and certainly not with him, but alone in a small crowd of people.

Thea didn't look back.

He wanted her to. He wanted her to flash one of those over-the-shoulder smiles that challenged him to be a better man. A better person. To notice that he was struggling because he was a jerk.

She didn't. She chatted with Mara and Keegan about birds and leaves and God, and when they got to the steps of the old stone church, neither kid was whining or complaining, and that was a first.

A line of people had formed a broad path around the church. Thea and Jazz paused with the kids at the edge of the crowd.

Eva paused, too. She looked sad. So sad, and Ethan felt worse for his foolish reaction. "What's going on?" she asked Thea.

Thea answered as Jeb moved along the crowd, handing out palm leaves. "Palm Sunday."

"Like I'm supposed to know what that is?" Her frown deepened. "And why is everyone outside? It's nice out but not that nice, and standing here's going to get chilly real quick."

"Won't be long. I promise," Thea told her.

From his vantage point, Ethan saw the minister walking through the milling people from the back corner of the churchyard, just east of the vintage cemetery. The minister moved forward, quiet and serene, waving to people as they cheered him on.

Ethan wasn't a churchgoer by choice, but he'd taken Early Christianity in undergrad, and Alexis had loved to talk about her faith. The minister was reenacting Christ's triumphant ride into Jerusalem days before he was put to death.

Did Jesus know his fate as he rode into town? Did he know what awaited him? Was he aware that one of his followers had sold him out? Did he know the hour was at hand?

A group of people followed the minister. Jeb was among them. Several women dressed in Biblical-style garb walked alongside. Maggie walked with them, hailing the minister with waving branches.

Children trailed behind, happy and joyous. When Mara saw Shannon wave them in, she grabbed Keegan's hand and they joined the children accompanying the young minister up the steps of the old church.

Women and children, following the prophet because he gave them a voice. He gave them hope. He met with sinners and tax collectors and shepherds and fishermen. Alexis had shared that commitment to faith often, how a good shepherd goes the distance for the lost lamb.

Jesus had dared to defy the elders. He'd sat with the unclean and offered redemption. He threw out the old rules and embraced a message of love.

Ethan had studied this not because he cared—he didn't—but because he wanted a good grade and it looked like an easy A for a guy who wanted to get into medical school. Alexis's take on it had helped, and that had been enough back then.

But now . . .

Seeing the people reenact the scene on the quiet Sunday-morning street . . .

He did care.

It had taken guts to stand up for the oppressed when those in power had the right to kill you for it. Or have you killed.

Shannie had taken Keegan's hand as they wound their way through the people, toward the front steps. As he watched, Mara reached out and took Shannie's other hand, the angst of grilling hamburgers shoved off for the moment.

Suddenly the emptiness inside him erupted in a stranglehold.

Why had he thought he could rise to the occasion of raising kids just because Alexis thought it was a good idea? The other grandparents had already raised two kids. They understood childhood development and character and normal kid stuff.

He didn't, and how was he supposed to know that a simple thing like barbecuing would tip a beautiful child over the edge? How could he fill that longing and emptiness inside a child who'd lost so much?

Then Thea reached back for his hand. The touch of her fingers was cool and small but strong. So strong. He looked down, and she kept her voice soft. Really soft. "You beat yourself up over so many things, Ethan, and you shouldn't." Facing him, she held his gaze with a calm, quiet expression. "Sometimes we just have to be patient and let time work its healing powers. Physical healing is the easy side of all this," she whispered as they began to file into the church. "Like your surgery. But the mental and emotional things take longer. Stay strong and funny and kind. The rest will come."

She let go of his hand and moved into a pew near the back, with Jazz.

He followed, and when the kids came looking for them, Keegan looked disappointed. "I really wanted to be up there," he explained in a not-very-soft voice. "So I can see everything. It's not fun to be way back here and just see grown-ups' heads and stuff."

He'd never thought of that, either. That the view for kids would be better up front, because he was more worried about keeping them quiet and entertained in the back. "Let's move."

"Really?" Keegan's smile was reward enough. "Come on, Mara! Maybe we can sit by Shannie!"

He turned toward Thea.

"We're going to stay here," she whispered. "There's not room for all of us up there."

"Eva?" With the crowded conditions of Palm Sunday, Eva had slipped into the pew behind them. She realized what he was doing and shook her head. "I'm fine here."

She didn't look fine, but there wasn't much he could do about that now.

He took the kids forward and squeezed into Maggie and Jeb's pew on the left side, with a full view of the altar.

A crown of thorns lay propped against a pile of nondescript stones. A purple cloak lay alongside, as if carelessly thrown there.

"That's what they put on his head." Mara pointed to the thorny crown. "They made him wear it and they made fun of him just because he wanted people to be good." She reached out and clutched Ethan's hand. She swallowed hard. "I don't know why people would be mean like that."

He didn't know, either.

"Folks like their power," whispered Jeb. "And when they have it—the power, that is—they don't rightly like to lose it. Having too much power or too much money can mess up a person's soul, that's for certain. Or too much pride," he added, thoughtful. "Thinking too much of ourselves makes it easy to get brought down."

Sage words from a smart old man. Ethan turned, wishing he hadn't hurt his sister's feelings. Wishing she'd join them up front.

She wasn't there.

He bit back a sigh because there it was, in a nutshell. Her moods. Her reluctance to be something. Anything. Her recalcitrance drove him crazy.

Should he look for her? Go after her?

The dancing notes of a flute kept him where he was. The service was beginning. Eva was a grown woman. She could take care of herself. And the children needed him.

He stayed there in the pew with them for the whole lovely service, but when they got back to the apartment nearly two hours later, Eva was gone. There was nothing but a terse note saying she was moving on.

And that left Ethan to question his judgment all over again.

CHAPTER
TWENTY-TWO

Max guided the saw through the silvered barn-board plank.

The wood had been strong once. Fresh and new. It had been hammered into place with care, and then 113 years of use had taken its toll. In the end, when the current owner had decided against putting a new roof on the old barn, the structure had begun to fall.

A little TLC and the barn could have stood another hundred years. All it needed, really, was a roof. But without those repairs, water and bugs had begun their crazy dance of decomposition. When he stood the plank up against the wall, though, he saw that this ten-foot section had been spared, ready to be used again.

Hale Jackson's patrol car pulled up next to Max's white pickup truck. Hale climbed out and headed his way. He didn't look happy.

"What's going on? Are you okay? Is your mom all right?" He'd talked to Jill an hour before. She'd called to invite him for supper, grilled chicken to celebrate one of the first nice weekends they'd had in a long time.

Hale frowned. "Ethan's sister took off this morning."

"Eva?" When Hale nodded, Max worked his jaw. "She's got issues. With herself and with the police. I got that vibe right off when she found out I was a retired trooper. But why are we this concerned?"

"No money. No job. No car. No life, really, and Ethan said she was upset."

"Upset by what?"

"She had suggested staying with Ethan when he moves and taking care of the kids for him instead of getting a job, and apparently he freaked out a bit."

"Painful and fairly stupid reaction."

"I believe he knows that now." Hale's concern deepened. "She surprised him."

Max understood the downside of over-the-top reactions all too well. "No idea where she might have headed?"

Hale shook his head. "None."

"Did you check taxis? Uber? Lyft? Buses?"

"Got nothing. How could she have gotten out of town so quickly without using some kind of service?"

"Either she's still in town or she hitched a ride. She was pretty proud of doing that to get here cross-country. She didn't tell me that, of course. Ethan did."

Hale's face darkened. "Of all the stupid things to do. Doesn't she have a clue how dangerous it is out there? Especially on the interstates, where traffickers can disappear in no time. We're not talking a minor problem here." He pulled off his hat and raked a hand through his hair. "We're talking about a documented racketeering-style industry that uses the interstate system to cross state lines and has been growing at ridiculous rates the last five years. And New York City is a known hotbed of trafficker activity."

"She's young and mad at the world for whatever reason and figures she can take care of herself. That's a recipe for disaster right there."

"It will be when someone grabs her and sticks her into a slave ring," agreed Hale. "My hands are tied, Max. She's not a minor, she's not a runaway, she's not a person in danger. So how do you protect someone who just plain does something stupid?"

Max thumped him on the arm. "You come to your friend, give him the facts, and let him look. You've got to play within the rules. I don't. I'll go see Ethan. Did he give you a picture?"

"Two, yes. Current ones. I texted them to you."

Max checked his phone and nodded when the pics came up. "Perfect. Less time wasted this way. I'm on it."

"I appreciate it. I'd like to see Ethan catch a break. Wouldn't you?" Hale asked as he moved toward the cruiser.

Max splayed his hands. "He already has. Multiple times. Thea helped save his life when his heart seized up. He's got two beautiful kids to raise, the opportunity of a lifetime. He's got a fistful of degrees, a great profession, a roof over his head, and plenty of food. I'd say he's had amazing breaks. Way more than some, right?"

"By that perspective, sure. But . . ."

Max turned off the workroom lights and closed the door. "It's not perfect, Hale. You know that. You've lived it." Hale had a brilliant NFL career yanked out from under him by a tragic knee injury nearly five years back. "But if you've got that rock-solid faith to shore you up, it doesn't have to be perfect or even close. Because you're not walking alone. Maybe that's a lesson the doc needs to learn." He wiped his hands on a towel and headed for his log-cabin home tucked into the edge of a large, wooded lot. "I'll go see Ethan. Call in some favors. We'll see what we can find out."

"Thanks, Max. I owe you."

"You don't. And never will. This is what friends do, Hale."

He hurried inside, grabbed his keys and a box of cookies because he hadn't bothered taking time to eat after Mass that morning, then headed into town. There were only so many ways to get out of Wishing Bridge, but proximity to I-90 made it easy once you got there. But a pretty young girl, traveling light, looking for a free ride, might find a whole lot more than what she was looking for, and the interstate systems offered a quick way to make people disappear.

They needed to find her before someone else did. Someone nefarious, with evil on their mind. Movies often portrayed traffickers and criminals as scumbags. Dirty hair, scruffy clothes, awful hands.

He'd been a cop long enough to know that a lot of criminals looked fairly innocuous in public. That made approaching or coercing their victims relatively simple. Until they had you and circumstances switched in a heartbeat.

Max sent a text to local members of Troop T, the thruway trooper patrol, with pictures attached. They'd send it east and west, putting everyone on alert. But with a bright spring morning and plenty of traffic buzzing at seventy miles an hour, it would still be like finding a needle in a haystack.

~

Thea took the kids to Maggie's house. The last thing the three youngsters needed was more angst heaped on their little shoulders.

Maggie had set up a back-porch table with juice and cookies. The three kids dashed outside, bright, normal, and full of life. Exactly how childhood should be.

"What's going on?" Maggie asked once the kids were running around out back. "I smelled trouble the minute you walked in the room."

"Ethan's sister ran off. He hurt her feelings and she left with absolutely nothing. No money, no clothes to speak of, and no help."

Concern creased Maggie's brow. "It's next to impossible to protect hardheaded young adults," she said softly. Was she remembering the beautiful daughter she'd lost to anorexia the year before? "So many take the hard road, rarely listening to advice. Lord have mercy, we've had our share of that in this family and this town, but we will pray this one to safety, Theadora. You and me."

She grabbed for Thea's hand as Kelsey came into the room. Without asking, Maggie took her hand, too, to finish their circle. "Lord, this one's on you."

Maggie didn't pray quietly. She was a full-force prayer person. She laid her concerns out in full voice and a matter-of-fact manner, knowing God would listen even if she wasn't sure how he would respond. Maggie's faith and bossy nature made Thea love her even more.

"You dealt with all kinds of folks over time. This one's no different and is tough as nails, but she's young, Lord. And headstrong. And hurt. You can just see it in her face, in her eyes, but way too stubborn to sit down and talk about it, so we need you, Lord. Bring her back to us, give us the chance to talk common sense and make her part of the family. Your family and ours. A body forgets how awful it is to miss a bunch of meals until it's staring them in the face, and this child's left with nothing. That puts her at danger's door right there. Let no harm come to her, sweet Jesus. Protect her for us, wherever she is. Amen."

"Hale went to Max for help," Thea told them. "Eva's an adult, so there's not much the police can do."

"Max has contacts," noted Maggie. "And he knows things, things that go beyond fixing houses and setting up storefronts. We're blessed to have him here. How are you doing?" Maggie turned her attention to Thea. She peered closer, then folded her into a hug. "Sweet girl, I wish I could make the paths clear and mend the broken road you've had to follow for so long, but I can't. And I won't say how it makes you stronger, because you already know that. But I will say that broken roads get tiresome after a while, and maybe there's a reason for that."

"To stop walking?" asked Thea when Maggie released her.

"Well, we can't do that," said Maggie, as if the idea of stopping was out of the question.

"Then how about this." Thea sat down. So did Maggie and Kelsey. "I'm going to make Becky an offer on the practice so I can stay in Wishing Bridge."

"Thea! For real?" Kelsey grabbed her hands. "I can't begin to tell you how much I'd love to have you here, but are you sure? That practice in Philadelphia sounded ideal for you, exactly what you've been looking for. That's a lot to give up."

How amazing was it to have such true friends, especially after all this time? Kelsey's love for her shined just as brightly as it had a dozen years before, at Hannah's Hope in Philadelphia.

"I thought so, too," Thea said. "Until I discovered I wasn't giving up anything, really. I was gaining something. A new viewpoint. A new focus. When I walked into Dotty Willoughby's place and faced the dark side of the moon, I realized it's not the location. That's just geography. It's the heart," she told them both. "And my heart is here. In this town. With you guys and Shannie and the people I've gotten to know."

"You're sure, Thea?" Maggie covered Thea's hand with hers. "A smart girl like you shouldn't toss her dream aside without a good deal of thought. Although I'm hoping you'll shush me and declare that you've thought this through and made a final decision. Just so you know where I'm leaning."

Thea laughed softly. "I'm sure. Wishing Bridge wouldn't have made the short list six months ago, but I think God put me here for a reason. To help Ethan, to help those children." The three kids' laughter punctuated her sentence just then. "And to help you and the town. So yes, I'm staying, one way or the other. If Becky and I can't come to terms, I'll hang my own shingle. Nothing wrong with starting small and starting over."

"Who'd have thought this could happen?" asked Kelsey. She grabbed a clutch of tissues and blew her nose. "But what about Ethan, Thea?"

What about Ethan?

Thea's heart pinched, but she put a smile in place. "He'll go on to Chicago and do his research. It means a lot to him. Seeing his brother suffer, watching him die of a horrid disease left its mark. And if trying to find answers in tiny chromosomal links helps Ethan heal, then that's what he should do."

Maggie didn't cut him that kind of slack. "We've got perfectly good research facilities not all that far away," she retorted. "Buffalo and Rochester, forty-five minutes either way, and then those children get to set their feet down in a normal town. Good as gold. And we don't need every smart person going off to other states, now do we? Jeb's been saying right along that it's time for educated folks to start settling here. He's not referring to that group living their fancy lives over the hill, tucked away so folks can't see them or talk with them."

Thea frowned. So did Kelsey. "I don't know what you're talking about, Maggie."

"Harrowsmith Woods," Maggie told them.

Thea pulled out her phone and did a search while Maggie talked.

"It's posh, private, and the folks there don't come into town if they can help it."

"I don't think I've ever stumbled across that neighborhood," said Kelsey. "But then my days are here, school, then here again with the baby. And the weather hasn't been conducive to exploring."

"There's no exploring there," said Maggie. "It used to be the Smith farm, way back. Passed down for a couple of generations, but then the last Alfred Smith got big into real estate. Not just here but all over. Made a fortune, maybe a few fortunes to hear tell, though I expect the current family has spent a good share of it. They're a troubled bunch."

"A trouble-causing bunch," said Jeb as he came into the room. "I'm fixin' a cup of coffee. Can I fix one for anyone else?"

Coffee with Jeb and Maggie sounded ideal. "I'd love some," said Thea.

"Me, too," added Kelsey. "So there's a posh section of Wishing Bridge? Where is it, exactly?"

"Not in Wishing Bridge," Maggie told her. "North of it, about fifteen minutes shy of the thruway. Close enough to get onto a highway really quick but far enough to be absolutely peaceful. And they're just above the school line, so their kids don't come to the village for elementary school, either. I expect most of them are in private schools, anyway. There's a couple in Batavia and more in Rochester, of course."

"Harrowsmith sounds delightfully British, doesn't it?" Thea smiled up at Jeb as he set her coffee down. "Thank you, Jeb."

"Well, it's not British, but it is snooty," Jeb told her. He fixed coffee for himself and took a seat. "They don't use locals for jobs because they think local workers will scope them out to find out who to rob when no one's home."

"Now Jeb, that might be gossip."

"It most likely is, but being gossip doesn't make it false," he reminded her. "Betty at the bakery overheard one of the women from Harrowsmith saying so last year, and Betty's not one to tell tales or stretch the truth."

"Maybe it's just one person, then," said Thea. "I can't even imagine a neighborhood full of people who snub this town. The history alone is worth loving, and if you throw in the present-day people and how wonderful they are, that's a total bonus."

"I'm not one to speak ill of others," said Maggie, and Thea knew the truth in her words, "but I don't think they see Wishing Bridge that way. They keep to themselves, and when they pull out of their gated neighborhood, there are few who head south toward the village. They turn north toward the interstate or the expressway, going off to their important jobs. Up here we keep doing what we've always been doing. Working. Minding kids. Supporting the church and each other. Although I must say, a bunch of us, me included, had high hopes when old Alfred sold that land for development. We thought it would mean more customers, more business. When all was said and done it didn't mean anything of the kind. I think that's when we all began to realize how quickly we were sliding downhill."

"But not anymore," said Jeb. "Not with Max fixing things here and there. New businesses opening up and folks with a little money put by are setting down roots. I think people are starting to see a reason to stay. We didn't nosedive overnight, and we won't recover too quick, either, but we'll get there. Just walking by that new general store and all the fun things Jill Jackson has to sell makes my day. And hearing Shannie laugh and run and play?" He sighed. "Music to an old man's ears. Mother, we've got that meeting with the reverend, remember? About Dotty?"

"I do now," she declared. "Good thing you mentioned it, because I was enjoying the chance to talk with the girls. And you gals are all right with the kids?" she asked as she reached for her favorite sweater. Its faded blue matched the pale blue of her eyes.

"Kids and coffee and praying Eva gets over her snit and comes back to us," Thea told her. "Because honestly, with the logistics of the thruway and interstate travel, God only knows how far she's gotten in a few hours' time."

"Then we'll leave it to the good Lord and Max's friends." Maggie looked way more confident than Thea felt. Max was a great guy, but he was one man. What could one man do in a case like this?

When Maggie and Jeb had left to meet with the minister, Kelsey grabbed Thea's hands. "I can't believe you're staying, but I want to believe it. So tell me again."

Thea smiled, then sighed. "I'm staying. I'm supposed to stay, it's like I've gotten that message loud and clear for the past several weeks. Now I just need to set my plan into action."

"Then let's go back to my earlier question." She meant the question about Ethan. There was no hiding her emotions from Kelsey, so Thea grimaced. "Trust me to have the bad sense to fall for a guy who doesn't share my faith, dreams, or goals. Oops. My bad."

Kelsey disagreed instantly, all the more reason to love her. "I've seen how he looks at you."

Oh, how she wished she could put stock in that simple observation, but a warm look didn't build dreams. It took way more than that to lay a forever-after foundation, and if she couldn't have that kind of a basis, she didn't want one at all. "I've grown on him, because we wouldn't have been having this conversation in December. He was desperate for help and I was available. I think the poor man spent the first two months we worked together trying to avoid me and therefore avoid confrontation. He succeeded quite nicely. For a while," she added, smiling.

"Well, he sure hasn't seemed to mind being in your way lately," noted Kelsey. "The phrase 'flagrant appreciation' fits perfectly, and I only see him once a week or so. And you did save his life."

She had. And the big jerk was still planning on leaving. Wasn't that wrong on multiple levels? "Here's the thing. Twenty-nine and a half is too old for a short-term romance, and until a month or so ago, the last thing on my mind was romance," Thea told Kelsey while the kids raced around the backyard. "It was work, work, and more work and then, all of a sudden, I'm mooning around like an eighth grader, swooning over the cool guy in class." When Kelsey looked skeptical, Thea changed things up. "Okay, the nerdy guy in class, but still super cute."

"Definitely more accurate. I'm sorry, Thea." Kelsey reached out and gave her a hug, a hug that felt really good. "I didn't come to Wishing Bridge thinking about God or faith or romance. I stumbled into this town and the rest just kind of happened."

"Because people are so nice? Or because it was God's timing?"

Kelsey shook her head. "I have no idea, except that a near-death experience makes you think about things like that. God's timing and how things manage to work out in the end. Maybe it doesn't really matter how it happens, but *that* it happens and we let it grow inside us."

"Like faith."

"Yeah. Like that," Kelsey admitted. "I used to think Mrs. Effel was simple because who could believe all that stuff and swallow it like it's the real deal? If there is a God, how could he let stuff happen like it did? Why would he let me and you get such awful mothers when the mothers on television were so nice and kind and perfect? I think I was more mad for what happened to you because of a lousy mother than I was for me."

"Luckily it wasn't a contest," Thea said, but Kelsey's honesty touched her. "I wondered that, too, when I was being held by those horrible people. Could God allow this stuff and exist? Or was it just because some humans were totally void of conscience? But when Sonny Geraci sacrificed his life to set me free, something changed inside me. No one had ever risked something for me before. Not my mother. Not anyone in my family. But this stranger did it because it was the right thing, knowing they might kill him. And he did it anyway, and he told me it was because God sacrificed for him and he was sorry things had gone so far."

"Thea." Kelsey took her hands. "You never talk about this."

"I never talk about a lot of things," Thea told her frankly. "Now I realize I should. That if we were more open about evil in the world, maybe we'd stand a better chance of fighting it. Knowing that Eva's out there all by herself, looking beautiful and vulnerable, brought it all back up, but not in a horrid way like it used to. In a way that tells me it's time to fight. Time to stand up and warn people about what danger lurks minutes or miles away."

"Then I'm even more glad you're staying," Kelsey told her softly. "Because if we fight those old dragons and demons together, we stand tall together. You. Me. And Jazz."

Keegan dashed through the door and up the kitchen stairs just then. "Gotta go!" he announced, then raced for the first-floor bathroom.

Thea stared after him. "I'm going to miss them, Kelse. All three of them." She met Kelsey's expression of understanding and stood as the baby began peeping over the monitor. "The Kleins are opening the ice-cream shop this afternoon. Let's take these kids on a walk and get them a treat once Hayley's fed. Unless you want to stay here and relax and I'll take the kids over."

"And miss ice cream?" Kelsey pretended horror. "Not on your life. Give me twenty minutes to feed and change Hayley. It will be her first walk to the ice-cream store." The thought made her smile. "A few months ago I'd toughened myself to the idea that she'd have her first everything with someone else. But here we are, the Soul Sisterhood, making our way in a tiny town. We wouldn't have imagined it or wished for it six months back, yet we're here. And I've never been so happy."

"Well, the handsome deputy-slash-former-NFL-player is a bonus," Thea mused, and Kelsey laughed.

"He is. But no more than having my two friends here with me. And I mean that with every fiber of my being, Thea."

Kelsey went to the living room to feed the baby.

Thea followed Keegan outside and spent the next twenty minutes running around with the kids. The upper yard had finally dried after the long month of cold rain. The new smell of green grass and fresh dirt filled the air. It was a spring scent on a gentler day than they'd seen in a long while. A day that would be more perfect if someway, somehow, they found Eva and brought her back.

But for the life of her, Thea couldn't imagine how that might happen.

CHAPTER
TWENTY-THREE

Ethan hated to tell his father about Eva's disappearance, but he had no choice in the matter. The call went to voicemail. He left a message to call back ASAP, then hung up.

Nervousness pulsed through him. Where was she? Was she safe? What did she think she was doing, going off on her own with no job, no plan, and no funds? Their mother had left her a small legacy when she died, but that was several years back. Would she still have fallback cash?

He hoped so.

The phone rang half an hour later. He jumped to answer it, then saw his father's number. "Dad. Hey. Thanks for returning my call so quickly."

"You sounded worried. Is it one of the kids? Are they sick? You might want to give Peter's mother a call and see if they're still interested in taking them. Tying yourself down to someone else's children might not be the smartest move you've ever made, Ethan, especially with your career on hold. Although I'm sure your sister meant well."

Ethan bit back a sharp retort. Maybe his father didn't have it in him to love more than one child, or maybe watching Jarod suffer and die had just drained the man, but he didn't need him harping about handing off two little kids who'd already been given a bad deal. "The kids are fine. They're playing at a friend's house right now. That's not why I called."

"Then why?"

He didn't ask about Ethan's health or recovery. That was typical, so why did it still bother Ethan after all these years? It shouldn't. "Eva left today."

Silence answered his statement.

"She got upset this morning and just took off with no money, no car, and very few clothes because she lost her suitcase on her trip east."

More silence greeted him, then his dad cleared his throat. "This isn't exactly unusual behavior for her, but you know that."

"I know she's a little scattered, but this could be serious, Dad. A young woman alone, with no money and no credit. Where will she stay? What will she do? Do you think she'll head back to your place?"

His father made a noise of disbelief. "Not likely. She's got no reason to come back here now that she's of age, Ethan."

What an odd statement. A lot of young people these days returned to their parents' place to regroup when their pie-in-the-sky ideas failed to produce a living wage. "Except she might want a fresh start. Maybe go back to school the way she talked about a couple of years ago."

"Well, that won't be happening here," his father replied. "I did my part. I went above and beyond already. Whatever happens now is on her."

"On her?" Ethan whistled lightly between his teeth so he wouldn't explode and say too much. What good would it do? "I know she's twenty-two, but we might want to cut her some slack, don't you think?"

His father's voice hardened. "You were getting ready for medical school in New York at twenty-two. Your sister was applying for a master's program at UCLA at that age. You two had your heads on straight despite all we went through with your brother, so if that spoiled-brat hippie kid thinks she can whine her way through life, that's her choice. Not mine."

Spoiled-brat hippie kid.

Ethan's heart had been feeling pretty darned good lately, but right now it clenched tight in his chest. "Dad—"

He started to argue the point, but his father's next words cut deep.

"She's not my kid, Ethan. I didn't make a big deal of it because your mother took off to New Mexico when we divorced, and I figured staying quiet was the best thing. You guys didn't have to mess with your mother or her kid very often, and you and Alexis were both on your way to being responsible. Believe me, there is nothing responsible about Eva, and when she showed up here as if I was her father, I set her straight in a big hurry. I let her live here, and I took the money from your mother's life insurance to pay for her room and board. Life here doesn't come cheap, as you well know."

Ethan was real glad the surgeons had done a nice job cleaning out his heart, because he was pretty sure it had just stopped cold. "You told her she wasn't your child?"

"Of course I did. I didn't want her thinking I'd be footing the bill for another college education, especially for a ditzy girl who barely made it through high school."

Eva wasn't his full sister.

His mother had taken her to New Mexico to raise her on her own because that way people wouldn't know. "You never told us."

"Wasn't anything to tell," his father replied. "By the time your brother passed away, your mother and I didn't have much to say to one another. Year after year of sadness and worry and emotional drain ruined whatever we might have had. I loved your brother but I despised what that disease did to our lives. To my life. There was no respite. I couldn't get away from it, no matter what I tried. There it was, a rotten, evil monster disease that ruined his life and did a number on everyone else's at the same time. It sapped the energy from all of us, day after day. I hated it. All of it. Not him, don't get me wrong, I would have done anything to make him normal, to let him be strong and vital and smart like you, but that was out of my hands. And I loathed every single minute of my existence with it."

There wasn't time to let his head spin the way he'd like to, because all Ethan could think of was Eva's face. The surprise, the sorrow, the anxiety, the utter sadness of her face when he told her she couldn't stay with him.

"Don't waste too much time worrying," his father went on. "She's your mother's daughter. She always manages to land on her feet. I'm sure she will again."

Ethan hung up the phone.

He couldn't bring himself to acknowledge his father's cool brush-off.

Eva wasn't his father's child.

So much began to make sense. Things that seemed wrong and weird for so long were now crystal clear.

Eva had spent over three years living with his dad. Being charged room and board. Three years of a precious teenage life, unloved, uncherished, uncared for.

He wanted to punch something. Anything.

How could his father be that callous? That cruel? And yet, hadn't he kind of known that all along?

He needed to talk to someone.

Or hit someone.

Maybe break something.

The doorbell sounded, and when he hit the intercom, Max's voice came through. "It's me, Doc. Can I come up?"

Ethan buzzed him in, and when Max entered, the first thing the middle-aged man did was take a step back, hands out, fingers splayed. "I don't know who you're mad at but please say it isn't me."

"It's not," said Ethan. "But the inclination to do bodily harm to someone is at the top of my list right now." He sank onto the edge of a seat cushion and indicated the phone. "My father. Who, incidentally, isn't Eva's father. And he made sure she knew it." He clenched his hands together. "We've got to find Eva, Max. Someway. Somehow." He gripped the back of his neck with his hand and squeezed. "I need to see her. Talk to her. And ask her to give me a second chance, because it seems like my family hasn't given her a chance at all. And here I was, on the other side of the country, living my own life, clueless. But I don't have the luxury to be clueless anymore, and with God as my witness, I'm going to save my little sister. And maybe wring her neck for scaring me like this. Then we're going to raise those two kids in something that at least resembles a normal house. Something neither Eva nor I could ever say we had. So how are we going to do this, Max? Because I need all the help I can get right now, and I'm not afraid to beg."

Max showed him the text he'd sent to Troop T and any friends he had along the expanse of the New York State Thruway. "If she got picked up going west, they'll be in Pennsylvania or Ohio by now, so my friends will send the message along," Max told him. "Going east, it's real easy to disappear when they get near the city, but that's a five-hour drive. If they duck down I-81, I don't have as many contacts there, and it's Pennsylvania and New Jersey for a lot of the way. If they take Route 17, it's part interstate and less traffic, so easier to spot, but that makes it a less likely choice. And fewer police on the road."

"It could be a nice person offering her a ride. Couldn't it?"

"The likelihood isn't in her favor," said Max. "Most folks are afraid to pick up hitchhikers, even sweet young blondes. It could happen. And make sure if she calls that you answer right away. Depending on circumstances she might not have much time on the phone."

Max was talking straight, like he always did, which only deepened Ethan's fear. "I'll keep it with me. Should I go looking for her? I feel stupid and helpless sitting here doing nothing."

"Then pray." Max moved toward the door. "Because that's what I'm doing. It's what Thea's doing while she watches the kids. And I'll bet Maggie has half the town sending up prayers for her return right now. You might not be a believer, but I've seen way too much in my years to ignore it. I only wish I'd figured it out when I was your age, Doc. And not ten years later." Max's phone rang. He hurried through the door and down the stairs.

The sound of the door clicking shut spurred Ethan into action. He tucked his phone into his pocket, grabbed his keys, and left the apartment. He filled the car with gas and grabbed some snacks to have on hand. And juice boxes. And fancy bottled coffee drinks that Eva loved and couldn't afford. If he had to make a mad dash across the state or multiple states to rescue his sister, he didn't want to waste one minute of time getting there.

He withdrew cash from the ATM, finished his errands, and spotted Thea and Kelsey walking down Franklin Street toward the ice-cream shop. The older kids skipped ahead, vibrant and free, laughing.

Kelsey was pushing the stroller. Thea walked alongside, talking, her hands dancing in the April sun's warm light.

Her light-brown hair glistened. She walked with an ease of authority that he'd envied when she first arrived. Not bossy, like he'd thought. Well, maybe a little, he mentally acknowledged.

She walked through life secure.

Which was crazy because she'd endured more in her life than anyone should ever have to face. After a traumatic start she'd grabbed hold of every lifeline offered once she met Jazz and Kelsey. She'd moved on to become a successful medical professional, and she'd just turned her plans inside out to stay here, in the small, embracing town.

Maybe her dreams aren't as big as yours.

He pushed the negative thought aside as he parked the car. Maybe it wasn't the size of the dream that mattered. Maybe it was the ability to adapt as needed. Wasn't it an inability to adapt that had felled the dinosaurs?

"Uncle Eefen!" Keegan raced his way but pulled up before tackling him, which made Ethan realize how much he loved being tackled when he was healthy. "I'm so 'cited to see you!" Keegan grabbed one of his hands and swung it. "We're going to get ice cream, okay? And you can come, too, because Miss Thea said it was too nice a day to *not* get ice cream so we're getting some, and she said I probally need a dish. Because I'm kind of messy sometimes."

"That's quite a speech, kid."

Keegan beamed. "I know. I'm a really good talker. And maybe you want a big ice cream," he added as they approached the others. "Because you're big."

Thea raised a brow to him. He shook his head slightly, letting her know there was no word, and withdrew his wallet. "Ice cream's my treat, ladies."

"That translates to a banana split for me," teased Thea, but she couldn't hide the concern in her eyes. "Thank you, Ethan."

"My pleasure." The ice-cream store had put out white-and-blue picnic tables in the small yard and along the sidewalk. "This is a real cute setup."

A middle-aged woman slid open the walk-up window. "It's nice, right? And nothing says spring in the north better than daffodils, new leaves, and ice-cream-shop openings. What can I get you guys?"

They placed their orders, and when Thea ordered a simple cone, he turned. "I thought you wanted a banana split. Don't downgrade because the boss is paying."

She smiled up at him, and when she did, the stress in his chest lightened. "I'll get that when we can celebrate Eva's return," she said softly. "Okay?"

"I'll look forward to it," he told her.

"Do you have the Super Hero ice cream?" asked Mara. "My uncle told me about it, and it sounded really special."

"Next weekend. That supplier doesn't deliver to me until Wednesday," she explained. "But I couldn't see missing a week with ice cream because a few flavors aren't here yet, you know?"

Ethan expected an instant meltdown. Mara surprised him. "Because something is better than nothing," Mara agreed. "Then can I have a vanilla-and-chocolate twisty one?"

"I'd like that, too," said Shannie. "I saw one on TV once and it looked so good."

"On TV?" Mara started to act surprised, then caught herself, and instead of making Shannie feel awful about her lack of experience, she seemed to accept it graciously. "I bet it looked good. And now we get to have one for real."

"I know!" Shannie reached out and gripped Mara's hand and, for once, Mara didn't pull away. "It will be so much fun!"

Ethan's phone signaled an incoming text from Hale. He pulled it out, then frowned. "No news."

A young couple strolled up to the newly opened ice-cream stand. Then a family walked their way from the next street over. Before Ethan and Thea and the kids had eaten their ice creams, more than two dozen people had taken the time to walk or drive to the little shop.

It was a small thing by city standards, one little shop making a difference. But in Wishing Bridge, it showed people looking after their own. Doing business in town. Sharing the wealth, even when there wasn't much to share.

He thought of his father, bilking Eva's money because she wasn't his biological child. His father wasn't hurting for money, he had a high-paying job, and he lived in a high-priced area by choice, not random selection . . .

He could have easily afforded to take care of Eva and keep the lack of relationship quiet, but he hadn't because he wasn't a kind person.

Ethan wanted to be a kind person, and when he considered that, he realized that's not exactly how he'd been behaving.

He needed to do better. Much better. He'd messed up by putting his dreams and goals above everything else. He'd seen his goals as paying something back, a way to help others, but watching Mara and Keegan eating small-town ice creams, he saw another way to give back.

These children.

Your children now.

He gripped his cone a little tighter. These were his children, and he needed to move forward with them. With their adoption, with their lives. With his life.

His phone indicated another text. This one was from Max. Sighting confirmed just west of Indian Castle service area. Wanna drive? Or I'll drive.

Ethan texted back quickly. Me. Let's do it. I'm at Village Ice Cream.

Be there in five, Max responded.

He motioned Thea over. "Max said she's been sighted, but it's about three hours east. Can you—"

"We've got this," she assured him, and he knew she did. "Go . . . and God bless."

"I'll call you."

She hugged him. And when she stepped back, Max was pulling into the small municipal parking lot. "Hit the road. And I'm going to be real happy to get that banana split, Ethan."

"I'll be happy to buy it." He hurried to his car and climbed in the driver's side. Max climbed in on the passenger side, and Ethan waved to the kids as they drove off.

There wasn't time for one of Keegan's adorable and long goodbyes, but hopefully they'd have plenty of time for that later. With Eva right in the middle.

CHAPTER
TWENTY-FOUR

Eva stared out the window of the upscale car heading east on I-90.

She'd find something to do in New York. Everyone found a job in the city, one way or another. Or Jersey, even. They had an aunt who used to live in New Jersey, and she loved it. With all the small cities and towns surrounding the boroughs, she'd find something once she got there.

"So, Tracey. Do you have family in New York?"

She faced the driver in the rearview mirror and lied, because a woman alone should never appear to be alone. She'd given them a false name and now she'd spin a phony story to match. "Several family members live there," she told him. She wasn't about to tell a total stranger that she had nowhere to go and no one to meet. Ethan thought her foolish.

Maybe she was in some ways, but one of these days she'd find a place to fit, a spot where she wasn't the round peg vying for a square hole.

"Parents there?"

She shook her head. "No. Siblings. And an aunt and uncle. A few cousins. They're in Jersey," she went on, hoping she sounded convincing.

"And they know you're coming?" asked Theresa, the woman at his side.

Eva held up her cell phone. They had no way of knowing the battery had died because she'd forgotten to charge it the night before. "They know I'm on the way, thanks to you and that older couple that got me to the Syracuse rest stop. This is actually a really nice road, isn't it? I haven't driven across this part of I-90 before. It's crazy busy but not quite as insane as I-5 along the West Coast. At least the traffic here moves."

"Our tax dollars and tolls at work," Theresa replied. She sounded dry. And bored. As if having a nice-looking husband and a high-class car was far too ordinary.

Eva could tell them what ordinary looked like. She'd had a mother who liked to whack out on drugs, before she died. Then there was the father who wasn't *really* her father, the man who'd helped himself to substantial room and board from what was supposed to be her college fund. Oh, yeah. She could explain ordinary in blunt terms. "Can we stop at the next rest area for me to use the ladies' room?" she asked. "Shouldn't have had that second soda at the last one."

The man—he'd introduced himself as Jason—glanced to his right. The woman replied. "The next one. We want to fill the tank and it's better if it's almost empty. You can hold out that long, can't you?"

A note of fear thrummed along Eva's spine. Tiny hairs at the base of her neck rose in protest. She was being ridiculous, of course. These people were about as normal as it got. Upper-middle-class America. People of means.

Why are people of means picking up a complete stranger and refusing to stop when asked?

Her pulse stepped up. She cringed slightly. "I don't think I can, actually. I'm so sorry. And I don't want to hold you guys up," she went on. "I can just get out, take care of things, and catch another ride. Don't think a thing about it."

Jason didn't change lanes even though there were only two miles to go before the Indian Castle service area. He stayed far left and picked up speed.

Her heart beat harder. Faster.

They weren't going to stop. And when she looked at the fuel icon, it noted hundreds of miles in capability.

A full tank.

They didn't need to go one more stop. They didn't need to stop at all. She was in the car, in the back seat, cruising an interstate at over seventy miles per hour, with no way out and no charge on her cell phone.

She thought of Ethan.

Would he even bother looking for her, or did he get home to that empty apartment and think "Good riddance"?

The kids.

Would she ever see them again? Would they remember her?

Stop. Think. Act. Act like this is all normal . . . fool them into believing you.

She couldn't. She didn't know how. Fear gripped her from the tips of her toes to the very hairs on her head, because Ethan was right and she had refused to listen. Why didn't she listen to him? He was smart. He was a doctor. He wasn't stupid, like her—

"Why are we slowing down?" The harshness of Theresa's tone snapped Eva to attention.

"I don't know." Jason scowled at the dashboard readouts. "The car's acting weird."

"You just had It checked," she fussed. "Don't let it die here in the center of the interstate. Pull it over!"

"Shut up. I've got this." He aimed a hard, cold look at Theresa, then eased the car over onto the shoulder as traffic whizzed by at an alarming pace and in close proximity.

The engine died.

He tried to start it.

No luck.

He glared at the dashboard, then his wife . . . or whoever she was. "It won't start."

"Duh."

"We've got company," he said then, in a low, deep voice. "A helpful trooper coming up behind in an unmarked car."

"I'm ready." Theresa's hands rested in her lap, but one hand was in the pink leather purse she'd been carrying.

The trooper approached the driver's side. Should she warn him? Was this woman hiding a gun in her purse? Could the trooper get Eva out of this situation? Of course he could, if they didn't draw a gun on him first.

"There's another one stopping. Pulling up behind the first one." Theresa kept her voice low. "A marked car this time."

Jason swore lightly, then hit the button to roll down his window as he painted a very convincing smile on his face.

"Car trouble?" asked the trooper. He leaned down to scan the occupants.

This was her chance. Her moment. She could jump out of the car and explain everything to the trooper. She was about to do just that when he gave her a hard look of surprise. "Eva Brandenburg?"

Her heart literally stopped in her chest when he said her name, because how could he possibly know her?

Jason glared at her in the rearview mirror. "You said your name was Tracey."

The trooper opened the back door in a quick move as the second trooper approached. A third one, lights flashing, was coming their way at a quick clip. "It's Eva Brandenburg and she's wanted for questioning a couple hundred miles back," the trooper explained. "Out of the car, miss." He took her arm as if about to arrest her while the other uniformed officer came up alongside. "Dave, can you escort this young woman back to your car?"

"Happy to, Ed." He reached for her arm, and none too gently, either. "This way, and step quick before we all get run over."

She didn't dawdle, because whatever they wanted to question her about couldn't be worse than being trapped with those two people with no possible escape.

The trooper tucked her into the back of the marked cruiser while the third car pulled to a stop behind them, sandwiching her in the middle car.

She watched through the windshield as the two other troopers spoke to Jason and Theresa. The first trooper's face showed concern and not a hint of suspicion. When he backed away, the shiny gray Lexus started up like nothing was wrong and drove away.

The first trooper came back to the unmarked cruiser. He got in, and when they had a narrow chance to move into traffic, he put on his lights and crossed all three lanes, with her trooper close behind. They pulled into the Indian Castle rest stop about two minutes later. The first lawman pulled up to the front, parked the car with the engine running, and got out, while her trooper did the same thing. Then the first trooper walked back to their car, opened her door, and motioned her inside. "Let's go."

She hesitated. He inclined his head with a stern look. She climbed out and preceded him into the stone-fronted service plaza.

"This way." The two troopers escorted her to a behind-the-scenes room and closed the door. It opened again quickly and the third trooper walked in.

"I didn't steal anything," she told them. She held out her purse. "This is everything I have, and it isn't much, but I haven't stolen anything since tenth grade."

The first trooper slid a picture onto the table, a picture of Jason Hammond, the Lexus driver. "See him?"

She nodded.

Then he slid another picture in front of her, a brutal picture of a deceased young woman.

Her hands went cold and she was pretty sure she was about to throw up.

The trooper indicated a narrow margin with his thumb and forefinger. "This is how close you came, Eva. Another two hours, or if you had fewer friends that care about you, you'd have been closeted in Brooklyn or the Bronx or Paterson and off the grid because these people don't play to lose. And once they hook you on drugs, it's just a matter of time before you're doing anything they ask of you to get your hits, which they happily provide. The FBI is compiling a case against them, but not too many folks risk talking about a pair like this, because they know what they're capable of."

"I don't do drugs. I don't do much of anything," she whispered, but the images before her told the story.

"They do it for you, honey . . . and it doesn't take long to be totally dependent, with no way out."

"How did you find me? How did you know my name?"

"A friend sent out your picture. Your brother's worried sick about you."

Ethan? Worried about her?

"And before you scoff, believe me when I say that this was a narrow miss and only by the good luck that one of our plainclothes guys saw you get into Hammond's car back in Syracuse. You matched the picture and he radioed ahead. We disabled the car via satellite so we'd have a chance to save you. If you're a praying woman, you should be thanking God right now because once they have you in a car, there's no way they're going to stop until they've got you sequestered and neutralized."

Neutralized.

Now she did need to throw up.

The trooper brought her a small wastebasket, and when she was finally done heaving, he'd taken the pictures off the table, but that didn't matter.

She'd see them forever. Jason's hard, chiseled face, and the warm smile that had seemed so sincere when they had approached her at the service plaza near the Central New York exits.

"Your brother's on his way. Please do the smart thing, young lady." The second trooper drew up the chair next to her. "Stay home. Figure things out. Get a job. Get two jobs if you need to, or go back to school and get your act together. Whatever you thought you were leaving behind is far better than what you were about to face."

She nodded.

Words escaped her, but when the second trooper got up to leave, she called out to him. "I won't mess up again. I promise."

He leveled her a straight look. "I believe you."

He believed her.

Would Ethan?

She didn't know, but when Ethan and Max came in nearly three hours later, she flew across the small room to him. And when Ethan wrapped his arms around her and whispered, "Thank God I found you, sis," her heart opened.

And then he held her as she sobbed against his chest, and Eva couldn't remember the last time someone had held her as she cried.

CHAPTER
TWENTY-FIVE

Ethan let Max drive home.

He sat in the back seat with Eva, one arm around his baby sister, holding her.

She couldn't stop crying, so he let her cry. He didn't shush her or promise everything would be all right. That wasn't his call. But he could make sure she had a place to stay and food on the table and love and encouragement, the things she'd missed out on by being part of a dysfunctional, angry family.

He'd been so busy wanting to save the Jarods of the world that he had forgotten about the Evas. The castoffs. The unloved and undervalued.

It was twilight by the time Max pulled up to the gracious old Queen Anne, but the second-floor lights shimmered through the clean, broad windows. "Hey, Eva." She'd dozed off about fifteen minutes before. "We're home."

She opened her eyes, startled and scared. Her gaze calmed as she looked around. "Thank God."

Ethan echoed the phrase inside.

He wasn't going to pretend he was sure about the whole God thing . . . although he and his buddies always used to come to the same conclusion a decade before, usually after throwing back half a dozen beers.

Something couldn't come from nothing. Matter didn't just happen. So there had to be some undefinable thing to get the ball rolling. Correct?

So was there a God? Was he a physical being, a spiritual being, an all-knowing being?

The thought was unbelievable for the educated mind, but then it rolled back to the basic property of physics: something never came from nothing.

So there had to be something, back then. At the beginning.

"Yup." He shrugged an arm around her and kissed her forehead as she climbed out of the car. "Thank God is right. And I'm thanking him for Max, too, because he sent out the alert."

"You did?" Surprised, she looked at Max as he withdrew the keys to his white pickup. "It was you?"

He nodded. "Not all cops are looking to get you into trouble. My experience says a lot of kids are really handy at making that happen themselves. I much prefer getting kids out of trouble."

"Thank you." She crossed the short distance and hugged Max. "Thank you so much. If I can ever help you—"

"You can," he told her, and when she gazed up at him in question, he pointed to Ethan. "Get your head on straight, get a job, work on that self-image. And I know just the guy to help you with all of that." He smiled Ethan's way. "See you tomorrow, Doc. I'll stop by for coffee after work."

"Make it supper. We'll have that cookout we talked about this morning."

"Calling for rain," said Max as he opened the truck door.

"I'll move the grill to the porch," Ethan told him. "See you then."

"I'll be here."

Max drove off.

Ethan didn't have to unlock the lower door. It buzzed from upstairs and he pulled it open, but when Eva started in, he grabbed her for one final hug before they met the others. "Whatever happens," he whispered against her hair, hair that smelled pretty rank right now, "I'm your brother. I'll always be your brother, and we can face anything together. Got it?"

"Yes." She swiped tears from her face with the backs of her hands and nodded. "I've got it."

He'd explain what he knew later. She'd been through enough for one day. So had he. And they'd have to figure things out because he'd had way too many curveballs lately, and for a guy who loved baseball, that was saying something.

But maybe there was a reason for the curveballs. Like Max said, sometimes the path stretches right in front of you, but you're too caught up making lefts and rights to see it.

He'd been too busy to read his little sister's pain. Too wrapped up in his own life.

He was tired. His body was sore but getting better, and he couldn't think straight to save his own life right now, but he'd examine his options more thoroughly tomorrow. Or the next day. Or the day after that. Right now, he'd gotten a second chance with his kid sister, a chance he was pretty sure he didn't deserve. But it was a chance he was determined to make right. At last.

CHAPTER
TWENTY-SIX

Jazz spotted the CEO of Rage Fashions, Inc., before he noticed her on Monday. Toren Hamblin, a man who had taken the grunge look to the extreme and almost single-handedly created a tough-girl industry with everything from torn jeans to slashed pullovers and flawed lace toppers. You couldn't walk into a department store or big-box store and not see either his signature lines or the cheaper knockoffs.

And if you browsed online and lingered on one of his staff's creations, his ads dogged your feed for weeks on end.

She'd worked for them until Bellisima had offered her a substantial hike in pay. She'd gone from teen-loving grunge to runway-model gorgeous and realized it didn't matter how they dressed you or made you up. The rules were the same. Don't eat. And barely drink. Because that size zero was not going to fit on a size four, and designers deliberately didn't make clothes with extra seamage. It was starve . . . or be starved. At least that's how it had worked for her.

Maybe that was her fault. Maybe not. But instead of taking the turn onto Main Street where Toren would see her, she cut through a couple of yards and hit the forest trails with firm, quick strides.

Toren hadn't stumbled into the quaint village accidentally. He'd come to Wishing Bridge looking for her.

Why?

There were lots of great models out there, and Rage's financials were soaring. Why look back? Why not grab some of the early-twenties and teen models that fed his consumer profile? Had she messed with his inflated ego by refusing calls and ignoring texts and e-mails?

She paced off the miles relentlessly. Nervous energy steamrolled her, and when she made the turn toward Harrowsmith Woods, she allowed herself the chance to slow down.

The predicted rain hit as she began the downhill approach to the pretentious neighborhood, and when she turned toward the winding sidewalk, her smooth-bottomed training shoes slipped on the newly wet grass.

She caught herself quickly enough to do a really bad dive-roll, but landed on her butt anyway, soaking her clothes.

She stood up, took a breath, and swiped her hands to her thighs, but the Dri-Fit leggings were too slick to be much help. The swipe only helped smear the dirt and grass covering her hands. Other than an ego hit, she wasn't hurt, and it wasn't like it was the first time she'd nosedived on a run in rough weather.

She resumed her course through the woven streets and turned onto the main road as a black limo came her way.

Trapped.

There was nowhere to go, nowhere to hide, and it wasn't as if this bucolic rural setting housed a lot of biracial supermodels.

The car stopped.

Toren got out.

He looked at her, at the pulled-up ponytail and the grime spattering her clothes, and the expression on his face went beyond priceless. "So. Jazz. How are things?"

Toren didn't do pretense like so many designers. He was an immigrant seamstress's kid from Brooklyn, he'd worked side by side with his mother and father for years, he'd made his own way in the eighties and never looked back. Thirty years in, he'd created a niche and made a fortune.

"Great, Toren. Unexpected to see you in these parts." She kept jogging in place for two reasons. She wasn't at cooldown yet, and she wanted him to know she wasn't giving him more than the few allotted seconds she'd give any casual encounter.

"I've learned to expect the unexpected in life, and when one refuses to come to the mountain . . ." He directed a look of exasperation her way. "Then the mountain is required to get on a plane and come to a postage-stamp-sized hamlet with no car service to speak of. Preposterous. What are you doing here, Jazz?" He moved forward and looked truly concerned, and he probably was because he wasn't a bad guy. He'd never been a bad guy. "If you need mental-health help, we'll get that for you. If you need a lighter schedule, I'll arrange it. You don't belong here. This isn't us, it isn't our people, our place, or our business. We survive by being busy. You know it. I know it. It's who we are, it's what makes us thrive."

"You thrived. I starved." She nailed him with a frank look as another car approached. "I'm done, Toren. Thank you for the interest, but I believe I've made it plain. I'm done."

She started to move away as the other car slowed down. She spotted Gus behind the wheel of the sharp, black Infiniti. Movement in the back seat meant Emerson was with him.

Toren reached for her arm. "You can't mean it. Not really."

"Can and do. Let go of my arm, please."

He named a figure that made her temples throb and her neck ache. "Tell me you can walk away from that, Jazz. You can't. No one can," Toren whispered.

"Miss Cinda!" Emerson's bright voice hailed her from the sleek car. "Are you okay? Are you all right?"

Gus had pulled his car off to the side of the road, ahead of the limo. He shushed Emerson and walked her way. "Trouble?"

She shook her head as Toren released her arm. "Fine, thanks. Just a chance meeting with a former boss."

"Where I come from, former bosses don't grab women's arms." Gus kept his voice low, but there was no mistaking the note of warning.

"I'm fine, Gus. Really. And I need to finish my run. Toren." She'd taken a deliberate step back from him. "Have a safe trip, and give my best to your parents. And I'm sure I'll see you two later this week." She directed the words to Gus but waved to Emerson, who was angling a look from the back seat. "Thanks for stopping."

She took off.

She didn't look back.

The sum Toren had thrown out as if it wasn't a fortune still boggled her mind.

Do you need more money?

She didn't. She knew that. So why the temptation?

Because you're human, and humans tend to think they never have enough, even when they have more than enough. It's a trap, one your therapist warned you about.

She had been warned. Back in Manhattan, where a huge percentage of people sought therapy as if needing therapy was the norm. Or maybe a badge of honor.

Her therapist had laid it out for her. They'd identified triggers, buttons, and emotions. Fear of poverty. Fear of being alone. Fear of too many things. And the temptation to be on top, all the time, in a very competitive and unhealthy business.

She was tired of being afraid and more tired of running the hamster wheel it took to make people in fashion happy.

But as she paced off the miles back through the woods, the number he'd offered still teased. That kind of money wouldn't just set her for life . . . it would enable her to help so many people.

There are other ways to help. Other ways to serve. You've got plenty of money.

She did, and she knew that, but the temptation to take one more chance washed over her, and that was exactly what Toren wanted. He wanted to plant a seed, and he was smart enough and patient enough to let it soak . . . to let it grow, tendril by tendril.

And Jazz was crazy afraid she wouldn't be strong enough to squash it.

CHAPTER
TWENTY-SEVEN

Thea stopped by Max's house after taking a fairly cooperative Mara to therapy on Monday. When he answered the door, she handed him a plate of cookies.

"For me?" He smiled down at her, one of those nice, fatherly grins she saw on TV shows. "I won't tell the doc if you don't," he added. The smile deepened. "I don't want any lectures about cholesterol or roughed-up enzymes. Whatever that means."

"The kids and I made them yesterday while you and Ethan went to get Eva. We wanted you to know how much we appreciated what you did."

He brushed that off swiftly. "Nice afternoon for a ride. No big deal."

Thea held his gaze. "It wasn't the ride. It was the connections. Getting word out quickly. I was in the system long enough to know that if you can prevent someone being taken, that's a whole lot easier than rescuing them once they've been tucked away. So thank you, Max. And don't go all humble on me. Just smile and nod."

"Ethan said you were bossy."

"He is correct."

Max smiled again. "Well, he's a lucky man, Thea. Me, too, because these cookies will be just the thing for our cookout tonight."

"Perfect." She glanced at her watch. "Gotta go. Meeting with Becky Wolinski in ten minutes."

"You putting in an offer?" He looked pleased and unsurprised.

"I am. I've decided to stay here. I love it," she finished simply. "It's not what I expected, but it's most assuredly what I needed, so here I am."

"Isaiah, chapter six. When the Lord calls, we answer."

"Yes." She studied him for a few seconds. "It was like that. And how does one say no to God?"

"I used to come up with a whole laundry list of reasons to say no," he told her. The admission made him look sad. "It was a long time before I stopped fighting and just started listening. And I did some pretty stupid things along the way. Thea, thank you." He raised the plate of cookies slightly. "I appreciate this. More than I can say."

"Well, the feeling's mutual." She climbed into her car and drove to Becky Wolinski's house, and when they came to very agreeable terms in less than half an hour, Thea was amazed.

Yes, she'd need a partner. She couldn't do this on her own financially or physically. Not with the patient load they had.

The partner would come. She needed to trust, and if too much time passed, she'd step up the advertising. Not every doctor wanted city access, but not every doctor was meant for small-town life, either. After all, when she'd wished for a place to call home, a small Western New York village hadn't made the list.

And yet it was the perfect fit.

She drove back to Maggie's, glad to have made a bold business move.

Ethan wouldn't understand. She didn't understand, not really, because a part of her longed to follow him and the kids to Illinois. Set up shop there. Be a part of a vital practice and pretend it was enough.

It wasn't. And when she'd come to faith years before, she had realized that. There was no way she could cut that devotion short now. Make it less important.

Patience.

The word dogged her, and being about the least patient person on the planet, she hated the reminder.

Jazz was at Maggie and Jeb's. Thea drove there and dashed through the new bout of rain. When she got inside, Shannie grabbed her in a hug that felt so good. Wondrously good.

Then Thea spotted Jazz's face across the room, a face marked with worry. Concern. Questioning.

Jazz masked it quickly, but Thea knew the drill from both sides of the medical equation. Something had tapped Jazz's triggers, and stopping her beautiful friend from a complete backslide just jumped to first place on the list of megaimportant things to do.

~

Thea didn't just look concerned when Jazz shared the encounter from that afternoon. She looked downright worried. "You're not considering this, are you? Not when we know how tough it is to maintain yourself mentally, physically, and emotionally? Honey, there's not enough money in the world to upset that apple cart on purpose, is there?"

"No." Jazz couldn't bring her voice above a whisper. "But I'm good at it, Thea. Really good. And I'm not much good at anything else worth noting."

"That kind of negative thinking needs to stop right now," Thea instructed. "You've got this foolish idea that you've been getting by on long legs and beauty for the last decade." She shot Jazz a *What are you thinking?* look. "What an outrageous notion. Thoughts like that negate the hard work and industry you've put into your job. Yes, you got blessed with the gorgeous face and body by a great genetic cocktail, but the effort and sacrifice was all you. Don't sell that short."

"I don't think being a puppet on a string is all that difficult, Thea."

Thea grabbed her in a hug. "You're wrong. So wrong. And there's a part of you that knows it, Jazz, but Toren's pushed all the right buttons, and he did it purposefully. He came all the way out here, making you feel invaluable."

Thea was right. He hadn't stopped at calling and texting. He'd flown to Rochester, hired a driver, and searched her out. The expended effort made her seem special. It had stroked her ego, and Toren was real good at that.

"He reminded you of how perfect you are in front of the cameras and how disappointed he was in what you're doing now."

He'd done that with just one sad look, disparaging her dirty clothes, her hair. Her face. Her.

"And he made you feel like he could prevent you from backsliding, from falling back into the food-is-the-enemy rabbit hole, but you know better, Jazz-ma-Sass."

Thea had called her that when they were teens in foster care together. When they had first promised to support one another no matter how the chips should fall. That pledge was what brought them to Wishing Bridge in December.

"Toren can't keep that promise. He can't because he's a busy executive with a lot of plates spinning, and he's not going to be there to fulfill his pledge. If he assigns those follow-throughs to someone else, how are they going to handle them? Easy." Thea shrugged. "They're not, because while he has a vested interest in you and likes you, hired help doesn't always feel the same way. Don't let him coerce you. Stop. Think. Pray. Let your life unfold a bit. Let time work in your favor. Not against you."

"You're right." Jazz walked to the turret window overlooking the quiet neighborhood. "I know you're right, but suddenly I was being bombarded with options and choices and fears. All because he showed up here. And if he did it once, he'll do it again."

"Probably. Or someone else will make the effort. And while that's a compliment of the highest order in modeling, it could also be a death sentence."

Jazz tried to swallow.

She couldn't.

The knot in her throat rose up to choke her because Thea was right. A body needed sustenance. And rest. When a compulsive nature faced the strictest of parameters, the tendency to go too far, to never think enough was really enough, skewed reasoning to unreasonable levels.

She set her forehead against the cool window and sighed. "You're right."

"I know I am." Thea crossed the room and laid her head against Jazz's shoulder. "Jazz, there are times I'd give anything to look like you. Tall. Exotic. Stunning. When we first met, I hated you. All that beauty, all that strength, it just oozed from you. But when you sneaked that dessert to me on a night when I'd broken the rules. When you slipped it my way and winked . . . I realized that looks are such a shallow measure of anything, because it didn't matter that I was plain and you were gorgeous. It just mattered that we looked out for each other."

"You're not plain, you're girl-next-door beautiful, and just hearing you say that makes me want to fight for you. And you for me. So here we are again." Jazz contemplated the outdoors for a few more seconds before she turned. "I *want* to be here. I do. So why do things like this grab at me? Why the major temptation?"

"I'd say the dollars and cents of the situation explain that one pretty well." Thea kept her voice dry and shifted her brows up. "And the compliment of Toren coming all this way. If he's as smart as you say he is . . ."

"Easily. And that ambitious."

"Then he's playing a hand. If he loses the hand, he'll grab some other gorgeous gal off the streets and make her life miserable. But that's how we learn, isn't it? By trying? Doing?"

"I'm tired." Jazz gave Thea a quick hug. "I'm done thinking. I'm going to put my earplugs in and sleep, and in the morning, I'll wake up realizing I'm in a much better spot than I was five months ago."

"Perfect."

She crossed to her bedroom, wishing she were stronger. Wishing she could face her dragons and slay them. Wishing she never had to think about modeling or thongs or plunging necklines again.

Maybe you don't.

The soft voice of her conscience nudged her as she tugged on granny-style flannel pajamas.

Be true to yourself, isn't that what Grandma said? "Cinda-girl, be true to yourself and the rest will fall into place."

Grandma.

Her mother.

Two strong women who had made do on so little and made it seem like so much, and then they were gone, so close together, leaving her alone to face a tough, hostile world.

Would they laugh at her predicament, two women who never had more than a bare-bones paycheck-to-paycheck existence?

The small plaque from her grandma's wall stood on her dresser. How many times had she read Isaiah's paraphrased verse and wished she faced life like the fearless women who had gone before her? "Be not afraid, for I am with you; be not dismayed, for I am your God. I will strengthen you and help you; I will uphold you with my righteous right hand."

Did she lack courage? Was that the basis for her fears and worries?

She went to bed, not praying, exactly. But not wishing, either, because one couldn't just wish for courage. One had to build it. Then embrace it.

So if she did pray, it was for the wisdom to gain courage, whatever it took, and when she woke up the next morning, she didn't consult Thea or Kelsey or Maggie.

She picked up her phone.

She didn't text Toren.

That was the chicken's way out.

She called him, knowing it was midday in London, and refused his offer. After thanking him for his efforts, she hung up the phone.

There would be more offers. Toren's surprise visit had shown her the likelihood of that.

But she'd placed one firm brick in her courage platform, and that didn't just feel *good*. It felt *marvelous*. And when she hung up, she called the Realtor and approved her to look for a solid local investment. Not in Rochester or Buffalo, but here, close to Wishing Bridge.

By midafternoon the Realtor had come back with two options. The lovely home in Harrowsmith Woods had been foreclosed on when the previous owners had divorced. It was available for under sixty percent of its actual worth, making it a no-brainer. She instructed the Realtor to place an offer right away.

The second option was for a plot of undeveloped industrial land between the village and the NYS Thruway. It was an eighty-acre parcel that had been sitting idle for decades.

"I don't get it, Trish." Jazz frowned at the land plot. "What's the draw here?"

"There might be none," the Realtor told her, but then she drew up a cable news website. "But then there's this, and no one knows the truth behind the implications. If this website is correct, and a major business player like Amazon or Walmart has narrowed the I-90 corridor between Rochester and Buffalo as a prime site for an eastern distribution center, this plot is part of a nearly three-hundred-acre contiguous parcel. This piece has the road frontage with the cleanest thruway access. If I had the money, I'd buy this myself. You, on the other hand, have the money to do both and set yourself up in a whole other kind of business," she told her. "Land sales. A lot of fortunes have been made and/or kept by knowing when to buy and sell real estate."

Buying and selling land.

Was she smart enough to cut deals?

Her heart said no, but then Thea's words came back to her. She'd hashed this out with her investment broker and her lawyer weeks ago, but the decision came down to her. *"I will strengthen you and help you . . ."*

Words of strength bolstering a courageous choice. She said yes to both and left Trish to draw up the paperwork.

If nothing else, owning something would feel good. Really good. And setting down firm roots into the ground around Wishing Bridge might be the anchor she needed to send the next offer packing with more confidence.

And if there were no more modeling opportunities ever?

That would be okay, too.

CHAPTER
TWENTY-EIGHT

Ethan handed Eva his debit card and the keys to the car. She stared at both, then him. "What's this for?"

"An Easter dress."

She frowned. "Hey, I can pick something up at the thrift store over in Mount Morris. I don't need this." She tried to hand the card back to him.

He went on as if she hadn't spoken. "There are malls right off I-90 in Buffalo and Rochester. Both are easy finds."

Surprise widened her eyes. Surprise mixed with gratitude. "You don't care if I drive there?"

"You've got a license?"

She swiped her palms against her pants. "Yes."

"If I could go with you, I would," he told her, then he pointed her toward the door. "Not to drive you, but to tell you how beautiful you are as you try things on. But I'm tied up this afternoon."

"Ethan."

He tapped his watch. "Kids will be home by four. If you're serious about helping with them, then get going. It's over a half-hour drive to the mall, and Easter's only a few days away."

"Thank you." She hugged him quickly. She didn't bother to change clothes or fix her hair and dashed out the door and down the stairs.

Within seconds his car engine sprang to life in the lot. He watched from the window as she cruised up Maplewood Avenue, past the big old colonial Max was fixing up on the opposite side of the street, and then took a left onto Main.

And she was gone.

His phone buzzed. He picked up the call, still watching Eva. "Dr. Brandenburg."

"Ethan, it's Thea."

He smiled instantly, a far cry from their initial meeting over three months before.

"Dr. Ayler from Travel Care is here. You wanted to be in on this meeting, correct?"

The itinerant doctor. Yes, he wanted to be in on the meeting, but he'd forgotten about it. "Be right there." He trotted down the stairs, glad to be feeling well enough to trot. Glad to be feeling fit. Glad to be feeling like himself again. Maybe better.

He walked into the office.

"Doc, how're ya' doin'?" Mr. Filiberti, an old-timer from Perry, seemed delighted to see Ethan when he came through the office door. "It's good to see you here. I told the missus there weren't much that would keep a young fellow like you down! She'll be happy I ran into you." The old fellow pumped Ethan's hand.

"Ethan, you look well!" Janice Nau, a middle-aged woman from the top of Warsaw Hill, came his way, too. "I saw you walking last week, and I can't deny I've been sending up prayers, but what a difference a week makes." She added her handshake to the mix.

"Lookin' good, boss." Sheila grinned at him from the far side of the desk.

"It's so nice to have you down here," added Laura. "And looking way better than you did last time."

"When they took him out on a stretcher thing," laughed the old man. He slapped his hat against his thigh, as if picturing Ethan on a gurney was all that amusing.

"Not so funny from my perspective," Ethan told him. He pretended to scowl.

The old man only laughed harder.

"I've got room three ready."

Ethan turned toward the unfamiliar voice. Then he paused. "Mrs. Hilbert?"

"Dr. Brandenburg." She came forward and shook his hand. "Welcome back."

"You're working here?" He noted the floral-print scrubs and the checklist in her hands.

"As of yesterday," she told him. "Thea asked me to come in part-time to get the hang of things while our youngest is in preschool. I start full-time at the end of the school year when my oldest is home to watch the youngest."

"Really?" Ethan said. Thea had come out of her office, and he aimed a purposeful look of question at her. She made a face.

"I may have forgotten to tell you that," she noted as he moved her way. "Busy few days."

"It has been, but possibly not too busy to tell me we had a new employee."

She looked miffed at the rebuke. That in itself was kind of fun for Ethan. "My apologies, Doctor."

He paused in front of her. Right in front of her. And when she was forced to look up at him, he made her wait for several long, drawn-out seconds. "Apology accepted."

Her eyes narrowed.

He ignored that and walked into her office. "Dr. Ayler."

The woman stood and put out her hand. "Dr. Brandenburg. My pleasure. I actually worked for Stilk Medical down in White Plains shortly after you left their practice to go to Montefiore."

"A nice practice."

"It was," she agreed. "Your patients at Stilk remembered you fondly," she went on. "They said you were short on talk but quick on cures."

"Two for two," Thea said.

He sat.

Then Thea joined him.

"So, Dr. Ayler, I don't know what Thea's told you."

"Quite a bit since you were ten minutes late." Eyes down, Thea consulted the notebook in her hands as if whatever she had written was of utmost importance.

"And you like to get things done," he said.

"Time is money," she reminded him, and he got a kick out of the scolding note in her voice. "Respect for time is vital in any small business, but certainly in medicine. I have a patient scheduled in twelve minutes."

"Then let's get to this."

Thea started in. "I was just explaining to Dr. Ayler that it's a four-week commitment, seeing patients here in the office and on-call commitments for a few days and two weekends."

"Although with crucial care and after-hours facilities, being on call here is quite different than when I first began practicing," Ethan told her. "Callouts are rare. Telephone consults are much more common."

"Times have changed," noted Dr. Ayler. "You said you might need time for interviews." She addressed Thea. "Are you adding staff?"

"I believe she's already done that." Ethan raised a brow in Thea's direction.

"I may be interviewing," Thea replied. "I'm buying the practice and it's not a one-woman operation. There might be interviews, there might not. I wanted you aware of the situation in either case."

"Not," said Ethan.

Thea turned toward him, exasperated.

"Interviews," he said when she sent him a questioning look. "Not needed."

"Except that if someone wants to interview, then—"

He reached over. Took her hand. And then he raised it up, to his lips, and kissed it. Right there. Right then.

Her eyes went wide. A blush stained her cheeks as her gaze darted from him to the new doctor and back. "Ethan."

"We need two primary care people here, correct?"

When she nodded, he glanced down to their joined hands. "You. And me. No applications required."

"This is your way of telling me you're staying?" Those eyes narrowed again, those pretty eyes that held so much past and so much future.

"It is."

"Ethan Brandenburg, I—"

She was at a loss for words.

Good.

Ethan was pretty sure that was a rare circumstance where Thea was concerned.

He got up and tapped his watch. "I've got rehab, Eva's out shopping for an Easter dress, and I promised Max and the kids we'd finally do our cookout tonight. We haven't had one since moving over here. So, ladies. Would you care to join me and my family for hots and hamburgers around six o'clock?"

Dr. Ayler begged off. "I'm going to get settled at the long-term hotel. But it sounds wonderful." She sent him a frank look of amusement.

"Thea?"

He turned her way.

She gazed up at him. Then she stood.

Watery eyes.

Multiple blinks. Chin down, she reached across the desk for a tissue.

"No crying. We have a rule."

She shook her head. "We don't."

"Then we *should* have a rule. Starting now."

She moved toward him.

He opened his arms, and when she stepped into them, when he closed them around her, there was no longer a question in his mind.

He was home.

She was home. Here. In Wishing Bridge.

He didn't know what the future would bring. He knew what he wanted it to bring, and that was enough for now.

Dr. Ayler slipped out of the room.

Thea leaned back, trusting his arms to hold her, trusting him, and met his gaze. "You're sure?"

"Positive."

"What about your dreams, Ethan? Your plans?"

"Don't you get it, Thea?" She blinked, long and slow, and that got her kissed. "My dreams seem to have changed. Plans, too."

"But—"

"I don't think there are any buts," he told her. He kissed her once more. "I think there's simply hope, Thea. For the three kids, for Eva, and for us. And if that's all God ever grants us, I'll die a happy man."

"Could you hold off on the dying part, though? Please?"

He laughed and tucked her under his chin for a few more seconds. "I'll do my best. See you for supper?"

"Wouldn't miss it for the world."

Sheila's voice came through the intercom. "Thea, your two o'clock is here."

"Thanks, Sheila."

Duty called. He stepped back. At the door she paused, then looked over her shoulder. "You sure you're not on meds I don't know about?"

He laughed softly. "I think the current prescription is faith, hope, and love. If I remember correctly."

Her smile set him longing for more. More smiles, more time, more everything.

But first . . . rehab in Mount Morris, followed by second-grade homework and hot dogs. It might not fit the norm for dreams-come-true for everyone. But for him—

Things were going to work out just fine.

~

"Would you ever, in your wildest dreams, have imagined this six months ago?" Thea posed the question through the three-part bridal mirror as she adjusted the lace-appliqued veil to Kelsey's hair and Jazz fluffed the gown's bouffant tulle train.

"Well, six months ago I was nearly seven months pregnant, deserted by a scoundrel, ready to give my beautiful baby up for adoption, and facing the toughest winter of my life. So. No." Joy and disbelief vied for control of Kelsey's features. "Not in a million years."

"Which is why the good Lord wants us to cast close-mindedness to the wind and be open to whatever he's got planned," Maggie told them as she and Jill ushered Shannon and Mara their way. The two little girls had been trying on matching flower-girl dresses, dresses that seemed to mushroom in volume as the children took their spots alongside Kelsey.

"Do we look like puffballs?" Kelsey shot Thea and Jazz a somewhat exaggerated look of fear as she met their eyes through the looking glass. "My goal is to not look like a giant puffball on my wedding day."

"On you, it's fine," Jazz told her. "I think the girls could use less volume," she went on, smiling. "It's a lot at their size."

Thea caught Mara's eye in the mirror.

Mara had been thrilled to be asked to share flower-girl honors with Shannon, but Mara wasn't exactly open to suggestions when she wanted something, and she'd fallen in love with the poofy gown the moment she had set her almost-eight-year-old eyes on it.

Mara touched her fingers to her gown. She twirled once, paused, then nodded. "I think you're right." She gazed up at Jazz, serious. "We'd have to walk like a pair of church bells all day long." She tottered around, swaying like a pendulum, and Shannon burst out laughing.

"We would look so silly!"

"And silly is the opposite of what we'd like for Kelsey's wedding day." Jill took Mara's hand. "Let's try the next ones on, okay?"

"Sure."

"All right!"

Jazz pretended to wipe her brow once the little girls were back in the closed dressing room. "Crisis averted."

"Who'd have thought?" whispered Kelsey. "I was set for the meltdown."

"Fewer and farther between now." Thea aimed a look at the dressing room before she shifted her attention back to Kelsey and Jazz. "She's still sad, of course. But now she allows herself to be happy from time to time. She feels guilty when she's happy. She told Ethan that, because how can she be happy when her parents are gone?"

"I remember that all too well." Jazz spoke softly. "When those we love are gone and our lives go on, it all seems so very wrong and makes no sense. But now . . ." She squared her shoulders and looped one arm around Kelsey and the other around Thea. "Now it's not wrong."

Thea locked eyes with her in the mirror. Then with Kelsey. "Not wrong at all. In fact, it couldn't be more right, could it?"

Jazz made a skeptical face. "Exactly what worries me, because how could this all be? How did it all fall into place, bringing the three of us here in the dead of winter? Then you falling in love." She pointed out the gorgeous multilayered tulle gown with a quick look. "Thea big-time crushing on the doctor and inheriting a beautiful little family. And me, jumping off a career roller coaster that spelled nothing but disaster. And don't be telling me that it's God's perfect timing," she scolded Thea. "There have been scads of imperfect things in my life, darling, and that means his timing only works now and again. You can't possibly tell me that's good for business."

Jazz and Kelsey both gazed at Thea in the mirror.

She met their eyes. Then she smiled. "Remember Christ, pulling that nasty big cross through the streets of Jerusalem? How he trudged up that awful hill to his death?"

"I'm not sure she's making this better," Jazz whispered with one of those gorgeous eyebrows arched up.

"But we'll hear her out because we love her," Kelsey whispered back.

"The broken road," Thea told them. "Life doesn't always come with smooth trails and easy choices. Sometimes it takes a broken road to bring us where we need to be. Our broken roads brought us to each other first. To Hannah's Hope," she reminded them. "And to this."

She let them think a moment, these two women who'd known her longest and probably loved her most. "It's brought us here. I don't know how or why, I just know it happened and it feels right. And being back together, seeing things work out for all three of us?" She smiled at them both, her faithful friends, the Soul Sisterhood. "That's enough of a gift right there."

"You are not supposed to make me cry with the dress on." Kelsey fumbled desperately for a tissue. "My mascara will run and—"

Jazz grabbed a tissue from a strategically placed "yes-to-the-dress" box. Thea did the same.

And when their hands met in the middle—with Kelsey's—Thea knew that's how it was supposed to be. Three girls, now women, friends forever.

With not one spot of mascara hitting that beautiful gown.

ACKNOWLEDGMENTS

When it comes to writing a book or developing a series, the final product is always the work of many hands. Huge thank yous to the wonderful developmental and editorial staff at Waterfall Press for working hand in hand with me to polish this story. I am so grateful for your hard work and advice. You've been absolutely marvelous to collaborate with from the very beginning. Kudos to Sheryl Zajechowski, Faith Black Ross, and Laura Whittemore for their efforts, and additional gratitude to the art team who brought these heroines and this quaint town to life in their wonderful covers. I couldn't be more pleased!

I count several nurses among my family and friends, and work on a board with several doctors. Big thanks to Kathleen Wessman, Barbara Maier, and Janet Elliott, whose nuggets of wisdom come to life in my fictional medical professionals. To Daystar, a foster-care service for medically fragile infants started by the Sisters of Saint Joseph of Rochester in 1988. Back then, the good sisters took in babies with low life expectancy and overwhelming needs and gave them the love and care and affection every child deserves. Thirty years and a lot of babies and kids later, it has grown to be a multifaceted facility that provides respite for kids with a wide range of disabilities. It's an amazing place, and I'm happy to give it a shout-out whenever I can.

A big part of the continuing thread for this series is the man who inspired Max Reichert's character. Greg O'Connell began rehabbing properties in Red Hook, New York, long before he moved to Mount Morris and started doing the same thing. A former NYPD officer, Greg has patiently developed the idea of great looks and low rents for businesses to get them off the ground. I wanted to shine a light on his work and those who emulate this idea in fading towns everywhere. It's a "teach a man to fish" mentality that works. Greg, thank you for all you've done, for what you do, and while Max is fictional (and there will be more of Max's story in book three!) the inspiration for his hard work and willingness to help others came from reading about Greg O'Connell.

To Carolyn Jones, MD, chief of Thoracic and Foregut Surgery at URMC, for her guidance as I pieced together Ethan's health issues. How nice that I picked the seat next to her when I joined the board! Any mistakes are totally mine, because she's far too smart to make them. And a huge shout-out to Steve Ward, Chris Muscato, and all the officers I've known throughout the years—my friends in blue, the first responders who advise me about protocol and action and how the two don't always meet. When I create characters like Hale and Garrett Jackson, it's you guys I have in mind. And to the Hilton Fire Department and Ladies Auxiliary for their fine work and dedication at all hours of the day and night. Your volunteerism helps create the backbone of our town, as it does in so many others. Huge thank yous for all you do.

And never last but always first, my thanks to God for the gift of my talents and the time to use them, a gift passed down from my mother. For multiple reasons, Mary Elizabeth Logan Herne never got the chance to let her words shine, and that is a sadness because she was an amazingly gifted woman. That makes me doubly blessed to have this opportunity.

And to my family, for their love and support and the occasional Abbott's Frozen Custard. I love you guys. You mean the world to me. Always.

Ruthy

ABOUT THE AUTHOR

Ruth Logan Herne is the bestselling author of more than forty novels and novellas, including *Welcome to Wishing Bridge*, the first book in her Wishing Bridge series. With millions of books in print, she's living her dream of touching hearts and souls by writing the kind of books she likes to read. The mother of six, with a seventh child of her heart, and grandmother to fourteen, she loves God, family, country, chocolate, and dogs and lives with her husband on a small farm in Upstate New York, where she can be found baking cookies, weeding gardens, wiping little faces, or prepping chicken eggs for local customers—who know not to say too much (or they just may end up in a book). Visit the author at www.ruthloganherne.com.